ONE MORE RIVER

ONE MORE RIVER

Mary Glickman

OPEN ROAD

INTEGRATED MEDIA

NEW YORK

For Frank and Freda,
who know all there is to know of love

CONTENTS

One More River to Cross

Oh, better love was never told
One more river to cross
Tis stronger than an iron hand
One more river to cross
Tis sweeter than honey comb
One more river to cross

Oh, wasn't that a wide river
River of Jordan, Lord,
Wide river
There's one more river to cross

Oh, the good old chariot passing by
One more river to cross
She jarred the earth an' shook the sky
One more river to cross
The good old chariot passing by

Oh, wasn't that a wide river
River of Jordan, Lord,
Wide river
There's one more river to cross

I

Vietnam, 1965

MICKEY MOE LEVY MANAGED HIS war, kept himself from going stark raving mad, by comparing every crazy, foreign, messed-up thing he saw or touched or smelled or heard to something familiar back home. He'd take those affinities and weave them around himself like a cloak in which he hid like a bandit or a child, and the cloak kept him whole. Sometimes this was challenging and other times not. He figured his age and experiences had something to do with that. He was the oldest of his platoon. Most of the men were ten years younger than he, baby-faced and raw at least for the first week or two. Mickey Moe was raised a country boy, he'd had his backwoods adventures. It helped that the sight of death, the smell of gunpowder were not unknown to him. He was glad he felt easy with Negroes, or blacks as they'd started calling themselves, even the ones from New York and New Jersey, who all talked like they came from the South anyway, using down-home expressions in accents that seemed as queer to him as the seesaw chatter of Vietnamese. And the ones who were dirt-poor farmers from anywhere at all, with those he felt blood brother to each.

It was just before Chu Lai, the first major bleeding of American troops in the war. All the men on patrol were jumpy. Everyone felt something was coming, and each mustered his nerve in his own way. Mickey Moe looked across marshland terraced in rice paddies, shrouded in fog, and conjured up Mississippi, conjured up the Pearl River in August at dawn, and it didn't seem so different. The bugs and leeches were the same, even in number. So was the heat, heavy and wet. He watched the women working the fields, their long shirts caught up between their legs, their small backs bent, their pointy hats tilted down hiding their faces, and he thought of Laura Anne: Laura Anne in her broad-brimmed garden hat the day they met, her sweet, lovely face smiling at his lame conversation, her butterscotch eyes large with good humor and kindness; Laura Anne bent over as she worked the vegetable patch back of Aunt Lucille's big house, the sun and her labor making damp ringlets of honey hair that clung to her cheeks and her neck. Once he got going on his wife, everything sang her name. The rain, the far-off rat-a-tat-tat of bullets, helicopter blades, boots hitting mud: Laura Anne, Laura Anne, Laura Anne, they sang until he had to stop it, until the method he'd found to keep from going nuts threatened to turn on him. He hit his helmet hard with his handgun. Clang, clang, clang. The Jersey boys, annoyed maybe, or worried about him, said, Your brains gonna stick to that thing, Crackah Mick. But he kept it up or he ran the risk of ending up like his daddy, dead against a tree trunk in a battlefield. He would not do that to his son. He would not leave him with a great question mark of a father. Not his son. Not that boy growing in Laura Anne's belly.

Mickey Moe's daddy died in the Ardennes, his hands too frostbit to pull the trigger when he saw the Nazi coming toward him, taking aim. Helpless, he watched the squat peasant legs rush forward. He saw the boy's bright blue eyes, wide with fear, the way he stopped, stock-still, to raise his rifle and shoot the daylight out of a G.I. too dang cold to squeeze his trigger and shoot him first. On such things hang the fate of man, Mickey Moe reminded himself. Not on courage or capability or even being right. Something like the weather, a thing that changes with the wind, can be the only reason a Bernard Levy fails to take advantage of the moment and blow out a Nazi's brains instead of suffer his own spread like a crimson flower over the pure French snow.

Nothing like that would happen to Mickey Moe. He wasn't going to die, not on this alien ground he'd related so much to home. Last night, as usual, his sleep was disturbed by hybrid dreams. He dreamt of Aunt Lucille's farm full of rice fields instead of cotton, of the battered mobile homes in his hometown's Negro village transformed to Vietnamese huts. Laura Anne was there. She wore black pajamas. She stood at the jungle's edge and pointed. When he followed her directive, he found that severed foot from the backwoods, the one he never got out of his conscious mind no matter how many babies he saw wailing at their dead mamas' breasts or buddies with bones poking out the side of their legs. In his dream, the foot nested in thick brown vine and palm fronds, not the oak and dogwood leaves of Mississippi. It floated in monsoon mud. It looked like it might right itself and walk straight up to him demanding in its dead severed foot way why he hadn't done more that night, that hot Mississippi night, to avenge itself. I did what I could, he told the thing. I did all that I could at the time. Now today I could do a lot more. Thanks to the Armed Forces of the USA, I've got the skills. But I didn't then, and there ain't nothin' I can do about it now.

When he woke, it confounded him that the severed foot waited until he was deep in country to pop up in his dreams. He never once dreamt of it back home. Maybe he didn't have to, it was so often in his mind.

Funny what haunts a man, he thought. Laura Anne and that

chopped-off foot. Two things on opposite extremes of human experience. Yet, they'd always be linked in his head and for good reason. The foot was a part of the life he and his wife shared. It was their first secret, one that pitched them head on against murderous Klansmen. They didn't have to speak of it. It was just there, uniting them, part of the changing times no one saw coming.

Mickey Moe wondered how Daddy kept his secrets during the life he shared with Mama before his war came, especially as he was a charming man by all reports, a talker. But Daddy's ability to keep a secret was so strong that he had to find out everything he knew about his father on his own. Finding out about Bernard Levy was the hardest thing he ever did, including going off to war, but in the end, since he wound up with Laura Anne, he thought that was alright. His wife was worth the price.

During the downtime of military life, he liked to review every second of his relationship with Laura Anne from glorious beginning to the painful separation caused by this insane war. When Sarge told them all to take a break while he conferred with the signal officer, he removed himself from the gripes and antics of the men and remembered the day he met his future bride.

Aunt Missy Fine Sassaport had arranged an afternoon tea so that the Sassaport men along with their cousins and neighbors could meet appropriate, marriageable women from all over the tristate area of Mississippi, Kentucky, and Louisiana. Mickey Moe, a reluctant attendee, kept apart from the festivities. He drank spiked lemonade from a mason jar and told the other boys stories from his sales route for Uncle Tom-Tom's insurance agency. He ignored the ladies. It offended him he was asked to attend the party at all. He was not some hard luck swain who couldn't get a girl on his own. Mama made him promise to go or else Aunt Missy would pitch a holy fit. He'd gone affecting an I-could-care-less manner until the moment he saw Laura Anne

Needleman sitting beneath a massive oak wearing a peach-colored dress and a large-brimmed straw hat. He didn't know it yet, but all the men of his family were suckers for love at first sight. True to his fore-bears, he took one look at Laura Anne Needleman, at her fine-boned face and figure, at her long honey hair, and his course was fixed. He could not have looked elsewhere if a horde of men yelled "Fire."

Unaware she had met her destiny, Laura Anne Needleman glanced up and caught sight of a handsome young man with a square jaw and a thick black forelock falling over almond eyes that studied her with a starstruck, puppy-dog gaze. She watched him turn red when she favored him with a smile. She patted the spot next to her with a slen-der hand, then fluttered fingers tipped in the same color as her dress, tapping them gracefully against the ground as if she were playing the piano. He nearly tripped over himself rushing to her side and seemed unable to catch his breath to speak, so she spoke first.

These get-togethers are awkward, aren't they? Whoever's idea was it to throw every young, unmarried Delta Jew of good family into a great lump on a sweltering afternoon in Hind's County and watch them knock together until a match or two emerged?

That would be my aunt, Missy Fine Sassaport, Mickey Moe said, his expression as serious as the grave. He feared her opinion of Aunt Missy might taint him.

She laughed outright. Her laughter, gently bubbling up from some warm, knowing place inside her, enchanted him. Between the way she filled out the peach-colored dress and that deep, soft laugh, he was a goner, plain and simple.

There was a pause in conversation then, a silence hard as a block of cement. His mama had taught him that too extended a pause in conver-sation was cruel as a slap to a young girl, so he began to talk and once revved up could not stop. All the while, he cursed himself for acting a fool, as if he'd never romanced a woman in his life, as if he hadn't had four lovers already. At age twenty-five, in 1962 Guilford, Mississippi, this was not a bad batting average, not at all.

Well, Miss . . .

He leaned over to study her name tag just as she leaned forward to study his. Their heads bumped lightly. When they looked up, their lips nearly met. He coughed to regain control.

. . . Miss Laura Anne, it's a fact that the folks over in Atlanta started this kind a thing, with that Ballyhoo weekend they got over there. Then Montgomery's got that Falcon weekend and Birmingham the Jubilee. It's also a fact that the members of our tribe are too spread out to meet each other on a regular, more casual basis. I think it's a sign of restraint that Aunt Missy organized these tea parties. I am deeply grateful to her that rather than requirin' us to spend the entire weekend in some stranger's house goin' to forty-two events in a row, all we boys got to do is make sure for two or three hours we don't get pastry crumbs stuck to our chin whiskers and don't spill tea onto anyone's party dress. Yes, it's a remarkable sign of restraint, a quality for which Aunt Missy is not known.

He took a deep breath, as he'd run out of air. Although a salesman of some skill, accustomed to spinning a spiel tailored to the situation at hand, he found himself at a loss in this woman's presence, and he could only guess why. Laura Anne Needleman put two incredibly soft fingers against his lips.

Hush. I am not interested in your aunt Missy. Everyone in the county knows a Sassaport or two. I take it your mama's another one? And Levy. Why, there are Levys sprinkled about in every corner of the South. I don't know if it matters much which ones yours are. I am sick of all this focus on the ancestors!

Mickey Moe considered for a moment that Laura Anne Needleman might have a rebellious nature. The thought excited him. The idea that he—a man of questionable family history on his daddy's side—might escape the culture's obsession with lineage, made him tongue-tied with gratitude. So he said, Pardon me?

My, oh my. That did come out funny, didn't it? I only mean I like to find out first about the person settin' right there in front of me, not all the old ghosts. When I say tell me about your people, I want to know about the ones closest to you in blood. What are they like? What do they do? I mean your mama, your daddy. Your siblings. You have siblings?

He told her about his three elder sisters, which didn't take long, because the first two, married and living out-of-state, didn't interest him and the third, whom he loved, lived at home and never seemed to interest anyone else. He told her about his mama and how it was his job to take care of her ever since his daddy died in the Battle of the Bulge.

She asked him the question he most dreaded. And before the war? What did your daddy do?

Buying time before he answered, Mickey Moe Levy looked down. He played with the blades of grass under his hand and sighed and told her what he knew and then, because he was a goner, what he'd come to suspect in his heart.

My daddy, he began, was a man of mystery.

Laura Anne straightened up at that. She leaned in close to him, giving him an intoxicating whiff of her scent, one of lavender soap and fresh linen dried outdoors in the sun. She regarded him intently. The gold flecks in her eyes glittered. There was a fierce heat in her gaze. It was like being watched by torchlight. When a sudden breeze passed by, her honey-colored hair lifted so that a few silky strands escaped the fetters of her sunhat to graze his cheek. It took all he had to keep himself from grabbing her right there in front of everyone and planting a smack, hard and wet, on that sweet little mouth this close to his own. To cover evidence of his struggle, he paused, mopped his brow and neck with a pocket handkerchief, and continued.

Daddy claimed he came from a prominent family in Memphis, but only three cousins of his, two male and one female, were in attendance at the wedding. Mama's family thought that pretty odd. He explained it away. Told them his mama and daddy had not finished the year's mourning for his granddaddy and would not attend a celebration, even their own son's wedding. Now, Mama's people had never heard of such a ban, but they assumed the Levys were more observant Jews than they were. Daddy told them his people were from somewhere or other along the Rhine, which from the Sassaport perspective, bein' of Portuguese descent, was so foreign a place the river might as well have flowed through China. In those days, people didn't have long engagements. Once a couple declared their affections, you married them off right quick before they had a chance to dishonor themselves.

Laura Anne shook her head in vigorous agreement. A wise program, she said.

Mickey Moe shot her a mischievous glance. Think so? he asked, wondering if her blood was hot.

She blushed, clamped her upper teeth against a plump lower lip. His hopes soared.

When my sisters and I were born, Daddy's family was invited for the name days and the bris, but no one showed. They sent letters and bank drafts, but that's it. Mama put it about that they were dismayed he'd married a girl out of their sect, a notion the Sassaports accepted, remarking it was a dang shame his people were so hard. Twice a year, Daddy traveled to Memphis to visit them, but he always left us home. Mama said he was pavin' the way, pavin' the way for our eventual presentation, which I believe she put some faith in. She shouldn't have. It never happened.

Then the war came. Daddy got killed sittin' in a foxhole half-froze to death. His buddy told us he saw that Nazi comin', but his fingers were so numb he couldn't pull his trigger.

Laura Anne reached over and pressed his knee in empathy, which felt so good Mickey Moe longed for her to keep it there. He swallowed hard to embellish his misery. He dipped his head to make his forelock graze his eyes, a pose he knew women found difficult to resist, and dropped his voice to a soft, sad, seductive hum.

. . . Mama hired a detective to track down Daddy's family so she could let them know their son and heir was dead. It was a considerable expense for a war widow with a sparse income, but she was hopin' for an inheritance. They wrote back and said they had no idea who she was talkin' about. There was no Bernard Levy in their kin or ken. Mickey Moe slapped his thighs with both hands in a gesture of finality.

So you can say everything I know about my daddy is a lie. I don't know who he was or where he come from. I only know the falsehoods he told. I don't remember him. But I have a feelin'—and there's some fact to this, because when I was a bit younger I looked into things— those Memphis Levys lied, lied as outright as my daddy, about who he was and where he'd been. He was one of them alright, but one of them they did not care to acknowledge. Why, I do not know. I like to think maybe he was a bootlegger. That'd explain a lot. Explain his so-called trips to Memphis and why the flow of money stopped once he was gone to war.

Laura Anne frowned and gave a little shrug in response to his conclusion, as if nothing more could possibly be said. Her eyes looked sad and damp. He was gratified his story moved her. Mickey Moe rose to his feet and threw up his hands, pointed them toward the moon that had begun to rise in the afternoon sky, boldly asserting itself just below the bright and burning sun.

I am a child of mystery, he said, but I am as easy to decipher as a semaphore waved from the deck of a riverboat on a sparklin' day in spring. I might take a little study, but there is no deception in me. I've made my life a devotion in plain talk and honest proposal to atone for whatever drops of my daddy's lying blood flow through my veins. Do you find this upsettin'?

And because love, wherever it happens, whenever it happens, is a miracle even when it is the most natural thing in the world and obvious to every fool in its purview, Laura Anne said, No. I do not. I rather think it makes me like you more, Mickey Moe Levy. A whole lot more.

Fates have been sealed on less.

Stuck in the heat of a Vietnam about to erupt in its first full-scale battle, Mickey Moe was reluctant to let go of his memories of meeting his wife. Reliving them brought her so close a sudden waft of tropical breeze felt exactly like her breath against his neck. It sounds like a fairy tale now, he thought. Who would have thought that summer day amid the sweet tea and little cakes that tribulation would be born? It should have been all Saturday night dinners and drive-in movies, but what we got were the sufferings of Job himself. Blood, agony, and loss all tied up in a bow. He shook his head, then smiled. It turned out alright, though, even if she did find out she was pregnant the day before I shipped out. We made it through the backwoods. We'll make it through this. But who would have thought? Who?

Crackah Mick! Crackah Mick! Wake the fuck up! his buddy called out. We're on the move!

Mickey Moe shook himself and snapped to with a big country grin. Sorry, Wiry, he said. I'm comin'.

He knew the boys thought him slow-minded when he was only a dreamer. Most of 'em were Yankees or city boys who couldn't figure him out with a map. Seemed to him they had very peculiar ideas of what a child of the South might be. When he was polite in speech, they called him a pansy-assed born-again. When he emphasized no, no, he was a Jew and proud of it, sometimes they just laughed, half unbelieving. When it came to things like skinning a wild pig someone shot to improve on the cees, they gave him the task of butcher when he'd never touched game his whole life. No one noticed how he'd tuck his head into his chest to hide the retch he choked down when he split some critter's hide, or how putting his hands into steamy innards made his eyes tear up. They jumped to conclusions. They thought him a good old boy, hard to blood and guts by birthright. He took on that role with courage for the sake of the unit, but in his heart he knew he was never anything but a good old boy, more or less. He wondered if he ought to set them straight, if their misperceptions made him a danger to others. In wartime, a man has to be who he is, no bullshit, stand up or stand down. Lives depend on knowing what another man is going to do and how he's going to do it. It wasn't his fault, he figured, that these Yankee blacks and Midwest whites stuck him in a round good-old-boy hole he didn't fit, a square-peg Southern Jew in the middle of a war no one understood, least of all him.

On that day, as they marched single file up the side of the latest godforsaken hill, he saw a woman in distress stopped by the side of the trail they patrolled, her belly big with child and a broken wheel on the cart she pulled. He left his line and walked toward her calmly, patting the air with his palms to reassure her, smiling, nodding his head and showing his teeth so she wouldn't be afraid.

Mick! his buddies yelled. Get your Jew-ass back here!

He waved behind himself to let them know he didn't care what they yelled, he was going forward and sure, it didn't make much sense, but after his reveries he wanted more than anything to fix the woman's wheel as a way of making up to Laura Anne that she was pregnant and on her own. What did the hippies call it? Good karma.

So he smiled huge with plenty of teeth just as he hoped people back home smiled at Laura Anne, when suddenly the Cong mama pulled an automatic out from under a bundle of rags in her cart. That's where he thought it came from anyway, but Oh Lord, he really didn't know where she pulled it from, it was that quick. Showing him her own pointy little teeth to scare him, she grinned then screamed a yell as hard, as high as any rebel yell his ancestors marching to Vicksburg ever let rip and shot him. He didn't even know where, it happened so fast.

Then everything got real slow.

He sank to his knees, keeled over on his side, and his eyes, weighted with iron bars, started to shut against all the will he had left. Before everything went dark, he watched her body flail helplessly about with the impact of his buddies' payback fire. Pop-pop-pop-pop-pop. Her legs went in all directions, her arms pinwheeled, her torso seemed to have a thousand joints as it bent unnaturally to one side and then the other. Drops of blood fanned out around her in spirals of fine, long threads as she rose up in the air then fell down in the dirt. Like firecrackers, Mickey Moe thought, on the Fourth of July or New Year's.

Stay with me, Mick, someone far away said.

How can I? Mickey Moe tried to answer from the dark, I'm here, and you're not. But his mouth didn't work or if it did, he couldn't hear himself.

From where he was, he wondered where the baby went, where the Cong baby went, because last he saw of its mama flip-flopping on a current of gunshot, she didn't have a baby-lump anymore. Maybe it was never there at all. Maybe he just imagined it, because he was that fresh from conjuring Laura Anne. Or it could have been where the gun came from. He pondered the options awhile, there in the dark, in the nameless dark. Why was it so dark in the middle of the day anyway? he wanted to know. And then he decided he liked it, this quiet dark place, this warm, pulsing cave you could burrow into deeper and deeper without moving a muscle. He hadn't known such quiet for the longest time. Certainly not since he landed in Saigon. He might have stayed there forever, but the medic injected him with some kind of happy juice and the drug took instant effect. Light broke through dark, and the world came back to him. He was in it again but apart also, as if he was watching from somewhere else. His buddies barked orders at one another and moved around very fast, going nowhere except in circles around him. Then he noticed that he could not feel his legs, which were covered in bandages leaking blood. He wondered if the cause of his paralysis was the injection or if two dead limbs would be his ticket home. Somethin' extreme has happened to my extremities, he tried to tell the boys as a joke, but all that came out of his throat was a high-pitched, hysterical laugh like a crazy person's. Then he heard the whup-whup-whup of the helicopter arriving from somewhere far off to evacuate him. On hearing it, whup-whup-whup, faint like wings of a bird in a summer's still meadow, his head, wherever it was, sang Laura Anne, Laura Anne, Laura Anne. The sound of her name made him feel that she was there beside him, and because she was so near he spoke to her. No, darlin', he whispered. Do not worry. I am not going to die here. You are not at all my mama. And I am not my daddy. We are ourselves. We could never be those two.

II

Guilford, Mississippi, 1931–1943

BEATRICE DIANE SASSAPORT'S LIFE DID not turn out in the manner she anticipated. The privilege and promise of her youth encouraged her to have expectations. First off, Mickey Moe's mama was hands-down the beauty of the Sassaport family, and beauty is its own calling card, embossed in gold. Beadie's eyes were Tartar eyes, hazel and widely set, framed by a pair of arched eyebrows delicate as a Japanese brushstroke. Her face was oval-shaped, sweetly rounding at the chin as if the hand of God had cupped it in its formative stage. Her nose was straight, assertive but modest enough to allow her cheekbones and mouth to make more prominent statements. Such remarkable harmony was enhanced by a head of hair considered a marvel of shining black density too well behaved to frizz up in the heat. Her parents kept her out of the sun. Her skin was a rich amber and if six rays of sun got to her at the same time, her complexion went a shade darker than was prudent for a girl-child to sport in Guilford, Mississippi, at that time. From the cradle on, her family called her the Infanta as she looked a proper princess of Portugal, from whence her people had come to the South more than two hundred years before. She developed the figure and carriage for the evocation as she grew. Under the weight of constant praise, she could not help assuming a regal manner. The woman had airs. Etiquette was for her the very substance of civilized existence, what separated man from beast. If she experienced a situation for which none of the customary cues of proper behavior applied, she became so distressed, she invented her own with determined and startling creativity.

Opposites attract must have been among her more conventional wisdoms. Mickey Moe's daddy had been a short, stocky man, round and hard as a stew pot, with a peddler's rough hands and plodding feet. If taken one by one, his features were handsome enough, but they settled in a bundle at the center of a globular head and were framed by a pair of jug ears. His large button eyes were capped by thick red eyebrows of a northward slant, and between them emerged a thin, straight nose that flared at the nostrils as unexpectedly as a trumpet vine in an arctic plain. Beneath that was a dainty but impeccably shaped mouth. All of it together made his adult face a tableau of something so innocent, so childlike that whomever he met in the course of a day could not help but look at him and smile. This was not the worst luck. Given a lifetime of genial regard from strangers and intimates alike, the man developed a radiant good humor that the Sassaports decided must be the source of his wife's attraction to him.

When questioned on the matter, Beadie would demur. I believe he's a good man, she'd say, and he's entertainin' and he's kind, very kind, to me. One of the things she liked best about him was that he was respectful from the first, unlike other men who'd come to call. Even after his death, when all the world discovered Bernard Levy was a bounder, she revered his memory on that score.

Unfortunately, their daughters had not turned out like their celebrated mother, being more on the pleasant-looking side if you were kind about it. When they complained about their flaws, she'd tell them not to fret about themselves so. Be grateful, she'd say. Beauty is a curse. Men everywhere bother you, even the ones who seem so nice before they get you alone. They're all hands and their eyes violate you a thousand times an hour. Now your daddy kept his hands to himself while we courted and his eyes where they belonged—on mine. That went a long way with me.

What she didn't say, perhaps because it never really penetrated her consciousness, was that beautiful women are often the most self-critical, far worse than their pleasant-looking daughters. In secret, great beauties demonize every blemish. When such a woman appreciates a funny-looking man or an ugly man, the unworthy one is so astounded his affections can veer toward worship. That's a heady tonic for an insecure beauty. Bernard's respect, his near knightly devotion, most likely won her.

Or it could have been his money.

Bernard Levy, grandson of the founder of Levy Agricultural Supplies headquartered in Memphis, Tennessee, looked to have heaps of money when he first came to town, bags and bags of gold coin in weights sufficient to seduce every Israelite girl in Hinds County, including a half-educated belle socially crippled by her innumerable requirements and borderline skin tone. Bernard's money worked its seductive magic for his son's generation as well. Despite his family connections, Mickey Moe might never have been invited to the garden party where he met Laura Anne Needleman if his family had not been from the swell part of town. No matter that Daddy and his money were long gone or that his six-columned house peeled paint from every slat and sagged on its foundations into mud that had never dried out entirely since the flood, their address was old, important. The very best people lived on Mickey

Moe's street. It was a street so fine that when his daddy first moved in, everyone in the town whispered Bernard Levy must have made a deal with the devil to wind up there. At the very least, he must have bribed or blackmailed someone. Imagine that. A Jew on Orchard Street, they'd said, what do you all think he's got on whom? No one could accept there was that much honest money in pitchforks, feed bags, and plow blades in 1931. In those days, farmers around sold their produce and cotton at bargain basement rates or saw them rot. They bartered what was left over for essentials they couldn't grow or raise. They didn't buy equipment. They repaired what they had or went without and tilled the soil the way their grandfathers did, with their own two hands and the hands of all their women and children, using the sharpest imple-ments they could scavenge, or jerry rig, or steal. They furnished their own seed and their animals, if they could keep any, ate what nature left around for them to find. Yet Bernard Levy made money hand over fist at the family trade. Imagine that, they'd said the day he moved in, inventing unsavory explanations for how a Levy might accomplish such wealth off the souls of the poor.

Of course, the public solution Bernard Levy put forth to the puzzle of his resources lacked the colorful drama of pirated land and dispos-sessed widows the good Christian men of Guilford made up. When Beadie decided to ferret out the source of his wealth on their second date at the Rialto Cinema all the way over to Jackson, she chose phrases she thought would flatter him into candor.

You're such a young man, Mr. Levy, she said, to have accomplished so much in the material sense. Everyone in Guilford is impressed by your industry. I suppose you worked after school as a child and all the summers from dawn to dusk, spending more time learning the art of commerce than your ABCs.

Bernard laughed and leaned back so hard in his fourth-row orches-tra seat it cracked, startling their chaperone, Beadie's brother Ben, into spilling soda pop all over the aisle. He commenced to lie as easily as a rougher man might cough or belch. I'm very sorry to disabuse you of that charming notion, Miss Sassaport, but the source of my riches is more mundane. I had nothing my whole life, and then one day my granddaddy died.

Beadie did not respond with the amusement his riposte encouraged. That's terribly sad, she said, then favored him with a studied look of empathy, peeping up through her eyelashes and rounding her luminous almond eyes. She'd practiced the pose in the mirror ever since she'd seen Norma Shearer perform the same trick in *The Devil's Circus* five years earlier. Beadie did it better.

It took all the self-control the man possessed not to gasp. No, Miss Sassaport, he managed, elaborating the falsehood that would steer his family for two generations, it is not. Granddaddy was ninety-seven year old and hadn't known his given from his surname for six years. It was a blessing.

Four months later, Beadie and Bernard were united in matrimony. Between that happy day and the bombing of Pearl Harbor, Beadie refused to investigate the source of her husband's wealth any further. Her reason was rooted in conviction. Beadie believed a woman's job was to feather the nest, a man's to provide the feathers. As long as Bernard allowed her to acquire dazzling plumage for the neighbors and relations to see, she asked no questions.

Bernard Levy may have been a liar and a scoundrel, but he was a family man, devoted and true. He loved his wife to distraction and for all the worst reasons. He loved her not because she was kind or accomplished, although she had at least a half-portion of each, but because she was beautiful. He loved her not for the quality of her spirit but for her bloodlines, which were as blue as a Southern Jew could possess. He loved her for her ardent application of rules for living, which from his perspective amounted to the same thing as the highest level of refinement. He was ignorant of society. His upbringing had been entirely rude. In short, he loved her because she was everything he was not.

 For whatever reasons she chose him, shortly after the honeymoon in New Orleans, Beatrice Diane Sassaport Levy came to love her husband for the best reasons, although ultimately, each was exposed as a sham. She loved him because he appeared industrious, trustworthy, and educated. She loved him because he was of a family nearly as old as her own, one arrived in Charleston a mere two generations after the Sassaport ancestors disembarked at the port of Savannah. Those were brief generations, too. People often lived lives fleet as a June bug's in that time, there was so much malaria, yellow fever, and pneumonia going around. Bernard's pedigree was particularly significant to her. She was enchanted by the notion that the two of them, she and Bernard, were a pairing of eagles. Their children, when they came along, would be ranked among the oldest families in society, a democratic America's equivalent of royalty. Accordingly, Ladies Sophie, Eudora Jean, and Rachel Marie, not to mention Lord Mickey Moe, were the joys of her young life, representative of an achievement not even her illustrious ancestors had achieved. Their offspring made her better than her betters, you might say, better than those Old World peddlers and shopkeepers, those family icons of everything admirable in life for the way in which they'd triumphed over the meanness of history, putting down roots in a hard New World, and blossoming. Great as they were, Beadie thought, those peasants never approached the elegance of the Levys of Guilford, Mississippi. The old ones never imagined this! she sighed to herself as she wandered the cool, vast halls of the big house on Orchard Street just before solid, satisfied sleep. None foresaw these linens, these fruit trees, these porticos and piazzas, these nods from the gentile neighbors, hats tipped and heads bowed!

 Bernard and Beadie were happy in their sumptuous nest. They were passionate. They were always laughing in the beginning. There were ripples of discontent, but these were minor, the breath of angels against still water. For instance, Beadie found it necessary to train Bernard in various aspects of social discourse. On one occasion in which she found him deficient, she straightened her back and spoke as sternly as she dared. Didn't your mama teach you anything at all, sugar? She sighed, shook her head just enough to disturb her marcelled curls, a gesture she knew made his palms sweat. I've been told that you left only one calling card at the Parkers' house when you know there are three adult women there. How could you insult them so? It's one per female, darlin', one per female! Bernard's round face blanched as white as the moon in full. Beadie's heart soared, thinking, how he regrets my displeasure! Her sweet chin, already aloft with pride, rose a little higher.

How could she know his discomfort was not from remorse at annoying his wife or riling the sensibilities of the Parkers but from fear of being found out? He was not one of those liars convinced of his own falsehoods. He knew what he was: a thief of hearts, a poseur, common as dirt. He knew his bliss was founded on an accident of bravery committed years before he knew Guilford, Mississippi, or Beadie Sassaport existed, an act committed amid enormous tragedy. He felt he could never repeat that act even if—God forbid—a similar occasion arose. What he had done had been a product of the moment, of the dark clouds, the thick air, the screams of the river that terrible day. His deeds that day were an act of nature much like an earthquake or a tornado, both of which occur violently without warning. His actions happened outside himself. He was as much a stunned observer of his own behavior that day as those who'd stared down the levee to gape at him. A wildness had swept through his blood, and it propelled his hands, his legs, the words out of his throat into an utterly alien place, exotic with terror. When he pondered that surge of ferocity, and he pondered it often, he determined that this was the way prophets of old felt. And since he never quite stopped feeling the awful rush of that moment, he absolved himself of his sins. A divine instrument is entitled to material compensation, he figured, or should be, and he overcame his fear and returned to the lie that was his miraculous life.

Like all the best lies, Bernard Levy's life was entirely plausible. Every weekday morning, he rose at seven and ate what his wife had their cook fix up for him. He left for his office by eight o'clock like every other vigorous man on his street. Upon arrival, he exchanged pleasantries with his secretary and entered his inner sanctum. There, he read the newspaper, telephoned his cronies, and crafted spurious correspondence for his secretary to type up and mail to out of state drops maintained by the scant handful of associates who knew his true identity. At least once a week, he ordered a transfer of funds from a secret place to his marital accounts at Sassaport Savings and Loan. The orders, written in a code his secretary could not decipher, requested things like: "Kindly ship posthaste seventy-two pounds of chicken feed, 20 percent protein, 32 percent filler, by rail to Fine Fellow Plantation, Greenville, as a sampler." By choosing secretaries more interested in reading *True Confessions* and *Photoplay* than raising livestock, he was secure none would question his curious percentages and arcane weights. Lunchtimes, he went home for a big meal of his favorite delicacies. For an hour or so, he played with his daughters and admired his infant son. Afterward, he often took a nap on the couch in his office, the door closed to avoid accusations of indolence. Other than that, his days were passed in schmoozing. He was a champion schmoozer. He could spin tales with the best of them and was an attentive audience as well. When that comical face of his went serious, he looked kindly and blameless as a picture book saint prompting people to tell him their troubles and ask his advice. And he'd give it, he'd give it gladly with a flair he'd learned from his daddy while perched upon that wastrel's knee.

Son, Bernard's daddy told him when he was no bigger than a hound dog pup, there ain't nothing a sufferin' man likes better than havin' a hope or two. Whenever you're givin' a brother comfort after hearin' the sad tale of his wretchedness, be sure to tell him somethin' that'll make him think everything's gonna be alright, even if you can see plain as day he's hurtlin' down a fast road straight through the gapin' gates of hell. Tell him his woman loves him unto death no matter how round her heels are and that little bump the doc cut outta his baby's face ain't nothin' more'n a boil. Tell him with a straight eye and back it up with a story you have on the best authority is God's own truth. Foreign stories work the best. I've found most people will believe anythin' you tell 'em if the principals hail from France or Brazil.

It was the most useful thing the man ever said to him. There might have been more, but Bernard's daddy disappeared downriver before the boy was six years old. Bernard did not remember much of him. He often thought the only way he'd managed to hold on to that particular memory was that the man's knee was exceedingly bony and hurt to perch upon. Pain wipes out memory, he told Beadie when she'd survived her first labor and wondered aloud how it was women ever decide to get pregnant twice. Then again, he went on, sometimes pain etches memory deep in the mind. But there's no middle. Why, I recall a man I met once. Good-lookin' fellah. Tall and black-haired with a handsome mustache just like John Barrymore's. Now he was from . . .

São Paulo? Beadie asked giving him that lips pursing, eyelash fluttering upturned look that never failed to slay him and was particularly fetching when beamed from her hospital bed with her hair framed in a satin headband the same color pink as her quilted bed jacket and tied up in a floppy bow at the crown of her head.

He warmed from his toes to his earlobes and kissed her cheeks one after the other.

No, not São Paulo.

Her voice went soft and low.

Marseille?

His went to a whisper.

No.

Then he kissed her again until he quite forgot his story of the John Barrymore look-alike. He kept on kissing her until the nurse came in carrying little Sophie who was squawking up a storm. Sophie. Born with a full head of hair. The nurses called her the mad Prussian because she hollered so much underneath that tall furry helmet. Pretty as her mama only with her daddy's chin, which is to say no more chin than a dimpled dollop just beneath her lower lip followed by a slope of skin from there to her throat, an aspect that undermined the overall effect considerably. The next two girls were more fortunate, as they had chins at least and their mama's eyes, but neither was graced with her aristocratic nose and instead sported bulbous ones. Only the boy, the long-awaited son, Mickey Moe, had features that mirrored his mama's physical harmony and his daddy's fair and rosy complexion rather than her darkish one. Once she had him, Beadie announced to her husband, Well, there he is, darlin'. Perfection. I see no need to attempt to surpass this achievement. Do you mind much if I pack it in, so to speak?

Four children was a respectable number in those days, earnest without being excessive. None of them were outright stupid, although Eudora Jean came close, and all of them were obedient and temperate. Since he was beginning to be concerned with the way childbearing had afflicted his wife's beloved body, which belonged to him, after all, and not those little suckers, Bernard Levy supported her decision.

At a family wedding held a few months after, when a handful of ladies burdened by the heat and the weight of their sixth or seventh pregnancies shared complaints, Beadie, out of the blue, bragged to the assembled that she possessed the most modern, the most ethically advanced of men. If you all would like, she said, I could arrange for him to drop a word of procreative wisdom into your husbands' ears.

He surely can explain to them that there is no reason in 1937, no reason at all, for a woman to have more children than she wants.

Although she intended to be helpful, Beadie's suggestion prompted a tidal wave of resentment in the hearts of her sisters and cousins. How dare she say we don't want our babies! they complained behind her back. What manner of unnatural relations do you all think those two are havin' anyway? They accused her of being more interested in amassing additions to her silver service than sweet Jewish souls brought forth to honor the Lord.

Suffice it to say, when Beadie's downfall eventually occurred, there were none but false sympathies from her kin. Pride goeth before, they whispered at the dedication of Bernard's gravestone, a marker one grade up from a pauper's. Happy to console the poor widow, their faces puckered in empathy while their hearts nourished a secret flicker of delight.

Before the war, they were more than eager to attend Beadie's family parties, especially the picnics on the south lawn of the big house on Orchard Street. They knew the repast would be elegant. The out of doors didn't cramp Beadie's style. She'd serve soup to nuts and everything just so. She'd hire entertainment, too, puppet shows for the little ones and, depending on the solemnity of the occasion, chamber quartets from Jackson or jazzmen from downriver for the adults. If the latter, the young people would dance, getting their dancing shoes grass-stained. Things could get quite humorous when the ground was a bit damp. Nobody cared. Those were high times. Everyone else in the family felt the pinch of the Depression. For some, it was a downright punch. But one could always expect a grand soiree at Beadie's, a throwback to the good old days when all of them were swells and felt confident about the future. There'd be champagne smuggled in from God knew where, fish with two sauces, and cuts of beef some hadn't seen since '29.

Something strange happened at one of these parties, an affair celebrating Rachel Marie's sixth birthday. Beadie hired a traveling company to put on a play recalling the new smash-hit film *The Wizard of
Oz*. The clan sat on folding chairs under a big tent watching the song
and dance of a man who could kick up his legs almost as high as Ray
Bolger himself. He flapped wet noodle arms and sauntered down a yellow brick road made of cardboard, which cut a swath through Beadie's
vegetable garden. Suddenly, just as he disappeared into the cornrows,
the man shrieked. A moment later, he slowly backed out. His expression was bug-eyed, afraid. Later on, he claimed he was merely embarrassed at being startled out of character.

Every soul in the audience gasped in excitement. They craned their
necks and straightened in their seats, especially the children up front,
expecting an appearance of the wicked witch or one of her minions.
The film had not yet opened in Jackson—everything Beadie did at
these parties was up to the minute—and no one was exactly sure what
came next.

Out of the cornrows emerged the tallest Negro any of them had
ever seen, with shoulders so broad they looked fit to carry Atlas's burden. None could interpret the interloper's gender. There was a distinct
femininity about the figure, its movement, swaying and silent, but the
size and shape was distinctly masculine. Taking center stage, the creature planted two feet in a wide stance, studied them with eyes like fire
bores seeking the truth, and bold as brass spoke in a flat voice that
further confused the matter of gender.

Where is the master of this house? I have business with him.

The world went silent. The uninvited's appearance had thrown
Beadie into a near swoon. After making sure his wife was safely seated,
Bernard Levy stepped forward. Here I am, he said. If you'll kindly
respect the natal day of my baby girl, we might step aside to discuss
whatever business you came to effect. The intruder nodded and fol-

lowed him to the bower and trellis at the east side of the main house where the two spoke intensely for some time, attracting more attention than the garden players. They waved their arms in the air, turned from each other, whipped back. They slapped their foreheads or put palms to their cheeks as if registering both shock and sorrow. An apparent agreement was reached. Bernard raised a hand and placed it on the giant's shoulder—he looked to stand on his toes to do so—then gave the stranger a strong, solemn shake of the head. Subsequently, the visitor walked, lead-footed as a zombie, to the front of the house, turned down the road without so much as a backward glance, and was never seen again as far as anyone knew.

Times being what they were, none of the Sassaports celebrating Rachel Marie that day noticed the reactions of the servants of the house to these events. Those attached to the house and the day labor were all on the back porch by the kitchen, serving drinks, enjoying the play. When the stranger appeared, they froze, drop-jawed. Half raised their eyes to heaven and prayed to Jesus. The other half poked one another in the ribs with their elbows, sharing a knowledge none of the white folks could possibly possess. Except Bernard.

Truth be told, help left Miss Beadie's employ with some regularity. It was difficult to keep up with her rigid formulations of behavior. Folks worked for six months or so and quit, often directly after one of her demanding parties. No one was surprised, it was not even worth comment, when the day after Rachel Marie's birthday, the cook and Bernard's right-hand man packed their bags before breakfast and left by noon. Everyone assumed they'd been fired. After all, someone had to pay for the humiliation the stranger had caused Beadie, and it was not unusual in that time for blame to be assigned collectively by race. Nor did it seem strange that those who replaced the banished arrived by nightfall. They were Sara Kate, a winsome young woman the color of milk chocolate, and her husband, Roland, a big, strong man, midnight black, with hands the size of hams. What was remarkable was that these two lasted decades in the Levy household. Not even the war or Bernard's death pried them from it. And not a single soul put two and two together to come up with the fact that their employment had something to do with the oddity in the cornrows. That is, not until Mickey Moe and Laura Anne Needleman put their loving heads together.

Despite the mystery and disruption of her household, Beadie gave the world a happy face the next day as part of a determined campaign to make everyone forget it. Those who plied her on the subject received a dismissive response. Oh, my husband's into all kind of business, she said, who can keep up with it all? Meeting the Chinese wall of her dazzling smile, the curious stopped asking questions after a time and life went back to normal. Bernard had made his explanations, his wife kept them to herself. From the outside looking in, Beadie was content, all her early expectations were fulfilled. Then the war ripped everything away. Just after the Japanese attacked in 1941, Bernard enlisted along with everyone else they knew who was neither too old nor unfit for duty. He left a padlocked strongbox stuffed with hard cash in his wife's care. In time, the box went empty, prompting Beadie to tap into her husband's bank accounts. She discovered there was far less there than she thought, and no fresh moneys came in apart from his combat pay, a matter of much confusion to all she approached about it. There are surely more accounts! she insisted in despair to her cousin Abie, the weak-eyed, flat-footed vice president of his uncle's bank. In a voice of command Isabella herself might admire, she issued fiats. Search for them! she directed. And do not speak to me until you have found them!

Lord, how she'd huffed out of Sassaport Savings and Loan that day. Her heels looked to sprout puffs of steam as she took her leave with head high and eyes narrowed to angry slits, her mouth pressed and pulsing. She and Abie did not speak for three years, until VJ Day, when the woman lost herself in the spirit of release that seized them all. Up

to then, it was silent Beadie, fuming Beadie, bereft Beadie, uncomprehending, miserable Beadie, alone with three little girls and a young
son, cruelly forced to deal with the rude practicalities of life.

The first casualty of her war was her beauty. She lost weight and
the luster of her hair. She didn't sleep much. Dark, puffy flesh circled
her eyes, while the corners of her mouth turned down. Her charm was
next. Dismayed and confused as she was, she was not an optimistic
citizen but spoke gloomily, even on days when the news was good and
the president promised victory. I do not expect to see my husband again
in warm flesh, she said to whoever would listen. I have seen his end
before me as clearly as I can see Stars and Bars flappin' there against
the flagpole at the post office. When the war news was bad and not
even FDR could gloss it, she advised the family to study German along
with enough evangelical phraseology to mask their origins. As a result,
most of her people gave her a wide berth. Who needed a pessimist during wartime?

Her masculine cousins deferred from military service or too young
for it avoided her company completely. This was unfortunate since
what she wanted, what she needed was a man, even a man manqué,
someone, anyone, who would take over the functions of the male in a
world that had not raised her for manly tasks yet thrust them upon her.
With no one else to depend on, she zeroed in on Mickey Moe, all of
four and a half years old at the time of his daddy's departure overseas,
calling him "my little man" and "man of the house," dressing him in
long pants straight away even in summer. Since everyone knew manly
men loved the outdoors and suffered inside, whenever he tripped and
tore holes in the knees, she sewed on patches in a hurry, popped a salt
pill in his mouth, slapped his rump, and sent her little man back out
into the sun to sweat.

As a result, Mickey Moe assumed a good old boy's rites and rituals
long before he had the tooth for it. He never once questioned whether

the role suited him. Since there were no able-bodied men around him for a time and since the ones returned from war were each and every one of them scarred in some manner, visible and not, he was left to fashion his own code of manly behavior from whatever instincts he could muster or from observing old or infirm white folk and the Negroes around him, too.

From Uncle Benny Lee, who suffered from asthma and the catarrh, he learned to cough and spit and do it only outdoors or in the proper receptacle indoors if such might be had. From Mr. Banning, the bitter old man from across the street, who dragged behind him the leg he'd mangled in the first great war, muttering a blue streak with every step, he learned how and when to properly swear. Roland, Mama's housekeeper's husband, a huge burly man black as coal and in the prime of life, was denied military service when he'd attempted to enlist, because the draft board determined that the womenfolk needed some brawn back home with all the men gone and that Roland, unlike some of them uppity bucks, was a safe bet, meek as a mouse due to being tongue lashed half to death by his wife. From Roland, Mickey Moe learned to hold his hat at waist level and study the ground to make himself look humble and small when the occasion demanded, no matter how he felt inside. Since Mama's car did not get any younger during the war, nor her hot water heater, Roland taught him about motors and how things mechanical worked. Many was the afternoon Mickey Moe trudged along behind him from basement to driveway, carrying his toolbox. He learned the function of the instruments within when Roland asked politely, Master Mickey Moe, might you please hand me the Phillips screwdriver?

Another black man he knew, old Bald Horace, sold vegetables and dairy products door-to-door from a hand-pulled cart. Bald Horace taught the boy all about livestock and when to pick peppers depending on what color you wanted them. He taught him how good Mississippi dirt smelled of a damp morning, how fine the rising sun felt on the back of the neck. All these skills were topped off with his mama's instruction in manners, making him a good old boy, more or less, by the time he was nine, except he couldn't shoot worth a dang and he didn't know what bravado was nor how to imitate it. He wasn't stoic at all, in fact, he was something of a secret crybaby. All those things had to come to him later on at a hard and high price. Until they did, he made enough of a show to fool most of the people he met.

That Mickey Moe, people said. Poor mite. No daddy, a half-crazed, sour old mama. Left on his own to grow like a weed in the wind. But it's a good wind from a proper direction, Lord knows. Look at him. He could pass for any Christian boy you care to name. A very good wind, indeed.

His daddy would have been proud.

III

Guilford, Mississippi, 1944–1952

EVEN AS A CHILD, MICKEY Moe Levy didn't remember much of his father and what there was was second-hand, formed by the stories of those who consoled him after the man was lost to time. There were photographs of a short, moon-faced man with round, innocent eyes, an improbable nose, prominent ears, and a fringe of ginger hair beating a fast retreat from the center of a shiny head. When he studied them, Mickey Moe often wondered what his daddy found so funny about cameras, since in nearly every shot his head was thrown back and his mouth was posed as if he were Santa Claus letting go with a string of ho-ho-ho's. Once, when he was seven, he tried to spend the whole day tossing his head with his mouth shaped in an O to find out what it felt like to be Bernard Levy, happy all the time, but Mama told him to cut it out at two in the afternoon as he was giving her the heebie-jeebies. He quit without achieving insight.

Among the stories he heard, one he felt the need to corroborate by the time he was twelve and doubts, great and small, had set in, was that his daddy was immeasurably rich, a Midas of sorts, a man with a golden touch when it came to all types of business, one to whom even the princes of the Sassaport family came for advice and support if difficult, contentious decisions were to be made. When the boy was old enough, he questioned this reputation, because Mama and his sisters cried poor day in and day out. One of his peers suggested to him that chests of gold might be buried in his backyard or greenbacks stuffed in the walls. Although he could not make a proper search without the women screaming holy heck, he dug enough holes in the garden to appall Bald Horace and poked sections of wallpaper in the upstairs rooms with a three-tined fork. He hadn't the nerve to deface the front parlor where the women received or the dining room where they sometimes entertained, deciding that if his daddy was sane, neither had he. He poked through enough flocked velvet to conclude there must have been an off-site location where the family fortune was stashed.

During his adolescence, he was preoccupied with determining likely locales. In summer, he spent as much time as his chores and paper route would allow parked in a hard chair at the public library. He figured if he studied topographical charts of all the undeveloped land between Guilford and Memphis along with maps of the populated and cultivated areas and the twists and turns of the great river as well, he might find an echo of a clue mentioned in his daddy's letters and personal papers that Mama kept tucked away in a cardboard box in her closet, the ones he sometimes read by stealth when she left the house. Why shouldn't there be congruities between the maps and the paperwork, places where landmarks were mentioned, Mississippi tributaries admired or feared, towns and roads visited and traveled over and over? He came up with an intuitive list grounded in the notion that blood must ever call to blood. If a particular spot of high ground near the side of a particular country road struck him as a likely spot to bury a strong box, then surely it was his own daddy's ghost who'd whispered such directly into his heart. Next, he traced maps onto tissue paper and transposed in a prioritized color code selected locales he planned to investigate as soon as he was old enough to travel on his own.

One fall, he discovered how much he loved girls. Few gave him so much as the time of day. He made a new study to determine which boys girls gave not only the time of day but their hearts and hands as well, concluding that sportsmen seemed to be granted the best of what a young girl might offer and still go to Sunday school with her head up. Lickety-split, he joined every team he could think of in junior high. In the course of a single year, he was a wrestler, a sprinter, a right fielder, and a tight end. As he'd hoped, his feminine classmates flocked to him, every kind of girl he could desire: short ones, tall ones, fleshy ones, skinny ones, girls with breasts already, girls with wide, luscious mouths, girls with hips that moved in a way that stole his breath, Jewish girls, of course, but Christian girls, too. When he went into the town, he noticed that Negro girls gave him shy, curious glances. By this he knew, as Uncle Dr. Howard would say, he had arrived.

The shameful secret was he didn't really like sports. He'd rather sit in the library pouring over maps or work in the garden or tag along after Bald Horace while he tended that ornery tribe of goats he kept in a rented patch of rocks and grass next to the village where the Negro folk lived. He much preferred the quiet study of river currents, the cheering sight of a tiny green shoot peeping out of the dirt to the crunch of bones on the thirty-yard line or the way his back hurt when he spent hours hunched over slapping a fist into his mitt, endlessly waiting for a ball to fly his way. He especially preferred pastoral occupations to the sharp jab of Bird Dog MacKenzie's evil-minded elbow in his privates when they twisted on the mat. Since Mama always said it was a man's job to make sacrifices for the women in his life, he considered his involvement with sports as well as the odd jobs he performed after school to help out at home his primary forfeitures in service to the fair gender.

All of this had the effect of basting an adult patina over the whole of Mickey Moe's boyish being. Weaker and younger boys looked to him for advice and protection. No Southern lad can resist the glamour of the heroic. He rose to the occasion every time.

Mickey Moe, a cousin or classmate might ask, I got a cranky chain on my bike ruinin' my every effort to beat my brother home after school. You help me straighten it out?

He'd spit and roll up his sleeves and crouch over the bike getting his clothes and hands smeared with grease as he carefully removed the chain, laid it flat on the ground to correct any kinks, and with any luck got it back on again. Such was his reputation among his peers, if he could not fix something, it was declared dead broke and tossed away. If the stubborn object was a bicycle, it might resurrect, reappearing on the streets under the conspicuous bottom of a Negro boy who'd scavenged and coaxed it back to use. Out of respect for Mickey Moe, the original owner would refuse to recognize it, at least in public.

Such deference was a burden to him. He felt it based on his participation in sports he did not like and a mechanical competence he only half possessed. He often felt a fraud, and yet he performed his role of good old boy in training with increasing prowess throughout his high school years, because it was what Mama wanted and what the boys at school wanted and heck, what the girls at school wanted, too. Sometimes, he needed to blow off steam when the frustration of what he was, which he could not define, and what he must be got too hot under his skin or when he was generally confused and dismayed by the people around him. On those occasions, he went to the village.

The first time he went to the village without being taken there by Bald Horace on one learning experience or another was toward the middle of the ninth grade. Ricky Baker, who should have known better, asked Mickey Moe to go with him and his boys over to Sassaport Hardware to help him pick out a new pocketknife. His old one had rusted up tight. It was his own fault. Ricky kept his knife dangling from his belt loop whether a heavy rain came upon him or not. He approached Mickey Moe for help because they were classmates and friends more or less. They shared a sandwich at recess or a game of catch once in a while. There weren't an abundance of happy times between them, but neither had there ever been any bad blood. Ricky Baker also knew Mickey Moe was a relation of the Sassaport family, and he figured maybe old man Sassaport would take down the box of long, flat blades reserved for older boys and grown men from its high shelf if he was in the company of kin. On the Thursday in question, after school was out but long before supper, Ricky Baker and four of his boys biked over to Mickey Moe's to ask what he thought of that old knife of his, aiming to rope him into a trip to the hardware store.

Well, lemme see that sticker of yours, Mickey Moe said. Maybe it's not beyond repair. Ricky showed it to him, making a joke of the struggle it took to get the knife open to demonstrate its ruination.

Mickey Moe ran his thumb lightly against the cutting edge. Now that ain't bad at all, Ricky, he said. We can fix that up with a little sandpaper and oil, maybe sharpen it up a bit on a stone or it might just need some work on a strap.

But Ricky had his heart set on the new one he'd dreamt up, one with a mother-of-pearl handle that would make him feel as dashing as if he sported a Derringer out of Zane Grey. He bristled at the idea that he would not get what he wanted. Get out, Mick. It's ruint, he said, his head down and his cheeks hot and red.

Mickey Moe, still intently studying the knife, did not notice the boy's reaction. No it ain't, Ricky, no it ain't. We can fix it up. Why spend good money on somethin' you don't need?

To the child of a widow forced by fate into parsimonious habit, this was the bottom line. "Waste not, want not" was the lullaby of his childhood, the words that tucked him in at night. He had no idea how adult this made him sound, how utterly foreign to a boy with his mouth watering for something that such mature consideration could snatch away from him fast and furious. So Ricky, red as rust, sputtering frustration said, Ah, you cheap kike. My daddy's right. You all alike. Why'd I think you'd understand? And he took off with his pals, all of them yelling, Kike! Kike! Kike! laughing uproariously as they steered their bikes in the general direction of Sassaport Hardware, as if the slur had stuck in their throats all their lives and letting it loose was a relief, a celebration, a cause for joy.

Mickey Moe stood there, in the middle of his mama's front yard, pop-eyed, stunned stock-still that boys he thought his friends had just gleefully insulted him over a rusted-up hunk of cold metal. He'd been lucky in the past, he knew that, the Jew haters had pretty much left him alone, no doubt because of his swanky address. Mama always said it didn't matter what people said behind your back as long as they were civil in public, but now things were squirming out there in the open where no one would ever be able to ignore them again. He felt a spike of anger stab him at the heart then a deep sadness, deeper than he knew possible, and he bolted like a startled colt, ran wild to nowhere to escape weeping in the street for all to see. He had no conscious destination until he stopped outside Bald Horace's rented patch of crabby ground next to the village, crept under its post-and-wire fence, and lay down on some rocks. Panting with exhaustion, the shock, anger, and hurt beat out of him for at least as long as it took to catch his breath, he watched the goats.

There were seven of them. A year or two before, he'd given them the names of Snow White's seven dwarfs. When he told Bald Horace, the man laughed because the goats were does and their kids. He borrowed a buck when he wanted to breed. It struck him as quite comical for his high-steppin' little ladies to have names like Grumpy, Sleepy, Doc, and Dopey although Sneezy and Happy fit, he had to admit that, and maybe Bashful, which was what Mickey Moe named the runt of the crew.

That Thursday, Grumpy lived up to her name. For no reason Mickey Moe could discern, she ran up to poor Dopey and butted her in her side so hard she nearly fell over. Staggering off, Dopey tried to keep her distance, hiding behind the stump of the herd's climbing tree. Grumpy saw where she hid herself and signaled with a flap of lip, a twitch of ear to Sleepy, Sneezy, and Doc. In a bunch, as if they'd been planning it all afternoon, the four of them charged poor old Dopey. They rammed her into the fence, and she bounced off bloody where wire cut into her. Mickey Moe could not endure the look in her pained little goat's eyes. Her predicament drove all thoughts of his own problems aside. Jumping into the fray, he rushed to stand between Dopey and the others to save her, poor thing, and they butted him just as they'd butted her, as if he were not human, supreme over them, the almighty author of food and shelter and milking, as if he were just another goat who did not know his place, a foolish goat protecting the eldest of the herd, the one who required driving out as nature herself commanded. If Bald Horace had not chanced to arrive just then and rescue him, they might have done him serious damage. As it was, he was scraped bloody. When Mickey Moe tried to walk, he limped, so Bald Horace took him home to clean him up. He made him sit in the three-wheeled cart he pushed with old Dopey tethered to a handle, skittering along behind them. Can't leave her with those bullies no more, he explained. I'll have to leave her in the yard no matter what Aurora Mae has to say.

Mickey Moe wondered who Aurora Mae was. He figured she must be Bald Horace's wife. It struck him then that he'd never heard anything about Bald Horace's family, which was curious, because Mama knew all the Negro folk around for three generations. She gossiped with Sara

Kate about their goings on and spoke of their dead, too. Surely this
Aurora Mae would have been mentioned some time or other. He would
have asked Bald Horace directly who she was, but the man was preoccupied instructing him in the habits of goats and the proper manner of
managing them without getting stuck in the middle of a losing battle.
It felt rude to interrupt. Mickey Moe only followed some of it anyway.
He hurt too much to pay considerable attention as his ride was hardly
smooth and each bump in the dirt road sent fresh jolts of pain through
his hip and into his ribs, which, he suspected, were cracked.

When they got to Bald Horace's home, a tar-paper shack not much
bigger than Mickey Moe's bedroom in the big house, there was no
Aurora Mae to be seen or heard. After checking Dopey's wounds and
determining they could wait, Bald Horace took the boy in, rolled his
pants up, and washed his cuts with warm water heated on the stove
and mixed with Epsom salts. Next, he bandaged him with rags from
a wicker basket that sat next to the stove as if waiting for that very
purpose. All the while, Bald Horace talked nonstop in words that only
meant something important later on.

You see, son, you can't give them goats the chance to gang up on
you, which they surely will if you let 'em. And it ain't always the smart-
est thing to get in there and think you can best a whole herd. You gotta
bribe 'em. Sometimes you gotta outthink 'em, because, let's face it, they
may be smart, but they ain't as smart as people, no, no, no, not by a
long shot. You might not have noticed today, but I had feed ready for
them critters, and that's the only reason, I swear, the only reason on
God's good earth they left you alone long enough for me to dump it
and get in there and take you and Dopey out unmolested. You under-
standin' me?

I think so.

Bald Horace shook his head from side to side while he tied a bandage in a snug knot just under Mickey Moe's knee. He was thinking

his own thoughts. He came to a decision that had little to do with the goats and everything to do with life as he knew it. He decided to impart some wisdom to this poor, fatherless white child, who obviously, if he'd chosen of his own free will to spend time with a mess of hardscrabble goats on a fine April afternoon, was in need of guidance.

Listen to me, son. Listen to me good. I knew your daddy. I knew him well. And this is somethin' I know he'd tell you if he could.

The boy's head jerked up. Daddy had been invoked. He must take heed.

Confrontin' somethin' head-on isn't always the best way. Sometimes you need to run around things to fool 'em, to distract 'em. You get what I'm sayin'?

Mickey Moe considered his experience that afternoon on the street in front of his house. It was an opening salvo, he knew that much. There would be more torment from Ricky Baker and his boys, if only to justify their prior cruelty. And miracle of miracles, here was his dear, dead daddy speaking through Bald Horace in order to tell him how to handle the situation. He shook his head with all the grown-up gravitas he possessed.

Yessir, he said, aware his mama would be appalled if she heard him address the man with an honorific reserved for white men. But Bald Horace had just rescued him from a brute tribe, patched him up, and given him a great and powerful gift to boot. The boy thought he deserved the respect due a white man. Yessir, he repeated for emphasis, Yessir, I do.

Bald Horace smiled wide enough for Mickey Moe to count the spaces in his teeth.

Well alright, then. Alright.

They nearly embraced, so powerful was their moment of man-to-man intimacy achieved amid an abandonment of class and race and age when another entered the house in a bustle of sound and fragrance. Mickey

Moe looked away from Bald Horace's melting eyes toward the front door and beheld for the first time the woman known as Aurora Mae.

Aurora Mae was, without a doubt, the most imposing, blackest woman Mickey Moe had ever seen, and that covered quite a lot of human territory. When she entered the room, she had to stoop a little to make it through the door. She carried half a dozen grocery bags, and once she was inside, she seemed to fill the place up. Her head near brushed the ceiling. It would take arms twice the length of his own—or Bald Horace's for that matter, as he was a spindly type, shrunken with age and hardship, more on a child's scale of being—to hug her all the way around. Her chest could feed nations, her nostrils suck up all the sweet air of a spring day, and her deep brown eyes with their brilliant flecks of yellow reminded him of the great river itself and the way golden stones glittered up from its bottom in places near the shore. Every inch of her was doused in Sassaport Five and Ten's violet toilet water, a scent his second sister favored. He'd only got such a strong dose of it up his nose once before, the time he'd knocked over a bottle she'd left on the edge of the bathroom sink and the contents entire spilled out.

The woman spoke. Could that be young Mickey Moe Levy I see there settin' at our table? she asked through a wide, curious smile as she bent over to greet Bald Horace with a kiss on the top of his smooth head. Her voice was deep as a man's but soft, caressing.

That would be him, darlin'.

Bald Horace filled her in on the details of finding Mickey Moe in the goat pen.

My, my, she said. And now it's gettin' on to suppertime. I better drive the boy home before his people send folks out lookin'.

Bald Horace agreed. Relieving her of the groceries, he told her he'd put up the peas and grits while she was gone.

Just don't touch my chicken parts, she said. I've got some clever ideas for them tonight.

Throughout all this, Mickey Moe sat mute as a stone and remained so until he was installed in Aurora Mae's Buick sedan, a sparkling boat of a car the color of old money. He was surprised a Negro woman drove such a remarkable vehicle. He huddled against the door of the passenger side, because she scared him just a little. A minute later, curiosity conquered fear. He ventured to speak.

Is this car your very own? he asked. Or does it belong to someone you work for?

Aurora Mae chuckled in her odd baritone.

Oh no, son. It's mine. All mine. And I work for myself, too. No boss over me, don't you know. None at all.

He burned to ask her what she meant, but her tone of voice shut him up quick. As far as he knew, all Negroes in those days in that part of the world had a boss. A boss or a landlord who owned the farm they worked. They rode in silence to the end of his street where Aurora Mae stopped.

You need to walk the rest of the way, boy. You can manage that, can't you? You ain't too mangled up?

Mickey Moe shook his head and exited the car.

I don't mean to be rude, she continued through an open window. But your mama doesn't exactly like me, and it might be best to keep knowledge of our acquaintance from her. If you don't mind. You owe Bald Horace that much, don't you? For lookin' out for you?

Mickey Moe screwed up his face in consternation. He'd never kept anything from his mama before. Nothing important.

Aurora Mae smiled her big, toothy grin.

You look just like your daddy that way. My, but that man knew how to mark a child.

The boy's chin dropped, as much for the mere mention of his daddy from out of that particular mouth as for the stupefying assessment that he favored him.

You knew my daddy, too?

I knew him better than anybody. Alive or dead.

Then quick as that, Aurora Mae rolled up her window, executed a perfect three-point turn in the middle of Orchard Street, and peeled off down the road back toward the village in a cloud of orange dust.

Knew him better than anybody. Alive or dead. The way she'd said it, the way she left so sudden directly afterward, informed Mickey Moe that he'd best not ask anyone what she meant, at least any white person of his ken whether within his family or without. He decided sure as heck right then and there that he'd seek Aurora Mae out again, at the earliest opportunity, and ask her exactly what she'd meant.

Unfortunately, his decision was as ephemeral as any other an adolescent makes. Within the next two days, he asked Sara Kate, Roland, and Bald Horace pointed questions about his daddy's relations with Aurora Mae. Each of them gave him a blank look and changed the subject. On repeated queries, they pretended not to hear. When he insisted, Bald Horace got up in his face. Son, I'd like to help you, but I don't know much. Aurora Mae comes and goes on the wings of birds. Even when she's here, she keeps her business to herself. On the third day, Cora Gifford gave him his first kiss and parted her lips when she did. The focus of his thoughts changed so radically that Aurora Mae took up residence in the deepest chambers of his consciousness for nearly a dozen years, until circumstances demanded that she burst forth with all the glorious might of Athena when she charged newborn from out the skull of Zeus.

IV

Greenville, Mississippi, 1962

LAURA ANNE LOVED HER DADDY. She was a good girl, had been all her life. She was a good girl because it was the way her mama raised her, but also in greater part because she loved her daddy, loved him to distraction, and craved his approval like a fat man craves grease. Good girls, he told her from the time she was small, was what he loved, and so a good girl was what she became. Still there was an agitation in her, an itch she'd noticed first around the age of thirteen, one that often came upon her unexpectedly, started deep in her throat and rose up slowly, inexorably to tickle the back of her teeth, which made her bite her tongue and the inside of her cheeks so hard they bled. It was a compulsion only relieved by a notion to do or say something that was not good. If she had to name it, she'd call it an evil inclination, which is how Mama referred to any temptation to wander from the path of righteousness whether that meant slouching in a chair or talking back. Sometimes the urge beset her when she was all alone and under no onus to behave well. Those occasions occurred when she was bored or fighting a frustration she could not name, one related to boredom and yet not boredom. During the seven years between thirteen and twenty, her current age, she fought mightily against the pull of evil inclination in order to continue being the good girl her daddy loved, believing her efforts bred strength of will. But almost from the very minute she met Mickey Moe, she dropped every bit of pretense, reluctance, fear, filial devotion, or whatever it was that kept her from scratching that itch. Overnight, she surrendered to impulse.

In fact, on their very first date, Laura Anne gave Mickey Moe such damp, smoldering looks he could not be blamed for thinking a gentle assault at the outposts of her modesty would not be unwelcome. Before either of them had time to process the consequences, he crossed the moat, scaled the parapets, and raided its innermost chambers, planting his standard at the heart of her vault of treasures.

Afterward, he raised himself up from the fine leather seat of the LTD Brougham he'd bought used from a chum to drive to Greenville to see her knowing the battered pickup he used for work would not do for such a girl and, with tears in his eyes, said, I'm sorry, Laura Anne. I am so sorry. I got carried away. I didn't mean to . . .

There were tears in her eyes, too, tears of wonder, tears of joy she told him, but since he knew she was a good girl, he did not believe her. The only thing she could do to convince him was wind her fair arms around his neck and pull him back down to her while sliding her hips against him up and down and side to side because, Lord almighty, as soon as her urge got satisfied, it started up again, twice as strong. It came to her twice more that night. In between, they took a stroll along the river to appreciate the moon and the stars and their great good fortune at finding each other.

She could barely walk straight in the morning but made a valiant stab at keeping evidence of soreness to herself. Mama was not entirely fooled.

Are you alright, child? You look like a little lamb lost today. She regarded her daughter with narrowed eyes, her lips pinched, her hands on her hips in that pose mamas everywhere use when demanding the truth from their girls.

I'm alright, Mama.

Are you sure?

It takes time for good girls to learn how to deceive. Laura Anne nearly walked into a wall trying to quit the kitchen and escape Mama's prying eyes.

Yes, Mama.

Well, I'm not. That boy try anything with you last night?

The girl's blood pounded so hard in her ears it wasn't difficult to pretend she didn't hear. She left the house in a hurry, calling back to Mama something about being late to work at her father's furniture store.

It was a clumsy dodge. It was a Sunday, and the store was closed to trade. There was no need for punctuality. Normally, she worked Monday through Thursday with half a day on Fridays and Sundays. Friday afternoons she took off early to help Mama get ready for the Sabbath, which she kept, sort of. In other words, although Needleman's Furniture was open Saturdays, she didn't go in. She kept coin in her pocket, spent it if she wanted to, used the television, the car, the oven, her curling iron, in fact, all manner of things electrical or requiring fuel. During the week, Laura Anne served as store accountant and worked the floor with the sales force. Her specialties were kitchen and bedroom furnishings. Most days, she put in long hours, but her duties were light on Sundays. She recorded the Saturday receipts and sent out invoices, monitored both incoming and delivery orders while her daddy did the payroll and inventoried stock. Laura Anne had an associate's degree in business administration from the junior college, but her real preparation for her job came from life with Daddy. She liked to think he taught her everything she knew. It was only rarely that she wondered what else in the world she might like to learn, but somehow her ruminations tended to lead to bouts of agitation, so whenever fancy chanced to visit she distracted herself by chanting one of Daddy's maxim's, "If it was that much fun, they wouldn't call it work," or lost herself in numbers.

Although the women of the house observed the Sabbath in their fashion, the patriarch didn't at all. Motivated by social obligation as much as piety, Laura Anne and Mama often went to services at Temple Ohabai Shalom, the largest Reform synagogue in three counties, while Daddy took Saturday mornings off to sleep in. In the afternoon, he went to the store. Sometimes, fresh from rabbinical exhortation, Mama resented his behavior and cajoled him to change his heathen habits on his way out the door. Daddy would respond, Dang it all, I have a living to make in Babylon. When in Rome, do as the Romans do. No one, especially not Laura Anne, dared criticize him or point out his amalgamation of empires. Nor did she think to complain that she and Mama were restricted by religious law solely because of their gender. In those days, there were many restrictions upon young women of both secular and religious nature. The rules of living in the Needleman household seemed as natural to a child of the river as breathing moist air.

That particular Sunday, she worked hard at keeping Daddy in the dark about her moment of truth the previous evening. Out of fear he'd know everything if he looked in her eyes, she kept her back to him as much as she could, pretending to be busy with lists and sales slips, responding to his small talk with pleasantries and noncommittal expressions like uh-huh and mmm.

Lot Needleman knew his little girl well. After half an hour of evasive chitchat, he made a phone call. Although he used a phone out of range of her hearing, she caught his tone and knew he'd called Mama. When he hung up, he pushed back his chair. It screeched against the linoleum. The sound sent a chill down her spine. He approached, put a hand on her arm, turned her around to face him, and looked her up and down, slowly, head to toe. It was like being seared in a skillet.

Lot Needleman, né Laurence, was so nicknamed by his employees not on his own account but for his wife's strange habit of glancing over her shoulder regularly while in ordinary conversation as if she were pursued by an army of avenging angels. It stuck because his proportions were this side of biblical. He was tall and red as a cedar post, a stocky man with a thick head of salt-and-pepper hair, a man who exuded an air of physical power much in contrast to the fragile figure of his wife, Rose, a hothouse flower, who struggled to support his every decision in return for the security he provided her. He wore a large gold-and-diamond ring on his right pinkie, the kind of ring that looked as if it could rip a nostril off the face it took aim at. Everything about him indicated he was a man with fire in the blood.

Accustomed to only the gentlest of looks from the man, Laura Anne liked to shake in her shoes. He said, That boy last night treat you right, baby?

O Lord, she prayed, give me strength. And her prayer was surely granted, for she lifted her head, batted her eyelashes as if entirely surprised by his question, and bubbled up an answer as fresh and sparkling as a mountain spring.

Why, of course, he did, Daddy. He was a perfect gentleman. In fact, I can't wait to see him again. He has such promise.

Daddy frowned. Promise for what, sugar? I thought he sold insurance for his uncle. Now, I'm not sayin' he isn't a good old boy, for all I know he's one of the best the Lord ever thought to make, but employment in a family concern doesn't exactly demonstrate initiative, does it?

It didn't occur to either one of them that by belittling Mickey Moe, Lot Needleman was also belittling his daughter. Laura Anne still took offense on her lover's behalf. My stars! she thought. I have a lover!

He's a very good salesman, Daddy. He was a football hero, did I tell you that? He could have gone up to Raleigh-Durham on scholarship, but he decided his widowed mama and sisters needed him, and so he let Duke go. Don't you find that admirable? And he doesn't intend to stay an insurance salesman forever. He's got his eye on some property near Guilford. He intends to buy it, lease most of it out, and then farm the rest for his pleasure. A gentleman farmer, he's going to be, like great-granddaddy Chaim.

Throughout her life, Laura Anne's ancestors had been held up to her as icons of virtue. She could not know that the redneck great-granddaddy in question had been coarse and miserly, tormenting Lot's own father with his mean purse and a constant barrage of criticism meant to mold his character. When he was growing up, Lot was told over and over how lucky he was to have a kinder rearing himself. He did not see it quite that way, since his daddy had a festering canker at the seat of his soul due to Chaim Needleman's hard hand. Lot was often the object of his father's compensatory wrath. From the instant of Laura Anne's birth, he vowed to spoil his little girl as a way of making his own childhood misery up to himself. Since he wanted her to be proud of her blood, he whitewashed the family history, praising both her intemperate granddaddy and skinflint great-granddaddy to the skies, creating for her an ancestry as imaginative as the provenance of his showroom's Queen Anne desk. Though the stratagem gave him a daughter who held her head high in any crowd of genealogical swells, it left him neatly hoist on his own petard in the current instance.

In the face of her enthusiasm, he had no other choice than to go silent. He gnashed his teeth. He scowled. He sputtered. When his frustration dragged on to a point that Laura Anne's expression turned to one of filial concern, he covered it with a coughing fit. Holding his right hand up, he signaled she should get him a drink of water even though the office bubbler was three feet behind him and all he had to do was turn around. Laura Anne sidled behind him swiftly, got him water in a paper cup, and watched him guzzle it down. Luckily for both, the phone rang. When Lot answered and made a show of involvement in an inconsequential conversation, Laura Anne took the opportunity to turn her back to him and return to her duties, raising her eyes to the heavens in thankfulness as she did.

That night after supper, she retired to her room early, leaving her parents to watch the latest escapades on the Ponderosa alone. As she knew he would, Mickey Moe called. She hopped on her princess phone at the first ring before her parents had a chance to hear it. The lovers talked and sighed together and made plans for the next weekend and the weekend after that. They shared a sensible discussion of how they must behave with decorum in front of Lot and Rose Needleman until enough time had passed for them to make their intentions known, intentions that had become crystal clear from their first kiss. They were meant to be together forever. They would marry as soon as possible, have children, live on a farm, die old and happy in each other's arms. But young lovers can talk all they like about being discreet. The eyes of those who care to notice always will. Laura Anne's parents took measures. The first of these was the subterfuge of hospitality.

On the weekend of their third date, Rose Needleman invited Mickey Moe to Sunday dinner. The boy was encouraged by this and did all he could to make an impression. Despite the heat of that August day, he dressed in his good seersucker suit. Minutes before he left Guilford, Roland cut a bunch of blue daisies and yellow mums from Mama's garden as a bouquet for him to take with. Sara Kate tied a damp piece of cheesecloth around the stems to keep them fresh during the ride. Mama instructed him before he left. Now you present these to the mistress of the house, she said. You were not invited by Miss Laura Anne but by her mama.

Two and a half hours later, Mickey Moe arrived at the outskirts of Greenville. Along the way, the LTD's air conditioner had broken down. By the time he reached Laura Anne's house, it was close to three hours since he'd left his own, and the blooms, no matter how carefully prepared, had wilted. The formerly perky petals of his mama's exotic daisies curled in. The centers of the mums had gone brown. He studied them sitting there in the passenger seat where Laura Anne ought to be. Was it an insult to give Mrs. Needleman flowers in disrepair? Was it a worse insult to arrive empty-handed?

Mickey Moe checked himself out in the rear view and wiped the perspiration from his face with his handkerchief. Dang the flowers, he thought. They either like me or they don't, and a lot of dang flowers ain't goin' to tip the scales one way or t'other. He picked up the bouquet and tossed it in the back. Then just before leaving the car and heading up Laura Anne's front walk, he had an idea. He turned around and plucked the freshest-looking daisy from the pile and stuck it in the buttonhole of his seersucker lapel. Ok, he thought, smoothing his collar, ok. That looks right smart. He went up the walk and stairs to the front porch with a bounce in his step. He rang the bell, waited there rocking back and forth on his feet, his straw fedora in hand, a goofy smile on his face, feeling confident and free and full of good will.

Lot Needleman answered the door all smiles of sweet welcome. At the sight of that beaming red face, Mickey Moe caught his breath. The salesman in him was trained to read the hidden intentions of others. Right off the bat, he saw the man's desire to crush him in his two hands and brush the pieces off into the four winds. Mickey Moe knew men like Lot. Knew them well. Every sugared look had a vein of arsenic in it. Those smiles were a call to arms. He straightened up, narrowed his gaze, and offered his hand. He was ready to fight for his woman. Let the games begin, he wanted to say.

Thank you, sir, for invitin' me this fine afternoon.

Lot Needleman widened his grin to show more of his teeth. He leaned in to take the boy's hand and squeeze the life out of it. It hurt like hell, but Mickey Moe would sooner perish than wince. He returned as much pressure as he thought respectful.

It was the ladies' idea, son. Thank them.

There were footsteps, light, sprightly as a dancing cat. Laura Anne popped around her daddy's bulk to stand at his side with her right arm around Lot's waist and her left hand on his bicep. There was comfort, love, pride in the gesture as if she were presenting Mickey Moe with a giant doll or a seriously overgrown child.

Lord, he thought, how she loves him! But then if a girl doesn't love her daddy, she can hardly love a mug like me so hard so fast. His heart twisted in his chest thinking how important it was to her that he and her daddy got along, how difficult it was going to be to make that happen. Maybe, he thought, it'd be easier to go at the old man through his wife. Women talked. At least he might be able to find out if there was more to the animus oozing from Lot Needleman than every man's desire to preserve and protect his little girl. A conversation with his wife would let him know if it was personal.

I'd love surely to thank the lady of the house, sir.

Well, come on in, then.

He thought his introduction to Rose Needleman went a lot better. He took her soft, damp hand in both of his and pressed it, bowing his head slightly like a European courtier. According to his mama, this was a profound sign of respect for a lady. She claimed it was the way the queen of England would wish to be greeted if she were permitted the indulgence of common intimacies. Rose Needleman blushed like a bride and stifled a giggle.

Mickey Moe cast a slant-eyed look at her husband. Touché to you, big guy, touché. The latter coughed and said, I'm as hungry as a squash bug in July. Let's go to table.

The foyer of the house was airy, impressive with its vaulted ceiling, checkerboard tile, and massive clay pots from which grew ferns, five and six feet tall, perfuming the place with an earthy, humid scent. Led by Rose and followed by Lot and Laura Anne, who walked arm-in-arm, Mickey Moe laid his hat on a table of marble and wrought iron, crossed through a receiving room, a hallway hung with family portraits, and into the dining room where a fancy table had been set with the Needlemans' best silver, crystal, chinaware, and linens. Thanks to the family trade, the table was luxe indeed. If Beadie Sassaport Levy had not acquired the same quality of items purchased during the glory days of Bernard's wealth and retained most of them throughout her troubles, Mickey Moe might have been intimidated by the display, which was, after all, its purpose.

This is a lovely table, Mrs. Needleman, he said. Are these family pieces?

Ah, he wooed Rose as easily as he'd wooed Laura Anne. Her scrawny chest inflated like a sparrow's when that little bird is about to burst forth at dawn with a night's store of song. She glanced over her shoulder as if there might be spies lurking about then leaned forward and spoke in the most cordial, confidential manner.

How nice of you to notice, Mr. Levy. Some of them are heirlooms, of course. Now, the silver tureen there on the sideboard belonged to my mama's great-aunt Esther. She carried it here all the way from Louisville when she married. They say her grandmama brought it with her from Jamestown and her mama brought it from England. Did you know our people were Virginian originally? At least on my side of the family, that is. Mr. Needleman's people are Mississippian, through and through.

Mickey Moe raised his eyebrows and tilted his head in an expression of interest though it was a ruse, a prime example of maternal instruction in politesse. He hated himself a little for his insincerity until he remembered a warrior uses whatever weaponry the campaign demands, even if he has to scavenge in a dung heap to find it. Why no, I did not know that, he said. Your daughter's been very modest not to tell me. . . .

Conversation continued in this manner. It may be difficult to imagine that from the soup right through the fish, there was not time enough to dispense with the bloodlines of Mickey Moe's sweetheart, but it appeared Rose Needleman could chatter endlessly about great-great-uncle so and so, who kept a famous journal during the War of Northern Aggression, and cousin this-and-that, who planted rice in Savannah long before anyone even considered whether cotton might grow there.

It was not until they were finishing up the brisket and heading into the salad that Lot Needleman asked the question all this was leading up to. Your mama's people, I hear, are Sassaports. That's a very old name and quite lustrous. But which Levys are yours, son? The Alabama? I hope not the Piedmont! Lot Needleman laughed at the thought.

Worse than that, sir, Mickey Moe began. Cursing this fetish everyone he knew had about ancestry, he related his usual story about Daddy and the mystery of his origins. He even incorporated a version of the speech he'd made to Laura Anne on the day they met, the speech that charmed her for reasons he was only just beginning to suspect, those having to do with the seed of rebellion in her, rebellion against the restrictions placed upon good girls of spirit, a rebellion he was happy to indulge daily for the rest of her life if she let him. I am a child of mystery, he said, as he had that fateful afternoon. I am a child of mystery but I am as easy to decipher as a semaphore waved from the deck of a riverboat on a sparklin' day in spring. Which means I might take a little study, but there is no deception in me. I have made my life a devotion in plain talk and honest proposal to atone for whatever drops of my daddy's lying blood flow through my veins.

Rose Needleman's face went grim, her color heightened. She knew all this, having both quizzed her daughter on the young man's background and done a bit of research with her Jackson acquaintances. With an introductory little cough, she commented in the manner she'd rehearsed and refined under her husband's direction long into the night before.

Ah-hem. Why that is a remarkable story, Mr. Levy. A remarkable story. A sad one, too. How difficult it will be to find a bride of good family in these parts with a history like that. How very difficult.

It was as if a bomb went off. Laura Anne jumped up and insisted her mother not insult Mickey Moe. How can you be so rude? she demanded, which caused Daddy to jump up and tell Laura Anne to pipe down or go to her room. His wife started to cry. Her chin jerked repeatedly toward her right shoulder. I tried, Larry, I tried, she mumbled between sobs. At which Mickey Moe excused himself and rose to effect a rapid exit to avoid being witness to or focus of a family squabble. Laura Anne held him back then confronted her daddy bravely, without hesitation.

Daddy. This man, this very fine man, does not need to search for a bride as he's already found one in me although I am not so sure how worthy my own family is after this day.

She told him this in a measured tone with a look sharp as needles. Lot Needleman's jaw dropped out of complete shock that his baby girl could speak to him in such a way. Feeling the fool, he shut his mouth then vented his anger at Mickey Moe.

Look what you've done, Mr. Levy! he shouted. Turned the sweetest creature on earth into a harridan in three short weeks! I want you out of my house!

Yessir. Excuse me, m'am. Mickey Moe again tried to leave, but Laura Anne blocked his way.

I'm goin', too, she said and spun toward the door. Pursued by a stunned and sputtering daddy, half dragging Mickey Moe along behind her, she quit her parents' house. They hustled into his car and took off.

Neither spoke. Mickey Moe drove without destination for fifteen long minutes with Laura Anne nestled into his side, her head buried in his chest. It concerned him that she did not quiver, nor did her cheeks wet his shirt with tears. She breathed heavily. Her eyes were round and wide as a frightened doe's. At last, Mickey Moe spoke.

I left my hat.

What?

I left my hat at your mama's.

So?

Well, she'll probably call up those New Orleans cousins she mentioned and have their maid put voo-doo all over it.

Laura Anne started to laugh.

It was a good hat, too.

And she laughed harder and harder until the tears came and then the sobs. Mickey Moe sighed a great sigh of relief, because he felt without knowing why that no matter what the battle ahead, if the girl shivering in sobs beside him could cry like that, they'd be ok. Where shall I take you tonight? he asked softly, hoping she'd suggest running off with him then and there. She stilled, picked her head up, and blew her nose into the monogrammed handkerchief she'd had tucked in the pocket of her poodle skirt.

To my married cousin Patricia Ellen's house, I guess. I'll have her call Mama so she doesn't worry. I cannot go back there tonight. Tomorrow, maybe. Yes. I'll go back tomorrow and reason with them.

Of course, darlin', he said, concealing the disappointment he felt. Cousin Patricia Ellen's. Show me the way.

And she did.

She told him to go home, she was alright, she needed to talk things out with Patricia Ellen, but he stayed on, sleeping on Patricia Ellen's couch. In the morning, her five- and six-year-olds woke him up by pelting him with Cheerios. It was a workday. He had appointments up and down the Pearl as there was a new flood insurance policy he was pushing. He called Uncle Tom-Tom from Patricia Ellen's party line and asked the office secretary to cancel them all.

I am at your disposal, he told a pale-faced Laura Anne when she descended the staircase looking so fragile and tragic his heart overflowed with pity.

Just take me home, Mickey. I need to face the dragons.

He drove her home, then waited for her at a diner downtown for three hours. As soon as she entered the place, he knew she had not fared well dragon-wise. They held hands across a table while she told him what her parents had to say.

Daddy said, Baby, the world is full of men good at courting sweet, inexperienced gals. They're all soft words and flowers and bowing when they open the door. Don't say peep about their character. Now, blood does.

That was a fact she was too young to know, but one her parents had witnessed with their own eyes time after time. How could they let her link her fate to a man whose people were a complete mystery? It just wouldn't be right. For all they knew, there were thieves and murderers and madmen in his line.

She reminded them Mickey Moe's mama's people were like royalty in the South. She stuck out her chin like a boxer, daring them to knock her down.

Daddy sighed in a manly way, letting out a great burst of locked up air with plenty of noise and whistle. There you have it! Only half the story! he'd said. I doubt very much the Sassaports would have allowed his mama to marry that pretender had they even a clue about his true origins. Which they didn't and still don't. Look. We give in to you on this one and, Lordy, one day you'll likely present us with three-eyed, one-legged grandchildren with a cruel streak. You have to trust your mama and daddy, sweetheart. You'll get over this boy. You've known him what, three weeks? It's puppy love you're feelin'. That's all it is. Three month from now you won't recall the sound of his voice or the color of his eye.

Oh, Mickey Moe, that's what he said but I don't believe him. I will love you 'til the day I die.

Mickey Moe listened to her story, knowing how it went before he heard it. Somewhere between thieves and murderers and three-eyed, one-legged grandchildren, a plan came to him. It was a simple plan, as all glorious plans are. He tried it on in his mind, and it fit him. Fit him so well he wondered if his love for Laura Anne was a mystical thing, a product of divine intervention, moving him down a path he'd longed to travel his whole life.

It's alright, darlin'. Don't you cry no more. I know how to deal with your mama and daddy. I know just what to do.

She picked up her head and gave him a wondering, tear-stained look.

What's that? They are not changing their minds. What can you do?

Go on a quest, he said. A quest to find my daddy's people. From everything I've heard all my life about my daddy, he was well mannered, educated, and rich. Surely his people were as noble as any, including that great-great-auntie of yours who arrived in Virginia clutchin' a soup bowl. There's a mystery to it, that's for sure. Whatever made him hide his origins, it must have been some misfortune of his own, not because his people were trash. I'm sure of it.

They were so elated by this plan that, before taking Laura Anne home, they stopped off at the lovers' lane along the great river where they'd made their first vows together and indulged themselves awhile in broad daylight.

All the way back to Guilford, Mickey Moe made plans. First thing, he'd have to arrange time off from work. Uncle Tom-Tom was a good man. He'd surely cooperate. He was his top earner, after all, with the roughest territory. Didn't that allow him some sway? What was it Tom-Tom always said about him? Mickey Moe considered his mama's big brother. He was short, potbellied, red-faced with a head of wiry white hair, a man who perpetually hooked his thumbs in his suspenders near the waist and ran them up and down their length while he talked. It was a habit he'd picked up from the 'croppers on his sales route. When he wanted to emphasize a point, he pulled the suspenders out wide and snapped them. The rest, all that twiddling up and down, was preamble. Whenever he introduced Mickey Moe, he'd rock back and forth on his heels while he twiddled and say,

This boy here may not have a college education. And sure as Pharaoh loved Joseph, he grew up in the town, not out on the Delta with his toes in the mud. But he's got a nose on 'im, a nose for farmin' and a nose for risk. I don't know how he does it or where he gets it, but he can tell you when the frost is comin' and when the flood. Yessir. (Snap.) He surely can. You just ask any old boy hoein' a row up by the Pearl. They all know 'im. And don't get me started on how he knows when the baby's takin' sick or where the fire's gettin' started. It truly boggles my mind but he knows that, too. Least it seems that way, judgin' from the checks I pass on to those he's signed up in the knick of time. (Snap.) You all listen to him. You all listen to him good. You will not regret it. (Double snap. The end.)

Uncle Tom-Tom was so convincing on the subject of his nephew's prognosticatory talents, Mickey Moe half-believed him himself. It was true that when he went out into the field cold without leads, he turned up buyers in unexpected places just by following his instincts. He could glance down an off-the-map dirt road and somehow know it'd take him into jam-packed Negro villages or crumbling old plantations no one knew were there except the lonely families who worked them, solitary folk who found Mickey Moe's sales pitch more entertaining than the picture show or the revival tent. They'd buy some kind of policy from him—usually Tom-Tom's two-bit-a-week life-and-fire combination plan—mostly because he made such good sense but partly to keep him coming back every month to collect the premium.

So it should not have been surprising that Uncle Tom-Tom gave his nephew a hard time when he asked for a leave of absence, probably just for a few weeks, actually for as long as it would take. But it was a great surprise to Mickey Moe. Shoulders hunched, neck shortened as if his head were about to disappear into his collar, he stood in front of his uncle's desk, mute and uncomprehending, while Tom-Tom rattled off his objections.

Whoa. Back up, son. Who you think I've got that can handle all those boys with dirt up their nose you sell to? Your cousins can handle the retail business and the town families, but you're the only one I got knows how to make 'croppers give up their quarters and smile at the same time. I'm too old to go down those hard roads myself. What makes you think I can spare you? (Snap.) Times are not so easy these days, you know that. Those flap bottoms lose their policies when no one comes by for collection, and who knows who they'll blame or what kinda trouble they might stir up. Now, I've given you a blessed livin', trained you, and set you out. You owe me this much. Times bein' what they are, I cannot let you wander off into the wide blue on a crazy whim.

Mickey Moe was quiet a moment or two, long enough for Uncle Tom-Tom to initiate a slow rotation of his swivel chair toward the office picture window where late afternoon sun streamed in. The old man thought, staff problem solved, he might as well catch a nap in the sun's warmth. Then Mickey Moe slammed two open palms down hard on the far edge of Tom-Tom's big cherrywood desk, making such a loud crack his uncle snapped to while the secretary in the next room let out an involuntary little yelp.

Sorry, Annie Caroline, Mickey Moe called over his shoulder without letting his steady gaze leave the other man's eyes. I'm just making a point here. And that point is this is not about some crazy whim. This is about winning the woman I love. This is about clearing my daddy's name of scurrilous speculation once and for all, and, as I ponder it, easing the lingering pain of my mama, too. I would think that's an objective you could get behind, Uncle Tom-Tom.

He paused to watch his mentor's cheeks go a tad redder than usual, but before he could speak, Mickey Moe continued.

No one can dissuade me from this path. You might as well forget tryin' to turn my feet off it. Now, I understand that somebody's got to collect the premiums on my route, and I understand I owe that not just to you, but to those poor souls scrapin' together their pennies to pay 'em. So every three weeks, no matter where I am on my journey, I will make every effort to return for my rounds and send on the collections to you by wire if I have to. I can promise you that, but I can promise no more. I will not make sales. I will not draw up new policies. Can you live with that, Uncle? I truly hope so, because it's the best I can do. If you do not accept, then we can shake hands and part ways forever here and now. When I've realized my purpose, I'll just have to find new employment. That'd be a terrible shame, but it's something I am prepared for.

In the face of his nephew's determination, there was nothing for Tom-Tom to do. He had to acquiesce, which he did with minimal huffing and puffing. Delighted, Mickey Moe left the office gliding on a jet stream of balmy air that led directly to his home. He parked the car in the rear and burst into the kitchen where Sara Kate was hunched over the sink washing glassware.

Sara Kate was in her early fifties by this time. No longer winsome, she was still handsome with the muscular build a lifetime of hard work grants and a strong face that masked her emotions when it had to. The most remarkable thing about her was the unexpected delicacy of her hands, which featured the long, nimble fingers of a violinist. As children, his sisters would watch in a kind of trance as those lovely hands went about their chores with astounding grace. Afterward, they'd run to their rooms and imitate her. The maid was lost in her own thoughts while she scrubbed. She didn't hear the car pull up or the slam of the screen door. Full of high spirits, Mickey Moe planted his feet and bellowed, Anybody here? She started, spun about, and dropped a crystal juice glass, which shattered in a discrete arc at her feet. Remorseful, Mickey Moe moved to pick up the pieces, but she was on her knees before he got there waving him away.

Lord, boy. I'm too old for a shock like that. Leave the house and come back in like a man instead of a beast.

He did so.

You alone here, Sara Kate? he asked, putting a hand on her elbow to help her up.

Yessir, I am. Your sister's at work, and your mama's takin' tea over to your aunt Missy's.

It was all he needed to hear. Not half a minute later, he was upstairs rummaging through his mama's bedroom closet, reaching behind hat and shoe boxes, searching for the one with painted pink roses joined by silver ribbon on the outside and his daddy's personal papers on the inside. It was so far in the back and under so many other boxes of old checkbooks and family photographs, he figured his mama hadn't looked through it for years, which was a good thing, because now she'd never miss it. He tucked the box under his arm and went to his own bedroom, the one he'd slept in all his life. After shutting the door, he jimmied up two worn floorboards to unearth his childhood chest of secrets, that is, one of his daddy's old briefcases, a battered thing of cracked brown leather and tarnished brass fittings. He opened it and plunged his right hand deep inside.

He removed the several dozen sheets of folded tissue paper, those sheets that mapped his adolescent dreams of buried legacy, with reverence. He carried them to his bed as a priest does sacraments, in the flat of his two hands joined together to make a plate. He tipped them, and the papers slid onto the bedclothes. He sat down, took a deep breath, and opened them one by one with the great care their age required. Once they were spread around him, he took letters from Mama's box of roses and placed them in the middle. Since there was no one else around, he allowed tears to form behind his lids and trickle down his cheeks. Daddy, he whispered, Daddy. Where are you? Who are you? And then he began to read.

V

Memphis, Tennessee, 1904

THE SINGLE MOST HELPFUL PIECE of information Mickey Moe did not yet know, could never know from perusal of that dusty heap spread over his comforter, was that in the old days, the days when his daddy was young, there were two Bernard Levys in Tennessee. It's possible there were more than two, although it can reasonably be assumed there were only two of the same approximate age in Shelby County. Levy is a common name among Jews. There's a whole tribe of them. Some of these came to the South in the eighteenth century, more in the nineteenth, and twice that in the twentieth. They were from everywhere, most notably from Germany, Holland, Paris, and New York. One of the two Bernard Levys was of an old Memphian family, originally Dutch, wealthy purveyors of agricultural supply. The other Bernard Levy, Mickey Moe's daddy, was of less fortunate stock. Bad luck dogged his people in Spain, France, Italy, and Manhattan before they swung south on a bone-headed whim just before the War of 1812 broke out, only to find bad luck barked at their heels there, too. Generations before, these Levys had been respected artisans, fashioning chairs, chests, tables, and beds with mythic creatures for feet and finials out of the hard woods of Europe. By the time Mickey Moe's granddaddy bore the name Levy, the blood was not so much thinned as completely wore out. That man could not give a good grip to a dowel, preferring as he did the sweet caress of waxed playing cards against his soft, uncallused skin.

Gamblers, con men, and actors—that's what Mickey Moe's immediate forebears were, the kind of gossamer-winged parasites the Delta hosted with a shrug of her verdant shoulder. They fed off the river and mined it for fools. They had good years and lean ones, traversing the same parcels of land their peddler granddaddies did. Just as the ancestors stopped along the way to set up shop and try their hands at settling down until war or drought or depression uprooted them again, these boys stopped long enough to marry and father children until they ran out of hard cash or fools, then drifted downriver once more, looking for an angle or a game, often finding a knife, a bullet, maybe a fever or snakebite instead. In any case, most times they never did return.

Mickey Moe's grandmama was of more steady stock. Her people peddled odds and ends of bent silver, cracked porcelain, and snippets of lace scavenged from the refuse of Yankee factories and impoverished estates, carried down country on the backs of cousins then sold door-to-door to Negro families planning a wedding or 'croppers looking to beautify their homes on the cheap. Generations passed. They settled on the outskirts of Memphis, opening up a notions shop with housewares sold under the spurious label ANTIQUES. They weren't rich. But they did alright.

When Caroline Stern met Harvey Levy she knew what he was straightaway. He'd come into her daddy's establishment looking for a linen handkerchief to replace the tattered thing flaring out of his waistcoat pocket. She knew in the time it took to catch her breath that he was a trickster from the tips of his spectator shoes to the crown of his dove gray fedora, a fly-by-night, a gentleman of no repute at all. But he was very handsome, lithely built with mounds of wavy chestnut hair, bright black eyes, and eyelashes as thick, long, and curly as her own. At the sight of him, her heart beat so hard against her chest she feared her buttons might pop. Harvé, as he called himself, accenting the name in the French manner and passing himself off as a native of New Orleans, was not one to pass by a pretty heaving bosom on which to lay his head for however long it pleased him. He saw her interest and all but twirled his mustache.

Poor Harvé. A week's dalliance, a mere seven days in—where the hell was he? Podunk, Tennessee?—was all he anticipated, all he planned for on that fateful day of lustful inspiration. He should have remembered the Bible training of his youth, spotty as it was. Six days was all it took the Lord God to invent man, woman, beast, and the Mississippi, along with the entire planet, the stars in their heavens, and whatever lay beyond. For Caroline Stern, ensnaring Harvey Levy required two days and a half.

The woman was a prodigy of love, that was the thing. Once she made her mind up, there wasn't a man alive who stood a chance. She'd been watching men, studying them, from the time she was six and her daddy installed her on a stool behind the counter to count out change for the customers. By the time Harvé wandered in thirteen years later, she'd witnessed the gender in every state imaginable and recorded in her mind what made them whatever they happened to be. For example, she'd seen men old and young, black and white gripped in the fierce and angry despair that comes when the woman they want does not want them. For the flyspeck of hope a faded silk posy or a cut-glass bottle filled with the perfumed water Mama brewed in the back might give them, they'd pay twice or even three times what the thing was worth without blinking an eye. Once their hands were on it, their palms would sweat or their skin blanch or their eyelids flutter like a girl's. Then they'd bound out the door leaving a wake of sweet hope in place of the sour scent of desire denied. A few months later, the object of their passion might stroll in alone, clutching a bruised arm and looking through Mama's medicinal shelf for the greenish powder that covered up a black eye or holding a protective hand over her belly, searching for the whitish liquid that helped with morning sickness. From such observations, she learned the lust of a man dwelt on a knife's edge, a knife that could cut a man's pride to slivers or excise his lust overnight to be replaced by loathing or neglect.

She figured there were two ways to catch a man. One was to deny him, wrap him in a shroud of ice, and the other was to yield to him with a passion he could not match. The first day, Harvé flattered her into a cozy spot by the river, she went for ice princess, and that worked pretty well. The second day, she tired of acting like something she was not and allowed her true nature, a cross between Bathsheba and Jezebel, to surface. Harvé, who'd expected to make a woman out of a child that day, was jolted to the core that a virgin—he had that part right at least—could behave in such a depraved, insatiable manner. He was a slave to Caroline Stern's appetites for the rest of his natural life.

A month later, they stood under a canopy together and took their oaths according to the laws of Abraham. It would have been sooner, but Caroline had to convince her parents their marriage was a good idea. They only accepted Harvé after he gave them his purse with every dollar he had to his name as a bride's price and signed a document stating he would work as their purveyor of dry goods for the ensuing seven years in return for two rooms at the back of the store where the young couple could make their home. Although the idea of buying a wife had already gone out of fashion, there were plenty of folk around who clung to the tradition so that neither Harvé nor Caroline felt abused by the arrangement. They felt lucky.

What a great and wonderful beginning it was! The two were mad for each other. They felt they had fallen into a honey pot, and they laughed in each other's arms as often as they moaned. After customers complained the store was locked up in the middle of the day or they'd heard such groans from within they'd been frightened to enter, Mama and Daddy Stern had to speak to them about the indecent hours they chose to celebrate their union. Then Bernard was born, and all of that more or less stopped.

It wasn't that they'd stopped loving and wanting each other. Bernard had the colic, and there was no peace for a few months. By the time it was over, Harvé had come to grasp the idea of paternal responsibility. Nuptial contract or not, he decided the only way he was to provide his family with security was to take to the river again and win his fortune. He was gone four months his first trip, but he wrote letters and returned with enough silver and gold coin to buy a little house for his wife and child independent of his in-law's establishment. He stayed around half a year and was gone again, this time for nine months. Again he returned with his pockets overflowing, so all was forgiven. This pattern went on for a handful of years until one day, true to his blood, he went downriver and didn't return. No one knew what happened to him, but all assumed he was dead. Harvé Levy was too much the family man for any other explanation.

Caroline Stern Levy was forever changed. According to religious law, she was an abandoned wife because she could not produce a corpse to prove otherwise. She was unable to remarry without the verifying signatures of a hundred rabbis when she only knew of two, one in Memphis and the other downriver in Greenville. She could hardly drag her young son around high country looking for ninety-eight more. Yet Caroline Stern Levy was a woman of deep natural longings and in the prime of feminine life when such longings become a gaping need. She took lovers in remedy, although never anyone particular for very long out of respect for Harvé's memory. Not only did Bernard grow up funny looking and fatherless, but his grieving mother took her comfort in drops of opium and transitory assignations with men eager to accept such limitations, that is, men of low quality. They were the kind of men who thought nothing of making Bernard their errand boy or giving him a gratuitous slap or boot to help him grow right. The only thing that grew in him was a hunger for escape.

When the boy first became aware there was another Bernard Levy around, a Bernard Levy as handsome as he was homely, as rich as he was poor, as loved and cherished by his mama as he was neglected, he was just seven years old. A truant officer arrived at his house and confronted the boy while he sat in the dirt in the front yard, gnawing on a raw beet as it was all he could find to eat and he was hungry. Where's your mama? the man asked. Bernard dutifully pointed him in the right direction, thinking this natty man in his trim black suit and polished walking boots did not look at all like one of Mama's usual boyfriends.

The man entered the house and Bernard followed behind. Miz Levy, he said, loudly. I am here for the boy. When Mama didn't stir from the chair where she sat dead to the world from the previous night's excess, he kicked its legs to wake her. She remained motionless. Calling on Jesus, the man grabbed Bernard by the collar of his shabby shirt and threw him into his Model T, eventually depositing him in a one-room schoolhouse that stunk of river mud and the school's two-seater next door.

Bernard stood at the front of the class while his twenty-seven classmates, ranging in age from five to thirteen, stared at him wide-eyed. He was barefoot and filthy as the rest of them, his ginger hair a mess of stand-up snarls, his prominent ears red-tipped with shyness, his eyes, nose, and mouth even more scrunched together than usual as he was scared to do other than squint at his surroundings. A tall, wan lady in a polka-dot dress, thick white socks, and sensible shoes stood over him.

She had a wooden pointer in her right hand that she slapped against the left's open palm each time a word came out her big, fleshy lips. What. Is. Your. Name. Boy.

He squinted and said, Bernard.

She asked, And. Your. Surname.

Levy, he said.

Levy? she asked, looking surprised.

Yes, I am Bernard Levy, he said.

Suddenly, all manner of raucous hell broke loose as all the children and even their teacher burst out laughing. Actually, hootin' and hollerin' might better describe the bent-over, foot-stomping earthquake of merriment that ensued.

Bernard Levy! Bernard Levy! they shouted between giggles and guffaws. Little girls, young as five, old as thirteen, came up and curtsied in front of him, one after the other, followed by boys who came up and bowed from the waist. All of this was accompanied by a chorus of jeers and catcalls. To a startled, confused Bernard, the reaction at least seemed good humored and he chuckled a little himself. Truly, not since the great unwashed of Paris crowned Quasimodo was there such a festival of welcome to an outcast.

At last, the lady grabbed hold of her better instincts. Drying her eyes, she told the children in a loud voice that enough was enough and they must settle down. When they ignored her, she cracked her pointer hard against her desk, repeating her demand in a near scream. Everyone finally quieted. Poor little Bernard remained in front of the others while they regarded him quietly now like a museum exhibit. They stared at him so intently he blushed and looked down his nose past his round, hard belly to the tips of his bare toes. The teacher, a worn-out, prickly woman named Miss Maple, took pity on him. She placed a hand on his back and guided him to a seat on a long bench that accommodated the backsides of the smallest of her students. She got him a piece of slate and a stick of chalk from the cupboard near the windows, told him to copy the letters of the alphabet that decorated the top of the wall all around like crown molding, and went back to teaching the geography lesson she'd been working on before the truant officer introduced Bernard to their midst.

At the end of the school day, Bernard followed his classmates until he recognized a street, then made his way back to the river house Harvé bought his family before he disappeared. Caroline Levy was just waking from the previous night's stupor. He told her all about his day, beginning with the truant officer's arrival at their home and ending with his journey into the world of education. Mama's eyes filled up as somewhere in her dim soul she contemplated her life's tragedies and failures. Her eyelids fluttered, she felt the need to justify herself, and although her mouth was exceedingly dry, she said, And what did you learn, son? What did you learn that your dear daddy of blessed memory and I have not been able to teach you? We taught you your letters and your numbers soon as you could talk along with the Bible of our people, which I swear is all a boy needs to know.

I learned my name is funny. They all laughed and laughed when I told them all my name. Even the teacher who is named after a tree, Miss Maple. What right, Mama, has a lady named after a tree got to go on after Bernard Levy? To let the other children go on, too?

His lower lip trembled as he relived his humiliation.

I swear, Mama, it was half an hour they went on, least that's what it felt like. I do not want to go back there. Do I have to?

Mama's eyes, all puffy from sleep and dissolution, went wide for a moment then narrowed into slits. Red and wet, they took on a shine as of fire. She jumped up from the rocker in which she had collapsed three-quarters of a day earlier, and without combing her hair or changing her dress, she grabbed Bernard's hand. For the second time that day, he was dragged to an unknown destination, which turned out to be his grandparents' store.

Granddaddy was out and his grandmama was behind the counter. That tired and disappointed woman gave her daughter a look that blended sadness, pity, disgust, and fear. She said, What do you want, Caroline? I told you a thousand times I am not giving you any more ready cash. Though if you want food or clothing for little Bernard, I will surely give you that, poor child.

She bent down then and worked up a troubled smile. Come over to me, little one, come on over to me, she said with her arms out. Bernard headed toward her welcoming warmth, but his mama jerked him back so hard he nearly fell.

I need your phone, Mama. Feelin' enough charity in your frozed-up heart to give me that? My boy here's been ridiculed at the school by his teacher, and I intend to give that anti-semit whatfor.

When she let go of her son's hand, he ran toward his grandmother who was now on her knees beckoning to him. When he reached her, she folded him up. She smelled like bread and candy and the magical waters she brewed in the back to sell to the desperate. He squirmed against her with delight, inhaling all these things, while his mama grunted at them as if they were two despicable idiots. She made her way to the far wall behind the counter, the one with the phone bolted to it. Once there, she coughed, picked up the conical handle of the phone, put it against her ear, and, nearly shouting into the speaking part, asked an operator for the phone of Miss Maple, who taught over to the municipal school house there on Devries Street. Once connected, she ranted and raved a blue streak about the insults her baby boy had endured. This was the very reason she'd kept him at home, thank you very much, because in the schoolhouse you never could tell what trash a child might encounter and what lack of manners might scar him for his entire life.

Then she was still, listening. It seemed to Bernard she listened for a very long time, long enough for Grandmama to get him a stick of sugarcane from a glass case and for him to suck at a portion of the top until it went smooth and round as a stone from the bottom of the riverbed. When at last she hung up the phone, she was much changed, as thoughtful as she'd been enraged previously.

Well, now. Well, now, she said. Mama, you know those other Levys, the ones with the agri business downtown? Did you know they have a boy Bernard's age, also Bernard?

Grandmama shook her head. I don't have time to follow what folks in town get up to. I got enough heartache keeping up with the needs of the mouth-breathers 'round here.

Well, they do. And he's as handsome as the day is long, they say. And he's always done up in silks and satins and high-button shoes. He never goes out without a blackie or two to be lackey to him. Miss Maple tells me his nose is so high up in the air if it rained he'd drown. Every child in the county that's come close to him, he's kicked off with a sneer or a shriek, and him only seven years old, remember, just like our boy here.

So when this one showed up at the school lookin' as he does and announced that he was Bernard Levy, they all just couldn't help themselves. But she's sorry, that Miss Maple is. She's sorry she couldn't help her own self, and she swears to me if I let Bernard go back to the school tomorrow, she'll make it up to him and treat him as if his feet were gold and his eyes pearls.

And that's exactly what happened. Bernard went back to the schoolhouse the next day and proceeded to live the life of teacher's pet, which had a happy effect on his classmates who decided, perhaps also out of guilt, to be sweet and kind to him. Things got to a state where school was his favorite place to be, better for sure than being at home with his drug-addled mother and her lovers, and even better than his grandparents' store. He knew without fully comprehending why that it was all due to this other Bernard Levy. The older he got, the more curious he was about his name-twin. He felt their fates were related, tied together, that one day they would meet, and discover themselves brothers in the soul. All that happened, but not remotely in the way the boy anticipated, not in that sunny skies, balmy breeze sort of way but in a way Bernard could not possibly imagine no matter how much heartache life had doled out to his young soul already.

VI

Guilford, Mississippi, 1962

THANKS TO HIS INVESTIGATION, MICKEY Moe was downstairs late for supper. He'd concentrated so hard, he did not hear the little silver bell his mother rang every five minutes he was late, summoning him. At his appearance, Beadie gave him a dark look.

I'm sorry, Mama, he said. Time just ran away with me.

Well, it's in the process of running away with the excellence of this meal Sara Kate worked so hard on.

Mickey Moe made to get out of his chair.

I'll go apologize to her.

No! Don't you dare interrupt the table any further than you already have. Your sister and I have been sitting here waiting for you for near a quarter hour.

I'm very sorry, m'am.

He turned and nodded to Eudora Jean, the sole sister remaining at home. Poor girl was completely dominated by Mama's caveats and looked sure to fulfill the spinster's fate of living cowed and servile to her mother's needs until Beadie was in the ground. She was quiet and thin and often wore Mama's cast-off clothes, so it was hard to see Eudora Jean as an individual. She seemed more her mother's shadow. Mickey Moe felt sorry for her and frustrated that he could not inject her with a little gumption.

I hope you all forgive me.

Beadie sighed in response and rang her bell for service. Sara Kate appeared hauling a huge tureen as nice as the Needlemans', from which she ladled out a cold potato soup seasoned with dill.

Isn't it a good thing we decided against a hot soup tonight, Sara Kate? Despite the fact that folks say a steamy broth is just the thing to cool one off on a summer day? Thanks to my boy here, it would've curdled before we all sat.

Yes, Miss Beadie. It shows you never lost your instincts.

Mickey Moe's mama was proud that in the old days she could always arrive at the choicest menu to suit a particular occasion. The compliment pleased her and she relaxed considerably. She turned to her only son to bless him with the restoration of her good humor.

Why don't you tell us how your trip to Greenville went? I imagine it went quite well, as you were invited the night.

That would be a misperception, Mama.

He told the story of his visit to the Needlemans' and held nothing back. Mama was shocked, then outraged, then excited, and at last, disapproving of his plans.

I don't know, son. I don't know what good would come of finding your daddy's people. Some rocks are better left unturned.

It never occurred to Mickey Moe that Mama might know more about Bernard Levy than she'd ever let on. He thought she was worried about his welfare. He sat up a little straighter and squared his shoulders. As Sara Kate had just cleared his place setting, he put his forearms on the table, clasped his hands earnestly, and leaned forward.

I'm prepared for whatever comes my way. You don't have to worry.

He lifted his hands and rested his chin against them with a dreamy look on his handsome face.

I will be a child of mystery no more, no more.

Hmph, Mama said. As long as you don't remain a boor with his elbows on the table.

That night he lay awake plotting the first campaign of his quest. He planned to drive to Memphis over the old roads his daddy had utilized back when. There was a faint scratch on his door. Eudora Jean entered in her long linen nightgown and sat on the edge of his bed.

Mickey, she whispered. Mickey Moe.

Yes, honey?

I want you to know I think this is the most romantic, wonderful thing you are prepared to do, and I wish you the Lord's own help, no matter what Mama says.

He sat up and kissed the top of her head. Thank you, girl, he said.

And because of that, I think you should know that on more than one occasion Mama has intimated to me that sometimes in private Daddy didn't talk at all like an educated man from Tennessee. I think he came from somewhere else altogether. Once she mentioned that the only person she ever knew who used the same turns of phrase was Bald Horace. You should go talk to him, if you can find him. He hasn't come round for more than ten year, you know. After the uncles opened up Sassaport Milk and Creamery, his little business went dry. I hear he got awfully frail, too. But it shouldn't be hard to find out where he's bein' kept and who looks out for him.

Her brother grabbed her then and held her tight. Oh, you are a very good girl, Eudora Jean. When I marry, I'll tell my wife you are the most darlin' woman in Guilford, and she will be the best of friends to you.

The grave tone of his words made his sister giggle, and as her laughter was a bit loud, she disengaged herself from fraternal embrace, clapped her hand over her mouth, and left the room. Mickey Moe stared at the ceiling. Sure doesn't take much to amuse a homebody, he thought. He pondered what she'd said. It made sense to seek out Bald Horace and, while he was at it, that sometimes wife of his, Aurora Mae, to boot. Both of them had known something about Daddy no one else did. They each said so, and they hadn't been lying. He was sure of it.

Later, he let fanciful images of the woman he loved guide him on the road to sleep. It proved a hard road, a rocky road, full of peaks followed by valleys, and then unexpectedly peaks again so that it was early in the morning before he fell sleep. Accordingly, he slept in later than he ought. When he woke up and went downstairs to find Sara Kate and a little breakfast, he was met with a most bittersweet surprise.

The kitchen table was full. Dishes of eggs with sausage and biscuits and gravy were spread all over. Sara Kate stood at the stove top fixing coffee and sitting down enjoying their breakfast were Mama and Eudora Jean and and Laura Anne Needleman.

Sweetheart!

Mickey Moe was too stunned to do more than utter the endearment and stand there like a dope with his arms raised and open. Eager to impress her future mother-in-law, Laura Anne daubed at the corners of her mouth with a napkin, smiled at Beadie and Eudora Jean with her chin drawn in and her eyebrows raised, nodding to each in turn as if to beg leave of the table. To her credit, she did not rise until Beadie nodded back.

The lovers shared a quick, chaste embrace.

What are you doing here? Mickey Moe asked. Because he could think of no explanation, he added, Is your family well?

I imagine they're upset with me just at the moment, but I could not help myself. I've been tortured since you left. So I weighed my loyalty to them against my feelings for you and decided to come to you to help you find your daddy's people. I left them a letter explaining my thoughts, took the late-night bus from Greenville, and arrived just after dawn this morning. . . .

She continued speaking near breathless of the most difficult part of her journey. She'd had to find someone at first light who knew how to direct her from the bus station to his home. She'd walked all the way in her white high-heeled pumps while carrying her hatbox suitcase.

I thought my feet might fall off, she said. But once I got here, everyone's been so kind, they feel almost normal now.

Mickey Moe noticed a pair of white high-heels sitting directly under her chair. Her feet were red and a tad puffy. Every bit of the situation was a marvel to him. Mama had welcomed into her home a young woman she'd on any other occasion label a low-life, wild-child vagabond for leaving her parents and showing up at a man's home uninvited just before she slammed the door in her face. It amazed him that Laura Anne was there at all. She'd announced her scandalous intention to accompany him on his journey in search of his daddy's origins when the original purpose of his quest was to provide their love affair a mantle of propriety. He was in awe that she loved him enough to defy her parents and that the police had not yet arrived to snatch her back. Looking at her was like looking at the sun, he thought, and who knew brown eyes could carry so much gold in them. There were more wonders before him, but they remained unarticulated and were full of sighs.

With the reunion of lovers accomplished and witnessed, Mama further amazed Mickey Moe by instructing Eudora Jean to take their guest to her bedroom and make sure the poor lamb had a good lie-down now that she had nourishment. Laura Anne thanked her and bent to kiss her cheek. While she did not flinch at the intimacy, Mickey Moe knew his mama well enough to capture the tiny squint of her eyes and infinitesimal wrinkle of her nose. Once the younger women ascended the stairs and their footsteps were heard in the bedroom above the kitchen, he braced himself for Mama's speech. And what a speech it was.

Delivered in the soft, measured tones of a woman reciting from a book of Christian poetry, Beadie Sassaport Levy summoned up all the lessons of her blood and training to condemn Laura Anne Needleman as either completely wanton or thoroughly insane in language as refined as it was laden with secondary, even tertiary meanings, none of them pleasant.

I suppose they do things differently in Greenville, she began, as that place has been a hubbub of craven commerce and production for as long as Eve's daughters liked apples. To my knowledge, there has never before been a woman of good family, which is to say character, who would leave her mama and daddy a note—my goodness! a note!—to inform them she'd gone off to wander the countryside in the company of a boy of whom they had already registered their disapproval whether warranted or not. Unless she is the Bard of the Mississippi, is that possible, do you think? Has that young woman prodigious talent in the written word, son? It must be so, since I did not raise my boy to fall for a hussy so vulgar and willful as to leave a note that reads, Mama and Daddy, gone to throw myself on the mercies of man and the river. Love, your baby girl. No, no, no. Imagine, Sara Kate—are you listening?

The maid stood behind them at the sink as she washed the breakfast dishes.

Yes, Miss Beadie. I'm hearin' it all.

Then imagine, Sara Kate, the divine phrases she must have used to soften the blow! A good girl would have to, wouldn't she? Or die of shame and guilt along the road. . . .

Mickey Moe did not interrupt. He needed a place for Laura Anne to stay the night while he organized their trip. He thought maybe if Mama had her fill of insults and insinuations, she'd calm down, and he could plead their case. But she went on and on.

. . .There's other explanations, of course, Mama said when she ran out of ways to imply that Laura Anne was a common slut. She could be a madwoman. What do you think, Sara Kate? She seem hatter mad to you?

Well, now, I don't know, as . . .

Don't bother finishing if you aren't going to agree. I wasn't really asking a question. I was adding it all up aloud and invoking your name the way I would use chalk on a board. And my tally looks as if two and two are not three as you were about to claim but four. The poor child very definitely has a certain glint in her eye. . . .

At last, as an act of kindness or because her head was starting to hurt from listening to Beadie's harangue or even because she felt insulted herself, Sara Kate turned around. In full view of Mickey Moe, who was facing her, but not visible to Beadie Sassaport Levy, who was not, she raised a dish of very fine china high in the air and brought it down hard against the countertop in a loud, satisfying smash. The sound of pieces of porcelain hitting the floor effectively ended all speech-making.

Good gracious, girl, Beadie said. Is this why my store of china keeps dwindlin'?

I don't know how that happened, Miss Beadie. It slipped outta my hand like a haint pushed it from above out of my grasp.

She crouched on the floor gathering shards.

Haints. My, oh my, now I've got to listen to haint stories the rest of the day, I suppose. Wait, girl. Don't you go throwin' that away, lay those pieces here, and we'll see if we can't glue that thing.

Mickey Moe took their preoccupation as an avenue of escape. He tippy-toed upstairs and rapped twice on Eudora Jean's bedroom door. His sister answered promptly. With a finger held up to her closed lips, she let him in with a wink and a nod, leaving him alone with Laura Anne as she shut the door behind her to stand watch without. The lovers kissed long and hard, then pulled away from each other.

Sweetheart, I can't tell you how happy I am to see you, Mickey Moe began, but this was not a wise idea, was it? I mean, the whole purpose of my quest is to find a way to make my family wholesome in your family's eyes. Even if I can talk Mama into harboring you here—which is doubtful no matter how kindly you thought she treated you this morning—how will your taking off from home to travel with me, unmarried as we are, accomplish that goal? And I don't know where exactly my daddy's trail will take me. Might be a host of locales dangerous for you to go. Look. I'm going to call your parents straightaway and tell them you're on your way home. Tell them I was shocked to find you at my door and that I'm sending you home. Yes, that would do. Make me look the hero to them, I'm sure.

While he spoke, Laura Anne's face fell. Her eyes welled up. She looked about to cry when suddenly she knit her brow and raised her chin.

Mickey Moe, do you have any idea what it took for me to follow you here? The struggle I went through, knowing I was closin' a door on everything I've ever been? Mama's good daughter, the responsible employee, the darlin' of my daddy's eye. Well, it was hard. Very hard. But I figured in the end that I would rather be a pariah in Greenville for the rest of my life than spend the same span of years the puppet of people who thought they knew my own heart better than I did myself, people who felt they could tell me where I could go, what I could do, and who I could marry. Haven't you followed the news at all? Women all over are startin' to stand up for themselves. Right next to the Negroes and the Chinese. My coming here puts me at the vanguard of a great and powerful movement that will change the world. If I have a pure desire, I ain't lettin' anybody else tell me how to satisfy it. Includin' you. I am not behavin' on simple romantic impulse, Mickey. This was a decision. Fully thought out and accounted for. I never expected your family to put me up or anything. I'm not a child. I've been working, you know, for a salary plus commission. I have my savings. You can boot me out of this house if you want, but I'll find someplace to stay nearby. I'll get a job around here if I have to. All I know is, I am at your side for the duration. Don't you even think of gettin' rid of me. You just try, and I'll hound you from one end of the Mississippi to t'other through mud, bramble, concrete, and swamp. I swear this on my very soul.

Her passion rocked Mickey Moe. He felt a surge of desire that started at his toes and went all the way up to his hairline. He groaned and gathered her in his arms again. They petted at each other as much as they dared with his sister just outside. Eudora Jean heard everything, of course. She was duly impressed. On that day at that moment, Eudora Jean Levy began to question her life. Perhaps it was a little late, as the woman was thirty years of age, locked in a culture where youth and beauty determined a girl's worth until she married, when charm, charitable instinct, and accomplishment at domestic duties confirmed her status. By the time Eudora Jean's liberation was fulfilled, the least anyone might say about her was that she made up for lost time. With a vengeance. And in a manner not even the boldly loving Laura Anne Needleman would consider. Some people said, that's her daddy's blood comin' out. Of course, by that time, everyone guessed just how common that blood was.

Mickey Moe realized that Laura Anne frightened him a little. Here was a woman outside his experience, a woman of vision with the resolve to achieve things. He had no idea what those things were and that was the scary part. But her passion filled up his heart, and he wanted more than anything to give her whatever she needed to be whomever she chose.

This was a revelation. He knew the Negroes and other minorities were clamoring for rights they might have trouble handling. He was one of those boys who thought change should come for the colored folk. The way the men got blamed for every little thing that went miss-

ing or broke, the way their women had to be careful not to catch the
wrong white man's eye was downright sinful, but the Negroes could
get themselves burned up in the process of everybody's adjustment if
change came too quickly. There were boys about, those Hicks in the
southeast part of town for example, and their cousins, the Turners,
who cheered like apes on a picnic whenever ugly news hit the papers
or the TV about civil rights organizers gone missing or some poor old
Negro found floatin' in the river whupped and naked. By contrast, he
hadn't heard a whisper about any movement afoot to free women of
their bonds. He wasn't aware they had any. Womanhood looked to him
like a free ride, at least until the babies came or there was a household
to run. He knew plenty of females who worked alongside their men
in shops and pasture, worked hard, too, and were good at what they
did. To his mind, they were good at what they did because the responsibility and the worry didn't lay heavy on their shoulders, which freed
up their energies to help them focus on the task at hand. Now, there
were obviously exceptions. His mama, for example, learned as a young
widow to take charge, because her daddy was feeble, her brothers
mostly off at war. There was no choice for her. She learned to grip her
domain in a stranglehold, so you either did what Mama wanted or you
choked to death. He'd escaped her fearsome ways in large part because
he was the man of the house, but not his sisters. After schooling them
in every nuance of domestic management, she'd picked out husbands
for Sophie and Rachel Marie, threw the genders together, and dared
them to defy her wisdom on the subject. They didn't, although they
did move out-of-state as soon as they could convince their husbands to
do so and were seen only on the most important holidays. She chose to
keep Eudora Jean to home as her companion, and look how that turned
out. Never was a daughter so much under her mama's thumb, thought
Mickey Moe. That sister of mine is the complete opposite of my darlin'
Laura Anne, who can be intimidatin', but who thrills me no end. She's

my belle, he thought as he nuzzled her neck, my very own belle. He decided right there while being stroked in a most pleasurable manner by the lady in question that his future bride could liberate herself to the limits of her imagination and he would not care, which was a provident decision.

As luck would have it, Beadie had her canasta club that afternoon. No event, not even the appearance on her doorstep of her baby boy's deranged paramour, could forestall canasta club. Better luck, it was not her week to host the game. Aunt Lucille picked her up at twelve-thirty o'clock, so she was out of the house not long after Laura Anne went for her lie-down. Before she left, she instructed her daughter to keep an eye on the couple during her absence to preserve the household's honor.

Not five minutes later, Eudora Jean found an urgent reason to leave, taking the maid with her. It was her first overt act of defiance in thirty years, and it felt good. She sped off in Mama's car with Sara Kate installed in the front seat beside her. There was a smile on her face as broad as a moonbeam when that old man is at full on a clear night. She went to the hardware store and bought a plunger in case she needed proof of emergency. Since they'd need to feed Laura Anne later on, they drove next to the butcher where she obtained an extra cut of chicken breast and another of brisket and had the man pack the meat in lots of ice as she didn't plan to go home directly. Instead, she took Sara Kate to the village to visit her people. Eudora Jean spent a good chunk of the afternoon drinking lemonade outside the shack of Annie Althea, the Negro dressmaker, while fanning herself with an out-of-date fashion magazine. There she chatted with the dressmaker's help, young black girls every one, whenever they took a break from the heat inside. They talked about innocuous subjects, about the weather, which fabrics the trendsetters of Guilford were planning to use for fall, who had a new baby, and who had passed. Nonchalant, she inquired after old Bald Horace, asked was he still alive and where he might be living these days.

Oh, he's mostly alright, she was told, with Mama Jo Baylin takin' care of him over to her house.

It was the most fun Eudora Jean had in a dog's age.

Meanwhile, Mickey Moe and Laura Anne made love for the first time in a bed. After the front- and backseats of his LTD and a blanket spread on the riverbank, such luxury was enough to send them straight to paradise. In a kind of dizzy euphoria, they drank the ambrosia of each other's kisses and inhaled the incense of each other's sweat, their expressions dazed yet solemn as the grave. It was a stroke of luck they heard the car pull up outside. Laura Anne quickly got into her underclothes and daytime shift. She made it to the hallway eons before he did, but that was alright. It looked as if she'd never even come near his room and had just risen from her nap in Eudora Jean's.

After all their hurry, it was Eudora Jean who had returned home, not Mama as they feared.

O Mick, his sister said, I found out where Bald Horace is. She told him where to go while Laura Anne freshened up a little.

Sara Kate made the lovers sandwiches they could take with to eat on the ride to the village, as it was getting on in the afternoon and it wouldn't be right to intrude on anyone's home, black or white, too close to suppertime.

Don't worry, Eudora Jean said. I'll tell Mama you're showin' Laura Anne the town.

They set off.

When they turned down the dusty dirt road that led to the village, Laura Anne said, Now it's startin' to look like home around here. I've been wonderin' where you all kept the colored folk. In Greenville, there's more of them than there are of us. Can't sleepwalk without runnin' into one. Why there must be four of them to every one of us, and black homes mixed in with the white on every street. Daddy's always jokin', what we gonna do if they decide to revolt? But here in Guilford,

I didn't see more'n five or six in my walk over to your house and all of them were in the bus station.

He stopped the car in front of a battered mobile home, a 1957 Spartan Imperial with sheets of tin peaked over its roof to run off the rain. There was an expando porch at the rear. Tall herbs, their leaves feathered or spiked, sprouted from window boxes bolted through the main structure's sides. Next to the front steps, there was a vegetable garden, green with spring growth under a chuppah's worth of chicken wire as protection against night critters. There was a separate fenced-off area out the back where a pack of skinny dogs barked incessant welcome, and some thirty yards beyond that were the remains of the tar-paper shack Bald Horace lived in when Mickey Moe was a child. It looked blasted apart by a rogue tornado, scavenged, and left like a war memorial in a twisted heap. Mickey Moe ascended the cinder-block staircase with Laura Anne holding the hand he stuck behind him and knocked with the other.

A tiny black woman answered, barefoot, dressed in a loose house-coat of carnation pink. Small as she was, her hands and feet were long and knobby. Her face was set with hard, sharp features carved into taut skin like initials on the trunk of a tree, etched there by a bundle of time and troubles. She swung the door open, stepped back, and dropped her gaze to study her caller's boots. This was a habit she'd lately acquired when white folk came by in case they were kluckers come to pay a nasty call. It was an invitation to misery to look kluckers in the eye.

Mama Jo, Mama Jo, her visitor said, look up, it's me, Mickey Moe Levy, come to say hey to Bald Horace on a Tuesday afternoon.

The old woman raised her head to see if this was true, if this was himself come knocking. When she saw indeed it was, her face broke into an expression of relief, lighting up as if a handful of holiday spar-klers had been set off all around her mean, dim doorway.

Oh Mr. Levy, how wonderful it is to see you. How kind it is of you to call. How fine you look, how grown-up, fit, and strong! She was in mid-praise of the wonder of his jaw, which had not softened to the naked eye, not at all at all and he was how old nowadays? Twenty-five? My, my, and him so polished, so mature lookin' when he interrupted in an effort to get her to cease her rambling flattery.

Mama Jo, I'd like you to meet my fiancée, Miss Laura Anne Needleman, of Greenville.

Now Laura Anne was in for the hyperbole bath.

Why, this lovely gal is going to marry our Mr. Levy? Well, ain't she just a princess fit for a prince, then. What eyes you have, child! They're like the glitterin' dawn of a newborn world.

More of the same came out of her mouth until Laura Anne burned to clap her hand over it to get her to stop. What she did do was plaster a grin on her face then push herself past the other two to gain uninvited entry into the trailer. She craned her neck to take it all in, curious as if she had entered a museum of the exotic, studying what she could glimpse of the chopped-up rooms within. Not looking where she was going, she twisted her ankle in a pothole of linoleum warped and ripped through by the elements, artfully concealed beneath a strip of plywood and a scrap of rug. Mercifully, her stumble startled Mama Jo Baylin out of her litany, and an entirely different woman emerged, one who took charge of every situation she found herself in because without her help the world hurtled headlong to ruin.

Lord Almighty, child, I might have told you to watch your step there if you'd given me a minute, she said, her irritation clear. You alright?

I think so.

The girl hobbled over to an easy chair, covered against dust and common use with a bedsheet, and sunk into it. An open Bible was on a reading table next to the chair's arm. Above that a portrait of Jesus in a pose of sacral suffering hung on the wall, hovering forgiveness over her as if she represented the whole of reckless humanity. Mama Jo hurried to the icebox, wrapped a handful of frosty shards in a towel, then sat on a footstool in front of the chair. She removed Laura Anne's shoe and placed her foot in her lap, pressing the frigid towel against her ankle.

Please, I'm sorry. You don't have to do that. I'm alright, I'm just havin' terrible luck with my feet today, Laura Anne begged, genuinely uncomfortable from the woman's ministrations, but Mama Jo ignored her. She bent over her foot and examined it from side to side, up and down.

You'll live, she said, you'll walk upright out of here. But set with me for a bit like this for safety's sake.

Mickey Moe was left standing anxiously in the middle of the room. May I? he asked, gesturing toward the couch and, gaining permission, sat himself down.

Mama Jo, I'm sorry to trouble you this way. Our visit is obviously ill-starred. But I was lookin' for Bald Horace. I had a mind to chat with him about the past.

Mama Jo's chin tilted upward in a prideful manner.

Well, he ain't here right now. Every Tuesday afternoon, I take him over to the hospital for his treatment. We're so regular, they don't even make him wait much. I pick him up after five. Then once he's home, he needs his rest.

Disappointment flooded him. The prospect of waiting another day for an interview with the man who could hold the key to his happiness was a torment. Impatience pricked his memory. A long-ago image of that sometimes wife of Bald Horace, Aurora Mae, who claimed to know his daddy better than anyone, came to his mind. The thought of her lit his imagination afire. Yes! he thought. Yes! Aurora Mae would be the key to everything, he just knew it. There could be no doubt. He swallowed his excitement and asked, as politely, as he could manage,

And Bald Horace's wife, is she still around here?

The woman's brow creased with puzzlement.

Bald Horace got no wife I ever saw.

Sure he does. Great big tall woman. Wide, too. Aurora Mae's her name, I believe.

No, no. Don't know anyone like that.

Mickey Moe's heart sank; the fire fizzled and smoked. His best lead was lost to time. It never occurred to him that Mama Jo might lie.

They stayed another quarter hour, making pleasantries. When they were ready to leave, Laura Anne got up and put weight on her foot without pain, but Mama Jo insisted on a treatment of herbs plucked fresh from one of her window boxes. She placed them in a ring around the girl's ankle to assure that swelling didn't kick in later then secured all with a plaited rag of haint blue to keep evil spirits away. Mickey Moe told her they'd be back the next morning.

When they got home, Mama was waiting in her front room with her mouth in a twist. Where'd you get that? she asked straight off, pointing to the rag on the girl's ankle.

Sara Kate never hesitated to bedevil Miss Beadie if she could get away from it. She piped up from a doorway. I put that on 'er, Miss Beadie. I thought it best if she was stuffin' those poor li'l feet back into her shoes so quick.

And it was so very kind of you, I thank you so much, Laura Anne quickly said, with a nod of gratitude to her co-conspirator.

Mama held up a hand to silence them. She had a pronouncement to make. She'd decided that Laura Anne Needleman could stay in the house for two nights and two nights only, so's they could get to know each other, but only on condition that she phone her parents immediately to let them know where she was.

Laura Anne did so.

Hello, Mama? She said into the phone as cousin Patricia Ellen snickered on the other end of the line but not loud enough for the hovering

Beadie Sassaport Levy to hear. Why deception is easy, Laura Anne thought, when in the name of a good cause.

Oh yes, the girl thought she was the most clever woman alive; the strongest, most determined, invincible female ever to walk the streets of Greenville and Guilford. She spent her time under Beadie's roof with her chin held high, a demeanor of unshakable self-confidence coloring everything she said or did. The phrase *noblesse oblige*, a phrase she'd learned from the educational channel on the TV, resounded through her head whenever she spoke with her future mother-in-law. She related to that woman with a winning humility that barely hit skin-deep but worked wonders nonetheless. For two days, she proved to Mickey Moe that she could be a bulwark of strength for him, a wellspring of support, a partner in arms. For two days, their plans went extraordinarily well.

And then her daddy showed up.

VII

Memphis, Tennessee–Saint Louis, Missouri, 1918–1923

BERNARD QUIT SCHOOL WHEN HE was thirteen. His grandmama made sure he had something resembling a bar mitzvah that year. The part that stuck was not putting his hand on the Torah while the traveling rabbi read for him, nor the sugar cake they all ate afterward, nor was it the astonishing sight of Caroline Levy up, washed, and dressed before the middle of the afternoon sitting in the front row of the Memphis synagogue with an alert expression in her eyes. The part that stuck warmed his heart so much his toes curled inside his shoes. Now you are a man, the rabbi said. A man! Bernard thought, a man! A man gets to go wherever he likes, make money, and keep it. A man doesn't have to fetch beer for Mama's friends or clean their boots. A man doesn't get cuffed on the ear unless he goes lookin' for it. A man kicks the man who kicks him back. Sweet dang. I am now a man, and now I am free.

The Monday after the ceremony, Bernard went to school to tell Miss Maple good-bye. She did not try to dissuade him. She gave him a good hug and wished him well. When she did, he clung to her longer than was manly and walked away with something hard in his throat. He went directly to his grandparents' store and told them his plan to go to the levee and get a job on a riverboat, any kind of job, stoker, swabbie, pot scraper. It didn't matter as long as he saw a wage and some of the world 'til he could figure out what to do with his life. Grandmama moaned and groaned and beat her chest, but there wasn't much else she could do about his decision. Boys younger than he went out on their own at that time. Granddaddy slipped him ten dollars on the q.t. If he was careful, the old man pointed out, it was a sum that would get him by for a time. He didn't have to take the first backbreaking, mind-numbing piece of work that came along. He could study things around him, ponder a bit before enslaving himself to a cruel taskmaster. Grandaddy also gave him a parcel of wisdom.

Son, he said. Don't forget you're a Jew. Things is easy for us most times here, that is true. Especially when compared to up North or in the old countries. But when there's trouble, folks always seek to remind you of what you are. You can bet on it. So don't forget. They won't.

It wasn't so long before that Leo Frank had been lynched by a mob in Marietta, Georgia, after Governor Slaton commuted his death sentence for the murder of little Mary Phagan, a charge for which he'd clearly been railroaded. The incident sent a shiver down the spines of every Jew in the South, including young Bernard's. He shook his head as gravely as any man and promised he would not forget he was a Jew.

Grandmama meanwhile packed him a kerchief full of food for the road. She knotted it, then stuck a sprig of sage underneath the knot for luck.

Big Bette used to do that for me when I was a child, she explained. I had to walk an awful ways through the woods to the only schoolhouse in two counties. She swore on all her ghosts that li'l piece of green gave the innocent a heap of protection. She'd put it in my lunch and after I ate, I'd stick it in my drawers like she told me. That, she'd say, is where a young girl requires fortification. I tell you, it itched some, but nothin' out there ever hurt me. So I suspect she was right on all counts. You, when you finish up what you got to et in this bundle, you stick it, I would think, in your shirt near the heart.

As he was about to leave, they told him to bow his head. They raised their hands over him and gave him a blessing as old as time. His eyes stung and the hardness at his throat got bigger, so Bernard was a fine mess by the time he went to say good-bye to his mother.

When he got home, most of Mama's mind was deep in opium dreams. It's doubtful Caroline Levy understood what was going on as he packed up a sack of clothes and his daddy's penknife, the pearl-and-ebony-handled artifact that was the whole of his legacy. She had trouble keeping her eyes open when he gave her his prepared speech about being a man and the river calling to him. All she said was, Well, you're one of 'em, ain't you, boy. Then her eyes closed again.

He could not rouse her a second time. Wanting some part of her to take with him—she was still his mama after all—he grabbed a hank of hair and sawed it off using his daddy's penknife. He twisted it, wound the twist tight around his palm to make a compact ring he stuck in his pocket, leaving his hand there, touching it, while he bent over to kiss her forehead and left her forever.

It was late in the year 1918. The war was over. The influenza epidemic was winding down. Both had done their damage. White men's jobs went begging often enough. Bernard took his granddaddy's advice and spent a few days wandering the levee, observing things. He noted which riverboats abused their workers, both black and white, which beat the Negroes only, which crews looked half-starved to death, which were manned by thugs with cold, darting eyes. He studied barges that carried freight, noting what kind, and ferries that carried people to and fro. He studied the destinations of all of them. Like his daddy and granddaddy before him, what attracted him were pleasure boats full of dandies calling to serving boys on the dock by waving straw hats in the air. They smoked cigarillos, their free arms draped the waists of blonde and redheaded women, who leaned over the rails and behaved like Mama on her worst days. Minstrels serenaded them from the docks, and they rained silver coin upon them. There must be piles of money on those boats, Bernard thought, and dozens of ways for me to get my hands on some.

Luck was with him. One of the biggest paddleboats on the river, *Delilah's Dream*, had a ship's doctor looking for an assistant. The doctor took one look at Bernard Levy wandering the levee and smiled the way most folk did. Then he wondered about that sweet assembly of button eyes, flared nose, and curlicue mouth so fiercely focused in the center of a wide, round face. Although he had the stature of a child, he looked strangely adult in posture and gesture. The doctor had the boy brought to him so he might study such a curious package. He gave Bernard a dollar and examined him from head to toe, measuring his skull, his limbs, the breadth of his chest, and even that of his behind until he was satisfied that this was no genetic abnormality but a normal thirteen-year-old lad. He examined his intellect next to see if impairment accompanied an odd physiology. Finding Bernard with all his senses intact and quick witted, he offered him the medical assistant job on a whim, thinking even a man in extremis would be cheered by the sight of him. He could produce him at his elbow whenever he had bad news to tell.

And so Bernard's first career, in which he learned a great deal useful in all the others, began. For nearly three years, he followed Dr. Grayson around, carrying instruments, medicines, slop buckets, and towels. After the first three months, he could clean up blood and guts without getting sick to his stomach, steel himself against the stench of pus, and stitch a knife wound as well as the doctor himself. He witnessed the exposure, pulling, and scraping of female parts he'd never known existed. Once, the doctor allowed him to extract a child's tooth. He learned about people. He learned that rough men felt fear, that women could bear pain, that a body could watch moonbeams dance on the river and go mad from the sight. He watched the gamblers and con men ply their trades to learn where a man was weak, where strong, when pushing him worked wonders, and when pushing him went too far. He fell in love with one bad woman, then another until he swore off any woman he did not buy, as buying them seemed more honest and less trouble. He came to know more cities and towns than he could fairly distinguish other than by their climate or the goods sold from their docks. He learned that nature was more unpredictable than all the bad women he had known put together.

The doctor was good to him. He gave him time off, room, board, and a decent wage. Considering the hardships and barbarities Bernard witnessed every day on the river, these were no small boons. He slept in the antechamber of Dr. Grayson's suite aboard the *Delilah's Dream*. It was a cozy spot, one he made his own. He had a straw mattress, fine cotton sheets, and a goose-down pillow set into an alcove originally designed for the storage of muddy boots and such. That left enough floor space for a wardrobe and one of the doctor's cast-off easy chairs with a brick under its broken foot to keep it level. When everything was quiet, he liked to nestle in the chair and read old magazines he found abandoned on deck or study the pictures in the doctor's medical books. After two years in service, Bernard experienced a growth spurt, and the alcove became too small for sleep. Accordingly, he converted that space to a shelf for reading materials along with a row of cigar boxes, in which he stored his collection of sentimental treasures, mostly post-cards and ladies' hair ribbons. He slept in the chair.

One Saturday night during a full moon, the doctor roused him with a hand on his shoulder. Hurry, boy, he said. Saturday-night special.

This was their code for yet another knife fight in the dance hall where ragtime swelled a man's blood until it begged for release at the edge of a blade. When they got there, a cut-up man lay crumpled in a pool of blood, as usual, and a woman was bent over him weeping, as usual. The doctor raised the woman up by her elbows and set her aside, as usual. Across the room, a drunk, swearing revenge on the weeping woman, swayed on unsteady feet, as usual. Bernard placed the surgical kit next to the wounded man and opened it, as usual. Then something unexpected happened.

There was a shot from a handgun, then a sharp clatter as the drunk dropped his weapon when he saw whom he'd shot instead of the harlot he'd aimed for. Dr. Grayson fell to his knees clutching his middle and slumped over the man with the knife wound. Bernard shrieked and pulled the doctor off the first victim. Dr. Grayson was gut shot, bleeding a river, his eyes rolling up in his head. The man previously underneath him skittled away on his heels to the far corner of the room, screaming more about the doctor's blood mingling with his than his own injury. As there was no one else to do the job, Bernard grabbed a scalpel from the kit he'd opened. Saying a prayer for guidance, his first heartfelt prayer since Mama declared his daddy disappeared, he took that scalpel and dug around inside the doc's gizzard looking for the bullet. Clink, clink, he heard above the wails of the woman and the scramble of the men trying to subdue the murderin' drunk. Clink, clink as metal hit metal, and he'd found his mark. Slowly, slowly, holding his breath, he drew the blade out of the wound, holding the bullet against it with slight pressure against the belly wall, but that was the worst thing he could have done. He should have used the compressor forceps, tied up the bleeders then cuddled up to the bullet with the forceps' smooth, soft sides. Because he didn't, all hell broke loose in the form of a slit intestinal artery. Blood spurted up four inches high at least, a gush that bathed Bernard in his mentor's life. Within seconds, no matter how much pressure he applied with his hands, Dr. Grayson bled out and died.

It was the worst moment of his young life. Bernard was inconsolable. He'd acted rashly. He should have just tried to stem the bleeding until someone got the ship's cook. Even that butcher would have been more adept at extracting a bullet. At least the cook knew where the major blood vessels were of most beasts, including a man's. Instead, he'd murdered Dr. Grayson as surely as the shooter. The captain was summoned. He ordered the crew to haul off the slobbering inebriate and lock him up until midday when they'd reach the next town. Bernard tried to follow, weeping, holding his bloody hands out in front of himself, begging for the cuffs and imprisonment for this evil he had done, his slaying of the one man in the world who'd been a prince, yes, a prince to a poor, fatherless river rat unworthy of every act of kindness received from those pale, lifeless hands.

Everyone ignored him. A pleasure ship without a doctor was as serious a problem as a pleasure ship without a bartender. The captain and his mates busied themselves on the wireless to see whom they might line up at nearby ports of call. No one noticed nor cared when, wracked with guilt, Bernard disembarked along with the murderer and the corpse the next high noon. He took with him the doctor's anatomy book as a keepsake, the wages he'd saved, and his old sack stuffed with clothes, a bar of soap, his daddy's penknife, the lock of his mama's hair, and his shaving razor, abandoning his treasures for all time. He did not know where he was going. He wandered. He wandered over dry land, he wandered through swamp. He crisscrossed the wild river on makeshift rafts. He wandered past shantytowns alongside the railroad tracks. He slept out in the open along the ribs of Highway 61. Whenever he'd a choice, he took the most difficult path, as his passage was a penance, a grieving, and he understood such should be arduous. When his purse went dry, he hired himself out as a layer of brick, a field hand, a scavenger of refuse, a hauler of wood and coal, a grave digger, any kind of hard and dirty labor he came across. From all that hardship, he grew wizened, lost much of his hair, and looked aged beyond his years. And he found himself making his closest human relations with black folk, the people he most often labored beside.

Whenever he hit a town and he had enough pocket money to sleep indoors, the first thing he did was inquire where the black folk lived, and then he'd head there, looking for lodging. He found hiring a room in a Negro home was cheaper than any white boardinghouse in the town, especially those set up for transient workers by the plantations, the railroad, and the highway department. The food was usually more to his liking, collards and chicken parts rather than corned beef hash, and the Negroes had the inside dope on where there might be day labor, how fast a man might expect to be paid, and which foremen pocketed half a laborer's pay.

When he drifted up by Saint Louis, he was directed to a settlement five miles off river to which he walked the better half of an afternoon in the hot sun. The first house he saw on the outskirts of that place was a sight better than the ordinary ramshackle, having both a front and a back porch with rockers and potted plants all around. He judged it must belong to a preacher or an undertaker. Out of respect, he went around back to knock on the screen door. Just as his balled fist was set to rap, his eyes adjusted to the light within and his fist froze, his breath stopped.

There, in the middle of a planked wood floor, was a great tin tub, and inside the great tin tub soaked a black woman extraordinarily long and lean of limb. Her legs bent at the knee and dangled outside the tub over the sides as did her arms so that both her hands and feet rested flat on the floor. Her back did not arch. Her breasts and stomach were submerged in the milky water. She had long black hair, it draped the floor, there seemed no end to it, and it was full of life. Its tendrils twisted and curled every which way like the brush of a tropical forest. He would not have been surprised if birds flew out of it singing. He'd never seen the like of that hair before, nor would he ever see it again, although years later, a lifetime later, he was reminded of that hair when he first saw Beadie Sassaport, and the reminder had more than a little to do with his attraction to her.

The woman's face struck him as exquisite, even though all he could see of it was an assembly of shadowed planes and soft rounds. It was like something carved from marble and meant for worship. The cheekbones were long and deep, the nose broad but straight, the lips so full they looked as if a man could bite them to discover a drink of sweet nectar that never stopped flowing. Her eyes, if he'd seen them open, might have turned him to stone, but as it was he could only imagine their brilliance beneath closed lids fringed in thick, soft lash.

She seemed asleep. She did not move for a very long time, during which Bernard, entranced, studied her with no thoughts but those of marvel at the deep shiny color of her skin, the length of her sinewy thighs, the slender fingers and toes with their purplish nails, which led to thoughts of royalty. He imagined a crown on her head, in that hair, maybe one made of plaited river grass. As he pondered and marveled, his left foot fell asleep. It crumpled underneath him and he went clumsily down on one knee on the porch landing, making a helluva racket. The woman, who did not move a muscle, opened her mouth and in a voice that for Bernard was like the sound of heavenly cymbals ringing from on high to jangle every nerve he had left, said, Horace! Horace! That better be you!

Sitting as he was on the porch floor in a humiliating position, flat on his ass, cross-legged, rubbing his foot back to life, Bernard had an attack of humbleness. He spoke the truth when a quicker wit would have jumped up and hobbled as fast as he could back to the cover of trees lining the road.

No, m'am, it ain't Horace.

There was a great sound of sloshing water as if a spring had burst forth in a desert. Bernard jerked his head, looked up, slack-jawed and pop-eyed. The goddess had risen from her bath in a rush. She'd been wearing a shift while bathing, which was often the custom in those days, but it was white and thin and clung to her flesh so that she looked nude, more naked than if she'd been undressed. He stared up at her graceful belly, at her round, high breasts. His eyes moved up, up, up— she was as tall as her long limbs suggested with a long torso to match— until they rested on her face, which was now alert and livid. Her eyes, oh! those eyes! black and glinting with impossible light! She glared at him with a fury he could barely comprehend, such was the heat in those eyes, and he thought his very soul would melt in the fire of her fierce beauty.

It happened so fast, he didn't see it coming. In a heartbeat, she burst through the door and had her hands around his neck, squeezing, squeezing, with the rage in her eyes unabated. Her knees were in his ribs, keeping him down, pushing the air up from his chest at the same time her hands at his throat kept the air from leaving him. A war went on inside his lungs. At first, he fought, but she was so much larger than he, the pressure was too great. It was a losing battle. He burned, every fiber of his chest was enflamed. He went faint, he ceased to fight, his vision went dark, his body began to float in the air, so that he felt a willing victim offered to an unimaginable deity, zealous and primitive, when a voice, faint but insistent, came to his ears.

Aurora! Aurora Mae! Stop! Stop! That is a white man you're killin'! You will bring down hell upon us! Stop! Stop!

And the torture ceased.

When he finished gasping and could breathe normally again, sight was the first sense that came back to him. Bernard's eyes fluttered, struggled to focus, and what he could see was a young black man with a head of hair as wild and untamed as the goddess Aurora Mae's. He leaned over him with a glass of water and a frantic expression on his perfectly plain, unremarkable features. He was dressed as they all were in summer, in overalls, shirtless, barefoot. Apart from the worry on his face, everything about him, from his medium build, to his brown eyes, his broad African nose and full lips, was normal, everyday, a fact oddly comforting to a man nearly choked to death by a giantess. He reached out a trembling hand and his savior pulled him up. With an arm around his waist, Horace guided Bernard to a chair in the kitchen, one close to the tin tub, close enough so that Bernard could smell the sweet scent of store-bought soap and hear its little bubbles burst as when one has come close to death and lives, the senses return with mythic sharpness. When his breath regularized, he spoke in a voice made ragged from strangulation.

I'm very sorry—Horace, is it?

The man's brow creased in apparent suspicion. His face went dead still, the worry masked by something darker. He slowly shook his head up and down twice.

I'm very sorry, then, Horace. I come back 'round here to see if you got a room to let or know anybody who does as I am passing through and need both work and lodging. I did not mean to disturb your wife. I was not intending to spy on her, but confronted as I was by the astonishing vista of her, I could not help but be hypnotized. I do hope you both forgive me.

Suspicion was now writ more distinctly upon his savior's features. His eyes were narrow with it. His head tilted to the side with the chin pointed out. The mouth was a grim, puckered line. Verbose apologies after nearly being strangled to death by a black woman was the last thing he expected out of a white man's mouth. He waited for the sucker punch that invariably followed sly remarks from these people.

My sister, he said.

Miss Aurora Mae is your sister?

Yessir. She is.

Now this was something Bernard thought hugely funny, and he laughed outright, startling Horace into straightening up and backing off. Forgive me again, he said. It's just that, well, you and I, we're no more'n bugs next to her, are we? And yet you are blood related? Oh dear, oh dear.

And he laughed and laughed as much from exhaustion as from relief that he was alive. Even more, he laughed because he acknowledged to himself happily—it was pointless to deny it—that he was immediately, hopelessly, scandalously, outrageously, probably sinfully in love with Aurora Mae, and she was not married or at least was not married to the man who'd saved his life. For his part, Horace stopped looking suspicious and erupted into guffaws himself out of relief, because he'd decided this strange, funny-looking white man was no kind of threat to him and his but simply, clearly a fool.

He had a room for rent, too. The one off the kitchen had been slave quarters back when white folk owned the house. It seemed fitting that a redneck, beggar idiot might reside there now that the house had come down to him and his sister. Their grandmama, Sybil, had been the original owner's slave and had been much abused in that room, first by her master and then by her master's son. When the war came, the two men went off with a Confederate regiment to die at Pea Ridge under General Price. The lady of the house took ill around the same time with the yellow fever. She was as strong as she was mean and lasted longer than other victims until finally, she died in extreme pain. Sybil nursed her to the end in that same room off the kitchen, because it was the closest to boiling water and such. Now death and suffering have a way of gentling people, allowing them to give voice to their guilt, which is what won Sybil freedom even before Emancipation.

After the war, there were no blood heirs left to the plantation. The former slave wrested a deed to the house and its lands from a court official everyone said she either seduced or ensorcelled. A little later, she married a freed slave named Roman, a farmer one generation removed from Africa. Roman was the powerhouse of a man who provided the genes that made Aurora Mae the marvelous creature she was and bestowed upon Horace a talent for making things grow. He invited a nation of cousins to come and farm the land with them as a community, the way he'd heard Negroes did in Africa, sharing all they reaped together in harmony. That effort was a disaster. What the family's own feuds and slights didn't ruin, the animosities of their white abutters did. Yet even though the farming didn't go too well, the community grew. Over time, more and more black folk put up houses in the fields. They plowed out roads that led from a cluster of one set of cousin's homes to the next. Eventually, the parents of Horace and Aurora Mae were born, lived their span, and passed, their daddy from too much hard work in the middle of a row of cotton, their mama from the Spanish flu in 1914. Sybil and Roman outlived them, but not by much.

Teenagers at the time, Horace and Aurora Mae stayed on. Though they did not have more in the way of material wealth than any of their neighbor cousins, they lived in the big house and took good care of it. They looked like kings on a hill to all the world below them. That striking residence coupled with Aurora Mae's stature, her imperious manner, and expertise in herbs, spells, and potions taught her by her grandmama, made the sister and brother leaders of the colony, high priestess and deacon to whom the others appealed for audience or favor.

With Bernard's arrival, it soon became known that the witch and her brother kept a crazy white man around as a pet. Small children charged a penny to guide others for a look at him through the kitchen window. On the days he wasn't making a living rendering lye or mucking pigsties, Bernard could be found there working by Aurora Mae's side helping her boil sweet gum or pickle mandrake root. And because just being near her thrilled him no end, his eyes would sparkle, he did all manner of jigs and pratfalls to make her laugh, and all the children so inclined felt their pennies well spent indeed.

Bernard lived with these two for more than a year. Never was he happier than when Aurora Mae might brush her hand across his head, rubbing him, she said, for good luck. He literally lived in her shadow, sharing in the devotion her brother, Horace, also felt for her. It was natural that Horace and Bernard would become best of friends. He might have lived there forever, high upriver, in obscure happiness had not cruel circumstance intervened to scatter them in urgent flight. He might have remembered his time there with the kind of hallowed reverence men save for their truest love, lost forever, had they not been thrown together again under yet crueler circumstances, and had Bernard not decided to stand up and declare himself in the most dangerous manner.

VIII

Guilford, Mississippi, 1962

THE DAY THE YOUNG LOVERS headed out to the village to interview Bald Horace, the weather appeared fine. Everything sparkled bright and fresh under the sun. Still, Sara Kate tasted lightning in the air. She went to the back porch to see them off, and immediately, her nose wrinkled. She smacked her tongue against the roof of her mouth twice.

The bite of gunmetal's in the air today, she said. You all don't linger outside too long. You'll be caught up in a storm for sure.

They promised they'd be careful, but once the car got them out of sight, they snuggled up to laugh together at the perpetual doom and gloom that issued from the mouths of old black women, every one of whom considered herself a seer when it came to weather or illness or babies or death.

Mickey Moe ordinarily took such predictions as gospel, but he knew Laura Anne, from the city of Greenville, was more sophisticated than he, and he didn't want to look ridiculous to her. Besides, he'd opened his eyes to the world anxious that morning. It helped to share a chuckle at another's expense. Took a sliver off the edge.

As they drew near the village, his anxiety bloomed. His heart thumped against his ribs, his breath came ragged. It seemed the limbs of trees along the roadway sought to close him in, which gave him the fidgets. Laura Anne disentangled herself from his arm and sat up, spine straight, close to the passenger door.

You ok, honey? she asked.

He thought about it, because the last thing he wanted to do was mislead her. It was of supreme importance to him that this woman know precisely what he was thinking and feeling at all times. He knew from his mama that the worst thing a man could do was lie to a woman. He took a moment to judge his thoughts, and when he spoke, he spoke slowly, precise in his choice of words.

I feel like my whole life has boiled down to just this moment coming up, he said. At last, I will find out the truth about my people. I never appreciated how important that was to me until yours made an issue of it. I decided long ago only women were obsessed with the bloodlines or I didn't let it matter to me, because in my house questions on the subject led to dead miseries. I took my pride where I was told to—in being half a Sassaport—impressive enough in these parts, but apparently inconsequential in Greenville and the rest of the wide world. I feel that if I find the right words to say to Bald Horace, the gates of heaven will open to me in all their fragrant splendor, but if I fumble, they will slam shut on ten of my fingers and ten of my toes and I guess yours, too. It's a terrible responsibility. Terrible.

The girl let out a huge, empathetic sigh. He admired the way her bosom heaved during its execution. You're very brave, Mickey Moe Levy, she said. You remind me of a hero of ancient times.

They were outside Mama Jo Baylin's house. He stopped the car.

She squeezed his hand, and he kissed her mouth. Fortified, they made their way to the dented metal door and knocked. Mama Jo granted them entry with all due politesse but without the excess of the day before. Once they were inside, she tilted her little gray head and made a sweeping gesture. Here, her arm said, is the man you seek, and there in the stuffed chair under the portrait of Jesus Christ crucified sat Bald Horace. He looked old and weak and blank of expression.

Hello there, Bald Horace, Mickey Moe said with hopeful enthusiasm, but the man did not so much as blink. Hello there, Bald Horace, he repeated only louder this time.

Nothing.

What's wrong with him? he asked Mama Jo Baylin without looking at her, his gaze stuck on the slack lower lip of the ruined man before him, the half-shut eyes surrounded by puffy circles the color of blackberries.

He's always like this directly after one of his treatments. Knocks him right out. But you keep talkin' to him. He'll come 'round in a bit, wait and see.

What kind of treatments are they? Laura Anne asked while her lover knelt down on one knee the better to grasp the man's hand and shout.

Hello there, Bald Horace, hello!

A drug treatment. Brand new, they say.

Her head tilted sideways again, and she sniffed as if taking a brand-new drug treatment were an honor, one she shared in by proximity.

He's one of the first humans to take it ever, they say, and it's got a name long as your right leg. He had the shakes somethin' awful before in his hand and head. Well, he don't shake now, but he got feeble. He's just not right anymore, especially the day after his treatment.

Mickey Moe shouted a couple more times, and Bald Horace seemed to come awake at last. His chin lifted anyway, and his eyes focused, staring directly into Mickey Moe's own. He muttered something.

Speak up, honey, Mama Jo Baylin said. We can't hear you. We can't hear you at all. You gonna have to do better than that.

Bald Horace coughed a little and spoke again. This time, Mickey Moe leaned forward to put his ear close to the man's mouth.

I know you.

Of course you do, Bald Horace, it's me. It's me, Mickey Moe Levy, come to call.

I know you.

Yes, you know me. You knew my daddy, too. 'Member my daddy, Bald Horace? You 'member Bernard Levy? You 'member him?

You growed.

The old man raised an arm. He wiped his red wet mouth on his sleeve. Oh my, thought Mickey Moe. This is going to take some time. His heart sank but he kept poking around in the darkness of Bald Horace's mind hoping to hit on something that'd bring his daddy to the forefront.

Yes, Bald Horace. I'm a fully grown man now. But when I was a boy, you looked out for me, didn't you?

Yes.

You taught me a whole lot of things I'll never forget. You taught me when to plant and when to pick. . . .

Yes.

. . . how to know the day ahead from the color of the moon. Even taught me how to manage ornery goats. . . .

I surely did.

. . . 'Member me and those goats of yours, Bald Horace? What good friends we were?

The old man gave him a big smile showing his teeth. The inside of his mouth looked raw, bumpy. There were angry white spots on his gums. A bad smell came up from his gut.

They messed you up!

He laughed, making a harsh, strident sound that only half made sense. Then out of nowhere a look of pain crossed his features, knitting them up.

'Rora Mae took you home. He looked Mickey Moe straight in the eyes. His voice grew soft. Took you home in the big car.

At that moment, there was a flash of light, then a thunderclap, loud, jolting, right over their heads. Everyone started. Laura Anne and Mama Jo jumped. Bald Horace shrieked. But that was nothing to the bolt of energy that burned through Mickey Moe's head. Aurora Mae! To think after yesterday's denial from Mama Jo that Bald Horace ever had a wife, he'd given up on finding her. Even in his compromised state, Bald Horace had brought her up like a divine message from the past, a prod to inquiry straight from the beyond. Oh please, Lord, he thought, please let her still be alive and in her right mind.

He shook her husband's shoulder as if in the shaking he might rattle some helpful thoughts together. Bald Horace, Bald Horace, where is your wife? he asked, but something had happened inside the man, something coincidental to or because of the thunderclap.

Bald Horace began to keen like a grieving widow, moaning, rocking back and forth, with tears running down his gaunt cheeks. He mumbled, 'Rora Mae, 'Rora Mae, over and over, as if the name were a prayer.

Another clap came, the furniture rattled, and Bald Horace covered his head with his hands and rocked harder, sobbed louder, mumbled faster and faster, 'rormae, 'rormae, 'rormae, like a Buddhist's chant. Then he broke out in a wail as high pitched as a train whistle.

Mickey Moe was in despair of what to do with him until Mama Jo Baylin clucked and said, He's plain terrified of thunder. Now the storm's come, you not going to have anything like sense outta him. Just pitiful, ain't he. Everything he ever was got bigger after the treatments started. He was always nervous around storms, but nowadays he goes clear out of his mind.

Mickey Moe put an arm around Bald Horace and patted. He tried to take one of his hands and squeeze it for comfort, but the man's fingers were clamped tight against his own skull, the nails dug into his scalp, while the palms covered his ears. At the next round of thunder, he leapt out of his chair to run behind a chintz curtain where his bed lay, to curl up there, hiding from the sound like a child.

Laura Anne said, Honey, we should go. She said it softly, with a gentle, kindly look cast in Mama Jo Baylin's direction along with a slight feminine shrug to indicate helplessness in the face of fate, a matter women of all colors understood. Mama Jo returned the shrug with one of her own.

Mickey Moe fought the impulse to reach in and shake Bald Horace back to himself. Confounded by despair, he stared at the curtain. His shoulders slumped.

Laura Anne nearly wept to look at him. She bit her lip. Her skin crawled with a strange irritation and a surge of power rose up from deep in her belly, a power born of a great, yearning need to protect. She turned toward Mama Jo, who was, when all was said and done, a black woman required to obey her. Words flew out of her mouth so rudely, so aggressively that she blushed at her own behavior. Oh, for God's sake! she demanded. Where is this man's wife? Tell us now!

The old woman took a step back as if struck in the face. A veil fell over her features, and she retreated within herself. In a flat tone that shouted to them "I knew you'd get like this, Miss Sweetness from Greenville. All you all get like this sooner or later," she told them that Bald Horace never had no wife, that Aurora Mae was his sister who lived in Memphis these days. Aurora Mae was a very private person and wouldn't like her telling anyone her business. Aurora Mae paid her to keep Bald Horace clean and fed and keep her mouth shut, which is why she'd misled them before. But since Bald Horace himself mentioned Aurora Mae knew Mickey Moe personally, she'd make an exception and get them her address if they'd just hold on.

Minutes later, they were back in the car, drenched by the storm outside. Carried away by the emotion and adventure they'd experienced, Mickey Moe drove as far as he could before he had to stop and hold on to Laura Anne. The ditches outside filled up with rain made filthy by the dirt washed in from the road. Every once in a while, the lightning flashed and they saw each other stark and white against the blue-gray air of storm and wind. In that harsh intermittent light, Mickey Moe gave his love a troubled look. What was on his mind was hard to express. He said, Honey, I know you were hard-pressed back there and upset for me that nothing was goin' well, but you needn't have talked up to Mama Jo that way.

No matter how gentle he'd tried to make his tone, the criticism amounted to a blow. Laura Anne gasped. Her skin went hot. She opened her mouth, closed it, opened it again, but nothing came out.

We just don't talk to the elderly that way in our house, he continued, digging the pit into which she felt like throwing herself deeper. Even if they're Negroes. Mama always schooled us to be polite no matter what the circumstances. And not only are we beholden to that woman for what she did takin' care of your ankle yesterday, we were in her home.

Thoroughly humiliated, Laura Anne burst into tears and blubbered contrition. Mickey Moe felt as badly as she did or at least he thought so. It hurt him to see his warrior love compromised. He took to stroking her back, patting her between the shoulder blades in an effort to comfort. Now, now, he said. It was an unusual situation. I know you aren't like that every day. Not my darlin' Laura Anne.

She looked up at him, sniffling. No, no, I'm not. I'm really not.

Just then, the storm let up and there was a break in the clouds. A shaft of sunlight fell directly upon her face. Her eyes shone with tears, her brows were lifted with hope of redemption, her sweet lips trembled. I believe you, he said. Now let's put this behind us. Look, the weather's clearin'. We can go on now.

He kissed her forehead. She gave him a weak smile. There remained a shadow between them, which he needed to remove something dreadful. So he started up the car and addressed it.

I guess we're going to Memphis, he said. It's good, isn't it? To know that Aurora Mae lives where my daddy claimed to grow up. She must be the key. She must know somethin' of his people. She must.

We?

He stroked her thigh.

That's what I said, girl. We.

Laura Anne beamed.

They didn't speak the rest of the way, but each was buoyed by the small success of the day. Mickey Moe had a lead, and Laura Anne had won his forgiveness. They were truly a team now, she felt. Partners in every way. They could suffer conflict and go on. Wasn't that vitally important?

She fell to imagining their future after this quest was over. She felt confident that Mickey Moe came from quality and that his daddy's identity was kept secret over some convoluted matter of honor that didn't matter anymore to anyone living or dead. Much as she claimed it was irrelevant to her, she liked to think they'd still marry properly under a chuppah in her mama's backyard with two hundred of their friends and relatives weeping tears of joy for them. They'd eat filet mignon steak and drink champagne. Her dress would have a train, but not too long, just long enough to carry comfortably after the ceremony, or maybe she'd go for one of those detachable ones. After the wedding, they'd work side by side on that farm Mickey Moe wanted, and he'd teach her everything Bald Horace taught him. She'd become self-sufficient, able to carry on should the world fall apart around their ears. That seemed an important, modern goal. There'd be children, too, when she decided the time was right. What a life. What a life. But first there'd be Memphis, where they'd stay at a hotel together as if they were man and wife already. They'd face down this woman Aurora Mae in whatever mobile home or similar hovel she lived and they'd stand firm until she gave up the information they required.

While Laura Anne mapped out both the immediate and distant future, Mickey Moe planned their departure for Memphis first thing the next day. There were a few loose ends at Uncle Tom-Tom's office he had to take care of, but Mama had laid down the law that two nights was all she'd house Laura Anne, and Mama always stuck with her decisions, right or wrong, so they'd have to leave in the morning no matter what. He had to tank up the car, check the oil and water, too, go to the bank, and get some travel cash. Maybe he could do that after he dropped Laura Anne back home and save some road time in the morning.

Out you go, he said to his lover, pinching her bottom playfully as she left the car, laughing as she squealed and turned around to slam the door at him. He watched her smooth her skirt and enter the house. He drove off, whistling, thinking all was well as well could be.

Neither of them noticed the tail end of the Lincoln Continental parked far up the winding driveway that ended behind the house. Mickey Moe could be excused for not seeing it. It was 90 percent out of his line of sight, and he was on a mission to get them started on the way to Memphis. His preparations were where his focus lay. But Laura Anne should have seen. She should have caught at least a glimpse of the vehicle out of her peripheral vision and would have if her head hadn't been full of wedding dresses and banquet menus and childbirth and tilling soil. If she had, she might have been prepared when she crossed the threshold to hear the dark hiss of a familiar voice.

So that's the kind of boy he is. Drops my daughter off in the street like she was somethin' common. Well, I suppose it's what she deserves.

Daddy!

Another voice, icy cold, chimed in.

You lied to me, young lady. Your people had no idea where you were staying, only fears and dark suspicions. I am going to have to ask you to leave with your daddy immediately.

Laura Anne faced the great hulk of an outraged Lot Needleman on her left and to her right Beadie Sassaport Levy in highest dudgeon with her arms crossed over her breasts, her chin drawn in, her face scrunched up as if the sight of her future daughter-in-law was a disgusting mass of decaying organics. Daddy grabbed her arm and held it tight enough to make her wince. He held her hatbox suitcase in his free hand as if he'd been waiting in the vestibule for his moment like an armed robber hiding behind a roadside bush.

You comin' with me, gal.

She wriggled, she wept, she cried out, she protested, she twisted to look back and begged Sara Kate, who peeped out from around the door of the next room, for help. Of course, that woman had no power in the matter. Frankly, she didn't care much about the troubles of white people she barely knew apart from the gossip value, which was why she was peeping, or if she could give Beadie a headache, but this event was far beyond the scope of her meddling. Eudora Jean was nowhere to be seen.

Lot Needleman hustled his daughter and her luggage out the door and into his car. He locked the doors and drove off while she pounded with helpless fists on the window, saying over and over, I'm twenty years old! You can't do this to me! You can't! You can't! I'm twenty years old!

It didn't do any good.

At a stoplight, she tried to jump out the car, but Lot pulled her back. He sped off before the light turned green to keep her in. He drove with one hand and kept the other wrapped tight as elastic bands around her forearm. By nightfall, she was badly bruised. Once they were outside Guilford and speeding along Highway 61, there was no opportunity to get away, and Laura Anne calmed down some. She whimpered a while, then blew her nose. For the rest of the ride, she worked to overcome her daddy's determination to keep her home and separated from the love of her life. She turned sweet and apologetic.

Daddy, she said. I am very sorry for alarming you and Mama. I would not have done it in a million, trillion years, except that I know you are wrong about my Mickey Moe. Please don't blame him for my lack of respect for your wishes. He didn't know I was coming to him. Surely Miss Beadie told you that.

While she said this and many other things, some true, some not, she put her hand on the back of Lot Needleman's neck, the way she did when she was a little girl and he drove her to the playground or Bible class. He started to melt.

You know, Daddy, he's on the very cusp of finding out who his daddy was. It's incredible. After all these years, he's found a clue up in Memphis that could clear everything up once and for all. And when he does that, Daddy, when he can tell you who his very fine people are, will you promise me that you'll accept him? Will you let us be together? Because if you do, Daddy, I promise, in return, to stay with you and Mama until that day. I will not cause another moment of distress for you. I will be cheerful. I will be industrious. I will be your good and darlin' daughter. . . .

She promised a number of other things she would be, all designed to maneuver herself back into his good graces. Slowly, the hard set of his jaw softened. She won his promise. He'd give Mickey Moe another try soon as he knew his blood. Her vows proved as ephemeral as morning mist. She tried. She tried to be good, but it didn't take a week before her lovesick mind fancied one escape route after another. In each, she met Mickey Moe in Memphis or wherever else he might be along the course of his quest, and her flight was funded by the whole of her bank account withdrawn in cash and fueled by the power of a free woman's love.

IX

Saint Louis, Missouri, 1925

THE THREE OF THEM SAT on the front porch of a warm night in March, smelling the green damp scent of woodlands coming awake to grow again. There were many stars alight in a big band that stretched rainbowlike over their heads. Every now and then, several would shoot across the sky. It was a natural time for making wishes.

I wish I could travel, Horace said. It would be good to get away from the cousins for a little bit.

The other two agreed.

Oh yes, Aurora Mae said.

Uh-huh, echoed Bernard.

Wouldn't it now? Sometimes, I swear, they about to make me go insane. All that wranglin' between 'em. The gossip and the backbitin'. The nip-nip-nip at the heels . . .

Hmm-hm . . .

You know it.

I wish I was handsome, Bernard said. He cast a sly look at Aurora Mae, hoping she would protest that handsome was not that important in a man, that character and the desire to work hard were. She was silent.

A night bird called its mate. A new star shot past. Aurora Mae spoke up.

I wish I could get me a sweet little dog.

At that moment, there were three dogs sitting on the porch. None of them was small, and none could be described as sweet. Mangy mixed-breeds they were, eighty pounders with fuzzy yellow teeth, fleas, and bad breath. They roamed the farm at will, guarding its perimeter, keeping their own brand of order. They were more absent than present on any given day, pretty much useless in terms of keeping watch or company at the big house. Bernard thought they all belonged to the dogs more than the dogs belonged to them. In that respect, Aurora Mae's need for something cuddly and devoted sounded justified to him. He squirmed in his seat thinking about it because nothing makes a lover happier than finding a way to deposit delight at the feet of his beloved. Horace asked his sister exactly what kind of sweet little dog did she dream about.

Oh, some kind of lapdog. One of those dogs with big eyes that sit at your feet pleadin' with you to pick 'em up. I believe the purebreds would cost a fair bit though.

She laughed.

Who would sell a Negro such a creature anyway? Oh, I'd be happy with any kind of soulful little mutt.

Then she looked at Bernard. Their eyes met and lingered in conjunction until each felt hot under the skin.

Horace scratched his wooly head with one hand and covered a yawn with the other. I do think I'll go on to bed, he said. We got to get up before dawn to work at the mill the morrow, and maybe old mighty mite here can handle that place with hardly any sleep and half a breakfast, but I surely can't.

He kissed his sister on her cheek and left the two alone. Not that he was looking for trouble, but he wondered how long those two could keep from consummating the feeling they had for each other. Bernard was pure besotted with Aurora Mae, he knew that. Whenever he and Bernard worked together, side by side, at the mill or the graveyard or wherever they happened to find day labor in tandem, their conversation was mostly about her. Bernard Levy asked him questions from dawn to noon about their childhoods, going all soft and trembly whenever Horace resurrected something funny or touching to relate. They'd break for lunch and eat whatever Aurora Mae packed for them, and then they went on 'til dark. Bernard asked him a pile of "ifs" that varied each time. If Aurora Mae could have a dress of whatever color she pleased, what color would it be? he'd ask. Or, if Aurora Mae could sleep until any hour she chose, what hour would it be? Naturally, Horace found it irritating and dangerous, a white man showing interest in his sister, but Bernard won his heart over time. Besides being a generally pleasant companion, he taught Horace how to read and gave him books, starting with that anatomy book from his riverboat days, but magazines, too, ones he bought at the millhouse store, *Life* magazine and magazines about true crimes, hair-raising stuff in both cases, especially to a backwoods man of color in that time and that place. He felt grateful to Bernard, no matter how much it rankled to feel gratitude to a white man. Horace felt amused by him, too, with his curious courtly ways, that ignorance of matters he thought white men came swaddled in from birth, things like arrogance and the worst offhand cruelty. It helped that Bernard got all colored up working side by side with him in the out of doors. There were days he looked as dark as any of the half or quarter bloods around. Horace almost forgot he was a white man.

Almost.

It helped, too, that Bernard considered Aurora Mae an angel of some kind, untouchable, existing only to be served. It helped he was a small, wiry man, just a button of a man, really, a man his sister could swat to his knees with one hand if he bothered her.

At the end of the day, he knew his sister had feelings for Bernard, and sometimes that worried him. She had her reasons, mostly because she was lonely. When they weren't begging her for help, the cousins feared her and kept their distance. Other black men thereabouts called her Woodwitch or Big Time for her healing powers and her size, but it wasn't in a respectful manner. There was ridicule in it. Bernard was present, and Bernard was smitten. That must have gone a long way with her. For the life of him, he didn't understand why those two didn't knock together the way they should, whether he approved or not. It wasn't as if anybody around their little parcel of Missouri would find out if they did. They were as isolated as a body could get up there on the farm, surrounded by family, trees, and the river. Unless the cousins kept them apart.

Horace paused in pulling a nightshirt over his head. It hung off him like a poor child's ghost costume for Halloween. He sat that way, drop-jawed, inhaling and exhaling his way through a variety of unwholesome conjectures about where the jealousies of Cousin Clyde or the avarice of Cousin Frances Marie might lead until a round wet spot blossomed at the shirt's center. Later, he tried to sleep, but the wet spot made him uncomfortable 'til it dried out.

The next day, by chance, one of Cousin Clyde's little children came up the back door at breakfast looking for one of Aurora Mae's powders for his grandmama's breathing troubles. Horace shooed him away empty-handed as he was cranky and sleep-deprived, angry in general at Cousin Clyde for betrayals the man had not yet committed nor for that matter contemplated until that time.

On the way to work the next morning, Horace saw Bernard carried over his shoulder a bundle on a stick, jaunty as a pirate's parrot. Once they were out of sight of the house, Bernard told Horace to go on without him as he had business in the town. He might not make it back that night, depending on how things went. Saint Louis was a fair walk away, and the road he needed to travel was populated mostly by black folk. There wouldn't be an abundance of cars or even mule-driven carts along the way. It was unlikely someone would give him a lift.

What you got goin' on, man? Horace asked.

Bernard's close-set eyes crinkled with mischief and mystery and he said, A surprise.

Horace let it go. A man's entitled to his own business, he thought. His sister frowned to see him come home alone. When he couldn't tell her where Bernard was nor when he would be back, she snapped at him over the way he chewed his food. She sat up 'til the wee hours, too, pretending to make up orders for her medicines by the light of an oil lamp as if pestilence were about to sweep through the neighborhood like marauding kluckers. Horace knew her stockpiles were in good order. There was no reason for her to be working late like that, except she wanted to be looking for Bernard.

Oh, there was something between them, alright. Maybe he was naive to think it was a pure thing, unconsummated, a thing of the spirit. Horace wondered if there were secrets flying about his house, phantom passions barely glimpsed, whizzing through the air like bats in the night.

No, he decided. No. It couldn't be. He shook himself head to toe to let some sense in. Neither one of 'em could fool me.

He was asleep long before Bernard got home around first light. Aurora Mae went to bed in the kitchen, because it was a hot night, she said, although it was passably cool. When she heard Bernard's footsteps, she went to the door and sighed with relief that he was in one piece, chipper even, given his springing walk, his big beaming smile.

She opened the door with one hand to let him in. Something squirmed around inside his shirt.

What you got there? she asked. You catch me a squirrel for supper?

Bernard pulled out a puppy, a tiny Cavalier spaniel, its soulful eyes and long, sweet ears the biggest things about it. For you, my lady, he said with a sweeping bow, popping the dog in her arms. She squealed, then gave Bernard a short, gracious hug. The top of his head barely reached her clavicle. He shared his brief nuzzle in paradise with the little dog she cradled between her breasts. The puppy licked his nose. He didn't care. It was the happiest moment of his life so far.

Where'd you get that dog? Horace asked as they walked to work.

I had a plan. It didn't pan out, then I had a stroke of luck.

Do tell.

Alright.

Bernard paused for effect then plunged into his story with gusto. He drew it out where he could, made it short and snappy where necessary, and imitated voices. He was more entertaining to Horace than Saturday night revival hour on the radio.

First thing I did was go to the river, to a spot I know close to the town but suitable private for what I wanted. It was a hot walk. I got there long enough after sunrise to bathe in the river without too many insects feastin' on me. There was no way I was gonna walk into Saint Louis with the day's dirt all over me. I don't know if you noticed that bundle with me this mornin'? My city clothes. After the river bath, I laid out on some rocks until I was dry and changed into 'em. Left my work clothes up a tree. I slicked down my hair, spit-shined my shoes. Topped off with a boater. From a distance, if you squinted, I looked as dashin' as any river dandy, you can count on that.

When he got to the outskirts of civilization, he went straight to the docks, boarded the first gambling boat he came across, and strolled about the deck with a confident familiarity of such places. He tipped his hat to the back of his head. As a protection against pickpockets, he kept his hands deep in his pockets where he fondled the five dollars and thirty-nine cent that represented his life's savings. He picked out a gaming table, intending to double his stake to achieve the grand sum of ten dollars, which he figured was what a fine pup like the one Aurora Mae wanted would cost. When he strode up to the Great Wheel of Fortune, he was supremely sure fate would be kind. He slunk away six minutes later utterly broke and convinced he was cursed beyond measure. One thing for certain, he could not return home empty-handed.

He made his way to the part of town where shops for every type of luxury item could be found, whether lace, silver, buttons, threads, hats, chairs, beds, pipes, or pets. He stood in front of a pet store window where a load of puppies frolicked together and caged birds chirped around them like cheerleaders. He sized up everything he could see through the window: the chipped countertop, the dirty window-sills, the stray clumps of fur, feathers, and pellets littering the floor. Alright, he thought, alright. A new plan came to him. It wasn't the best, but it wasn't the worst and it might work out. It was worth a try, anyway.

He went into the shop and thanked God a woman was behind the counter. She looked at him quizzically, with almost a smile on her face, a middle-aged entirely forgettable woman with mud-colored hair and rust-red eyes. He took a deep breath and called upon all the fast talkers and gamesmen floating around in his blood to help him out here, help his ugly self the hell out here. He needed to charm this woman into giving him what he wanted, what he needed so bad. Primary among the solicited was his daddy. On the love you once bore for my mama, Harvé, when she was a good girl who cared for you alone, help me find the words I need to make this woman bend to my will.

And his daddy, along with all the other great, dead river men of his people, complied. For ten minutes, Bernard leaned on the countertop and chatted up Miss Loretta, the owner of Buck's Pet Shop. He professed his dearest love for animals of all kinds, particularly little lapdogs like that cute-as-two-buttons-in-a-row puppy over there. He bemoaned the loss of his savings on the pleasure boat, fool that he was, as one thing his daddy's helpful spirit whispered in his ear was that a little bit of truth was the anchor to every successful pitch, and that was his. He suggested to Miss Loretta that her place was in need of some cleanup—not that he faulted her housekeeping, but the cleanup required was heavier than a lady should do. Surely she was a widow woman, he could see that, in need of a man to help out some. He told her that in exchange for one of those pups, he could make her place shine as if it were a new-minted penny out of Denver. Within ten minutes of walking through the door, he got the job of sprucing things up. The puppy was all but a few drops of sweat away from being his.

He gabbed for all he was worth while he worked, engaging Miss Loretta in small talk. Once she opened up, he offered her truckloads of empathy as she related the tale of her dear husband's death two years earlier.

He was a good man, who knew all about every kind of critter you could imagine, she said, from bugs to snakes to chickens all the way up the ladder to that prince of beasts, the dog. He was an expert breeder, groomer, and trainer, and built up his business from scratch. Before he died, she bragged, there weren't a huntin' man along the Mississippi who didn't know the name of Dudley Buck. Why, people came from as far away as Lake Charles, Louisiana, for a look at his stock. Imagine that, she said, people seeking dogs long-distance when there were dogs of every sort available on every square foot of Delta you can name. That's how talented Mr. Dudley Buck was. Then, one day, on a Sunday, he jumped into a confrontation one of his bitches was havin' out the back with a rattlesnake, and he met his end accordingly. Things hadn't been the same since. Oh yes, I need a man to help out, she said. I'd pay quite well to keep one, too. Look what happened to this place since his death, she continued, as if Bernard had been around all along and wasn't simply a down-and-out stranger who'd wandered in the door hankering for a pup. It was a shame, an awful shame, wasn't it?

Bernard agreed and tsked, tsked wherever he could to sound sincere, all the while jittery to finish his job and grab that pup before Miss Loretta figured out she was getting robbed, jittery to head back home to where his own beloved was waiting, alive and blooming. By the end of the day, he had the place in tiptop shape and then Miss Loretta made him a plate of sustenance as she called it. Of course, he was required to eat and compliment her on her cooking and her kitchen as well. Finally, just after sunset, he was out the door with the pup in his shirt.

Miss Loretta said as he left, Why, wait. I have been so rude, I never asked. Forgive me, but what is your name?

And he said, Bernard, m'am. Bernard Levy.

It was the strangest thing. Just like all those years ago in Miss Maple's classroom, the mention of his name caused an eruption of robust hilarity. Miss Loretta laughed and laughed until she turned purple and looked as if she might keel over. He went back into the store and helped her to a chair while she caught her breath.

Oh, forgive me again, she said, but one of our very best customers in the old days was a Mr. Bernard Levy. From Memphis. And if you could note the difference between the two of you . . .

A creeping sensation came over Bernard's scalp as if a tide of lice crawled all over it. Later on, he wished dearly he'd paid attention to that feeling. It was prescient. At the time, he just wanted out of there with his prize so he ignored it.

Well, that was odd, Horace said to him when he remarked on the unexpected invocation of his name-twin and his scalp's curious creep. That was indeed odd.

Yes, it was, Bernard agreed.

Three weeks passed, three weeks during which Aurora Mae was in a constant state of contentment, due to the addition of Maxine, or Maxie, as she named the pup, to the household. She held the little thing in her lap whenever she sat to work at her potions and sewing and such. She stroked her head and murmured to her. She got quite dexterous at using the one free hand for her chores. Whenever Bernard was in the room with them, she cast him gracious looks or held Maxie up from under her front legs to show him the elegant line of her limbs or her sweet, round belly and did everything but call him the dog's daddy to her mama.

When the three of them sat on the front porch at night, Maxie was always with them, cooed over by the humans, nestled somewhere in Aurora Mae's person, whether licking her hands or lost in a snoreful nap. She looked like a furry wood elf sitting in the lap of a giant, a sight that amused Horace so much that one night while in his cups he decided to pull a prank. He stole the dog as his sister dozed in her rocker and dressed Maxie in a pair of his sister's knickers. The wee head with its snub little face and comically long ears emerged from one leg hole and the short, plump legs, squared up with a piece of hair ribbon, came out the other. He took her finest handkerchief, tatted all around with lace, and tied it under Maxie's chin then gently draped the whole canine bundle over his sister's shoulder so that it looked for all the world as if Aurora Mae had a most peculiar-looking baby there, one who needed a good burp. It didn't take a minute for Aurora Mae to wake up. She was startled but once that dissipated, she laughed as hard as her brother. The sound of their gaiety got Bernard out of the privy. He ran across the yard to the house, pulling up the shoulder straps of his overalls. When he got close enough to see what was going on, he, too, broke into a funny fit.

Here, Daddy, look at your baby here, Aurora Mae said in all good humor, handing him the wrapped-up spaniel pup, which he made a great show of tenderly accepting and cradling in his arms.

There was a full moon that Saturday night. It never occurred to them that anyone would be watching or listening to their foolishness, but it so happened that Cousin Clyde was coming home from a visit to a 'cropper's farm down the road. He crossed in front of the big house from a distance, so they didn't notice him. They weren't looking anyway. Cousin Clyde was drunk enough to see what he thought he saw, and hear what he thought he heard. He had enough lingering meanness over the refusal of his mama's cough medicine for him to develop conviction and decide to blab about it.

By Sunday morning, half the cousins heard that Aurora Mae had a baby by that funny-looking, little white man she kept around, a baby as homely as he was and as much a freak of nature as she. Naturally, they were all scandalized. Whoever knew she was carryin'? they asked one another until someone offered that a woman Aurora Mae's size might carry high and hide it quite well.

A handful of cousins liked to go Sunday mornings over to the Jesus Christ of Abundant Mercy Pentecostal church, because they had a white preacher there, a man with more fire and brimstone under his tongue than the Black Baptist and the A.M.E. preachers combined. One of those cousins couldn't keep her mouth shut on a morning buzzing hot with the shock and spice of fresh-cooked gossip. When the white preacher asked her how that heathen cousin of hers who bossed the colony like an old-time overseer was doing and was Aurora Mae any nearer to Jesus, she told him. And didn't that cause an unwholesome crop of unexpected problems.

It's unclear how the story of Aurora Mae and Bernard's baby got around so fast, unless you accept as gospel that white preachers have big mouths when it comes to the sins, real and imagined, of black folk. It's more unclear why no one ever corrected the story. It didn't take half a day for the cousins to learn Clyde had been mistaken. They all had a good laugh about it by Sunday supper, but the news never did make it out into the wider world.

Two nights later, Bernard went out hunting with Horace as the larder was light. They walked a long way into the woods before they could find game that didn't spook the second the hunters sighted it. It was as if the critters close to the house knew something evil was up, and they'd withdrawn deep under brambles and rock to escape humanity. Eventually, the men took down a scrawny pheasant too old to hear them approach and a possum in similar condition, then gave it up and trudged on home.

Not two hundred yards from the front porch, they found the yard dogs, all three of them, bleeding out from gunshot and writhing their last. They ran to the house. The door was open. Maxie was dead on the floor. The wall next to her battered little body was streaked white, rust, and gray with the pup's bashed-in brain matter. Everything else was a mess of shattered glass and busted-up wood. Aurora Mae was nowhere to be found.

The cousins told them what they knew. One of them, Cousin Mags, was at the house selling some roots she'd gathered to Aurora Mae when they heard gunshots outdoors, followed by the whimpering of dogs. Cousin Mags took off out the back but was afraid to go farther and risk being seen, so she hunkered down in the bush. She heard the whole thing and saw parts of it. She told Horace and Bernard what happened.

Five night riders came up on horseback looking for an ugly half-white baby borne out of blackest sin, a child of the devil. From behind the door, Aurora Mae bellowed at them. There ain't no baby here!

But they didn't believe her, so they broke in. She fought 'em, Lord love her, she fought 'em hard, but there were five of 'em, to her one and only self. Didn't matter how big she was, they had shotguns and knives, too. Over and over, they beat her to make her give the baby up. When that failed, they cut her. They hurt her so bad after a while maybe she would have given that baby up if she had a baby to give, but she did not, so they tortured that poor li'l dog to make her talk, and by then, she could not. Then they tore up the whole house looking for the child of the devil. At last, they started in to rape her, and when they were done they took her away with them, because, they joked, there was so much of her she weren't half used up. The one with the biggest horse slung her over his saddle like a piece of damn meat, Mags said, and bim, bam, boom, they was gone.

Throughout the telling of Mags's tale, Horace moaned and trembled and bent over double with grief. Bernard shook from his toes to the top of his head. Buckets of tears poured from his round, close-set eyes. For the next month, the two tried to find out where the night riders had taken her. They combed the woods, the farms, the city of Saint Louis. They put about to everyone in their ken to check with everyone in their ken, especially those Negroes who worked in the town in private homes and businesses, for sightings of her or gossip about the night she was taken. They tried mightily but could not find her nor any information about where she might be. So they gave up, heading east away from the river, not so much toward a new life, as life felt pretty much over for them both, but because neither could stay in the big house anymore, not without her, not with the sight of little Maxie's brains splattered on the wall burned into their memories, not with the images that sprang up in every corner of the house and in the yard, images of Aurora Mae's torments accompanied by the everlasting echo of her screams.

X

Greenville, Mississippi, 1962

EVERYONE AT NEEDLEMAN'S FURNITURE TREATED Laura Anne differently after her daddy yanked her back to Greenville. The men looked at her longer than they should. Whispers warmed her back each time she passed two or more of them together. The women smiled too broadly when they said hello and took too much interest in what she wore, remarking on the length of her skirts, the fit of her blouse. If she dared to wear a fabric that wasn't coarse or a color that wasn't dull, she'd overhear them criticize. Look at the way that silk lays against the skin, they'd say. I bet it feels like it's not even there. Can you imagine? Walkin' around in public feelin' naked? And that yellow is bright enough to wake the bees on a winter's day. . . .

All this was from her coworkers, many of whom she'd known since she was a baby girl when Lot would take her into the store as his "chair tester," when he'd set her down on something hard and then something cushiony and ask her to pass judgment on how they felt. The customers were worse. As she approached, her face tarted up in her would-you-like-some-help-smile, they turned on their heels, tossing her the insult of a sidelong glance before they walked away with chins up in the air. It got so bad, she quit working the floor and spent her time in the office banging about trying to find enough to do. Lot did not like having her at close quarters. He couldn't curse his suppliers or tell racy jokes with his daughter right there at the next desk. He couldn't have his best salesmen or the shipping crew in to share a shot at the end of the day. There were times he considered firing her.

Out on the street, things were better, but only if Laura Anne chose neighborhoods where people didn't know her. Otherwise, she was stared at, pursued by wolf whistles so rude and sharp they made her jump. If she walked to the drugstore to take her lunch at the counter, men sitting next to her exchanged winks and got their arms and elbows in her way or brushed their thighs against hers. In short, her public life had become that of a fallen woman, a consequence of her behavior she'd never considered when she was occupied with being heroic and in love. There were other consequences, too.

What she'd done to her mother, for example. Rose was a wreck. Her twitch was as fierce as it ever got, including the time she suffered the shingles and spent three weeks in constant agony. Her hair was a mess, she wore the same housedress every day. She kept herself in to avoid others. She would not answer the door. She couldn't look anyone in the eye, not even the help. The only gaze she met was Laura Anne's. Her daughter suffered each wet-eyed, red-rimmed stare like a knife to the heart.

Supper times were the worst. Before she'd run off, supper was an occasion of intimate pleasures, of boisterous fun. Daddy cracked jokes and put on the airs of fine ladies outfitting their boudoirs as he told stories about his business coups of the day. Mama might relate some whacky domestic incident, interrupting herself with giggle fits. Often

Laura Anne leavened proceedings with a report of something she'd read that informed them all, and conversation would take a serious turn while the family leaned forward on their elbows after coffee to solve the world's problems. Laura Anne grew up looking forward to supper as the best time of day, but since she'd come home, she hated it.

Mama picked at her food and ate little. Daddy overate and drank, too. The whole meal was silent but for the blessings Daddy made over the wine and bread and fruits of the earth before they ate and the thankful blessings Mama led after they finished. They'd never had the habit of all those blessings before unless it was Friday night or a high holiday. These days, Mama made sure they did so every night as an act of repentance. They'd raised a wanton and must to apologize to God, each other, and the community at large. If she thought to ask the cook for some, she'd have worn sackcloth to table and piled ashes on her head.

One morning after the prodigal was home a scant few days, Cousin Patricia Ellen phoned just after Laura Anne left for work. She gave Rose a coded message that communication had arrived from Mickey Moe and she'd call back with the lowdown after supper. Never had a meal dragged out so long. Laura Anne's nerves were in a fix. Every sound was magnified. Whenever someone swallowed, her spine tensed. The smack of tongue over teeth irritated more than a cloud of gnats. She broke.

Lord God in heaven! she said and threw her napkin down over her plate. If you two don't stop acting like grandmama was buried alive under the floorboards, I won't run away from here again, I'll kill myself instead!

With heavy tread, she trooped upstairs to her room muttering like a petulant child of thirteen rather than a twenty-year-old woman of the world. Thankfully, they did not follow. She imagined them sitting drop-jawed before Mama started to weep and ask Lot what she'd done to be punished with the company of a cruel, unmannered brute, and where had her precious good girl gone. Since Laura Anne remained a good girl, through and through, despite her parents outdated morality, an avalanche of guilt crashed down upon her, not guilt for loving Mickey Moe nor even for running off to him, but for losing her temper. She started to cry herself and was bawling away when the phone rang. She jumped on it. It was Patricia Ellen.

Whatsamatta, honey? You sound terrible.

Laura Anne dissembled. I'm gettin' the most awful cold.

While she waited for news of her lover, her heart leapt around in her chest like a rabbit with its tail on fire. Cousin Patricia Ellen, whose domestic life was by turns dull and harried, enjoyed the drama of her go-between role so much she doled out information in excruciating bits and pieces.

You know I must say that boyfriend of yours has the most lovely voice, she began. It's got a little rasp to it, but it's deep, the way a man's should be. Not like my Ruben's. His is just a tad thin, don't you think? It has a tendency to screech when he gets excited, and I mean when he's joyful excited or angry excited, either one. . . .

Patty-cakes! Laura Anne interrupted, employing the woman's baby name, which she knew annoyed her, to get her attention. Please!

Alright, alright. You don't have to shout in my ear.

Laura Anne apologized, groveled a bit even, because she needed her cousin's cooperation or she would be lost, truly lost, in this wasteland of opprobrium, formerly her most happy home. Ruffled feathers smoothed, Patricia Ellen spilled.

He was not in Memphis yet. That surprised. How long could it take for a drive of a few hundred miles? After he'd finished his premium collections, it seemed he'd stayed on the back roads, following his daddy's old route as well as he could piece it together, not for any reason that made sense, but because a voice in his head told him to. He'd met with a few mishaps, a flat tire, a washed-out road. In the latter case, a tumble into a ditch caused him to pause a few days in Littlefield, Tennessee, a town so small it was not on the map but near enough to Memphis that soon as repairs could be effected to the car, he could arrive there the same day. He was staying at the home of the garage mechanic. Cousin Patricia Ellen gave her the phone number, saying that Mickey Moe would love it if she could manage to call. His host was a good old boy, who enjoyed talking religion. They spent the night discussing the virtues of Moses versus Jesus. She wasn't to worry. If she was unable to call or failed to find him, she was to understand that his love had not faded but grew stronger each moment they were apart.

Laura Anne hung up the phone in a fog of love and amazement. Littlefield, Tennessee. Of all the places Mickey Moe should wind up. It was a miracle, something to do with that voice in his head, she was certain. She wished she could tell Mama. How could Mama object to Mickey Moe when the very voice of God was guiding him? Littlefield, Tennessee, was the birthplace of J. Henry, the janitor at Daddy's store. A sweeter colored man didn't exist on the face of this earth, she was sure of it, and every weekend he drove his old rattletrap of a Chevrolet coupe up to Littlefield to visit his ailing mama. Why, she could pay him to take her along. Since the next day was a Friday, she could be with her man in two short days, and no one would know, no one could find them, no one could fetch her back this time. Never again would she be bedeviled for the crime of loving Mickey Moe Levy. The two of them could resuscitate their original plan. They could travel in company to Memphis, confront Aurora Mae, and return to Greenville with Mickey's roots rehabilitated for all time. If that wasn't enough for Mama and Daddy, she and the man she loved would give up on propriety and get married by a justice of the peace. The thought gave her a twinge of pain—the dreams of young girls die hard—but she bit her lip, bid good-bye to the wedding dress lodged in her mind's eye, and renewed in her heart the vows of liberation that got her into all this trouble in the first place.

The next day at lunchtime, she went to the bank and drew out her entire savings, cashing out ten dollars of it in quarters, nickels, and dimes with which to call Mickey Moe from a phone booth. Then she cornered J. Henry and told him she had urgent business in Littlefield, that she would give him fifteen dollars to take her with him when he went up in the morning. J. Henry knew better than to ask a white woman what her plans were in a godforsaken place like his hometown. The way people talked about Miss Laura Anne, he knew she was wild. She was trouble. Her plans could have just about any definition at all. But fifteen dollars was fifteen dollars, so he told her alright, he'd do it, only next week. I got some springs busted in the backseat, he said, and I don't want to think what a mess some of them old roads might make of your spine. The following week when he'd had time to fix things up was better. He'd do it then.

Laura Anne would not let comfort stand in her way. Filled with the heady spirit of emancipation and recalling that she'd some redemption to do after insulting Mama Jo Baylin, she said, Don't be silly. I need to go tomorrow or not at all. I'll ride up front with you if need be. It don't matter to me.

J. Henry was a middle-aged man, slim and small, nut-brown with a face flat as a tin pan. He had no artifice in him that Laura Anne ever noticed. Just now, his discomfort was palpable. He looked at his feet.

No, Miss Laura Anne. I can't have that. You ridin' up by me might reap the whirlwind in them woods. You just don't know.

Then twenty dollars.

No.

Twenty-five.

No.

They say every man has his price. J. Henry's was thirty-five dollars.

It wasn't really fair, offering him that amount. It was a fortune in his eyes. He could hardly say no, no matter what his misgivings. They made a plan to meet in the morning at 9:00 a.m. on an access road near the town dump, an hour's walk from Laura Anne's home. She'd have to leave the house at eight, which would surely raise suspicion, but she agreed anyway, afraid that if she threw any obstacles in J. Henry's path, his will would become priceless.

That night on her way home from work, she stopped at the drugstore and called Mickey Moe from the booth at the back. He wasn't there. She told the man who answered the phone to tell him she would arrive in Littlefield the next afternoon. He promised to deliver the message. She stressed to him that Mickey Moe wasn't to call her back. She didn't want her cousin involved in this. Once she was determined gone again, Patricia Ellen's house would be the first place her father'd look. There remained the problem of leaving the house early. She puzzled things out a while and came up with the perfect excuse.

Where you goin' so early? Mama asked at quarter to eight on Saturday morning. Since she hardly slept anymore, she'd been up hours.

To temple. To services. I'm catching a ride with Rebecca.

Mama was incredulous. To temple? Really? To temple?

Yes. I feel as I need some prayer about now.

Rose Needleman's head twitched to the side three times. Her daughter was dressed in a light blue cotton dress of modest cut and length. She'd flats on, not her customary high heels, along with a straw hat with bunches of plastic cherries sewn on the back over a light blue grosgrain ribbon tied in a bow.

You look . . . you look . . . like your old self. Don't you think that pocketbook is a little ostentatious, though? For temple? Honey, it's huge.

Laura Anne had anticipated everything. She patted the bag with a slight, deprecating smile.

I needed some room. My siddur's in there.

Lord, Mama thought as she watched her daughter leave, she's carryin' a prayer book? Her weary, grieving spirit lifted. Could penitence be far behind? Thank you, Lord, Rose Needleman cried out with her hands clasped under her chin and her gaze raised to the heavens, thank you!

As soon as Laura Anne turned the corner of her street, she ran. She ran in her flat shoes all the way to the access road by the town dump. Somewhere along the way, her hat flew off. She left it behind. Her lungs felt like they might explode, but she made it to the meeting place in forty minutes. Her dress was soaked through under the arms. Her hair was plastered to her head. That's ok, she thought, patting her purse, which held a pair of blue jeans and a fresh shirt along with her makeup, her nightgown, her hairbrush, toothbrush, and wallet. She'd change when they stopped for gasoline.

She looked at her watch. She'd have to wait twenty minutes for her ride to arrive. Twenty minutes to work herself into a panic royale. After five, her head felt light, as if it were about to float off her neck. After ten, her knees went wobbly. Be calm, she told herself, be calm. She reached inside the bag to feel the item she'd thrown in there at the last minute in case things were as perilous in the backwoods as J. Henry feared. Ah, there it was. Her fingers wound around the barrel of Daddy's pistol, and her strength returned. She wondered if it was loaded. She'd never stopped to check. She reprimanded herself. Checking whether or not a gun was loaded was the very first lesson Daddy taught her about firearms.

Her thoughts drifted back to when she was only ten and Daddy first put a gun in her hand to show her how it worked. A gal needs to know how to protect herself in this world, Daddy said, and proceeded to show her how she might do exactly that. It was always hot at the gun range. The place had a smell she didn't like. She only ever went enough to make Daddy happy. She was alright with a gun, but never great. Still, she knew her way around a variety of weapons.

Her ride arrived in a cloud of dust and a world of noise. The paint was so worn, the car had no color but gunmetal and rust. There was a clean round spot as big as a head in the front window over by the driver's side, and the glass everywhere else was covered with a film of Delta mud thick as a widow's veil. Leaving the car running, J. Henry popped out, went around the side, opened the back door and ushered her in. The seat was piled up with hand-stitched quilts over pillow ticking stuffed with straw.

I put these down for you, miss. They oughta help smooth the ride some.

She wondered why he was still so concerned about her riding up front. Given the condition of the windows, it'd take a midnight owl to see in and figure out who was riding with whom, but she figured they could argue on the road if it came to that. The important thing was to get going. She got in back and settled in. With a great rumble and a jarring jolt, they peeled off the access road. Her torso jigged up and down with the chassis of the car but not so badly that her head hit the roof. The quilts and pillows provided a measure of comfort. Thank you, J. Henry, for setting up the backseat, she said, it's very cushy back here.

The driver rattled on about his wife gathering pillows and quilts from the neighbors so they'd be sure she was comfy, but Laura Anne wasn't listening. She kept her mind focused on seeing Mickey Moe by nightfall. Whatever she suffered along route was nothing. She would be amply rewarded by his loving mouth and warm embrace.

A jug lay on the floor at the left side of the dividing hump next to a wire basket covered by a towel. Suddenly, Laura Anne realized how thirsty she was after that hot run and her twenty-minute wait in the sun. J. Henry, might I have some of whatever's in this jug? she asked. I'm painfully dry.

The driver's eyes crinkled with pleasure up there in the rear view. Why, of course, Miss Laura Anne. That's just water. I packed it for you and you alone.

That was kind, J. Henry.

I got my own by me, so you just do whatever you like with that all.

Very kind.

There followed a lot of quiet but for the gospel music and preaching from the car radio. Laura Anne complained about the air, which was close to the point of stifling, but when they rolled down the windows more than an inch, the dust from the road billowed in and gave them both coughing fits.

Hours passed. They traveled Highway 61 awhile, then took an exit, and before long were deep in the countryside. They passed hardscrabble farms carved out of forest and rock. Every once in a while, there was a great manse near the river or some other body of water, a lake or a pond, and there'd be acres and acres of cultivated land, and where the spreads ended, clusters of cinder-block hovels with outhouses and barbecue pits. There were shacks made out of all kinds of scavenged wood pounded or lashed together with wire, and old washing machines and car parts strewn over what passed for lawn. There were dirt paddocks populated by goats, a lone cow, or a mule. In short, they passed terrain much like every other piss-poor patch of land Laura Anne ever saw outside the immediate environs of Greenville, only there was much more of it.

How much longer, J. Henry?

Oh, you just relax and enjoy the view, Miss Laura Anne. We'll be there directly.

This meant anywhere from three to six hours. She wished she'd brought a book or some knitting. Anything to pass the time. She tried talking to J. Henry, but they had nothing but pleasantries to exchange. The landscape bored her. They traveled deeper into nowhere by the minute as far as she could determine. She realized at one point she hadn't seen a home, rich or poor, for nearly an hour. Her stomach growled. She'd forgotten to pack something to eat. Like he was reading her mind, J. Henry stopped the car next to a spot of cleared woods and declared they should get out and stretch their legs, have the box lunch his wife packed.

Laura Anne gave him her biggest, toothy smile.

Why you thought of everything, didn't you, J. Henry?

Thank you, miss.

J. Henry got out his side of the car and looked in every direction as if he was searching for something before he opened her door. He took one of the quilts she'd been sitting on and spread it out over a patch of grass. He set the wire basket on top of that.

You come sit here, he said. This here's for you.

She did as he suggested, lifted the towel off the basket, and found a china plate, cutlery, no doubt J. Henry's wife's very best cloth napkin and, sitting on a square of brown paper, a plump fried chicken breast, a little tin of black-eyed peas in sauce, a square of cornbread, and an apple.

Oh! This is divine, she said. But it's much too much. Aren't you going to sit down and have a bite?

No, no, no, thank you very much. I'll stand here and keep watch. I can eat these here legs I got standin' up.

Keep watch for what? We're nowhere in the world at all. I don't mind if you sit by me. What are you so afraid of?

J. Henry sighed. Miss, you don't know these woods like I do, that's all.

Laura Anne couldn't comprehend the stubborn fears of Negroes. How could a people so remarkably strong be so timid? She guessed it was just the way they were made, and she was too hungry to think more about it, so she set to and ate her fill, enjoying the soft, fresh breeze that blew about her hair and up her skirt. When she was done, she would have liked to take just a tiny bit of shut-eye in the shade before continuing, but J. Henry was obviously agitated by that idea. More no, no, no's from him, and they were back in the car on their way.

Laura Anne felt frustrated and decided to complain.

Why on earth are you so edgy about traveling with me, J. Henry? Do I scare you so very much?

He'd had enough. He slapped his steering wheel with one hand in a way that made her jump.

Lord, miss! Are you truly so innocent you don't know what's been goin' on 'round here? Don't you know there's been mangled bodies drifting downriver and young folk disappeared 'round here all year long? Yes'm. There have. Two last August, and another in February. Ever since those Yankee lawyers came down here to help that Meredith child, the boys in these woods been fired up and ready for blood. What 'xactly do you think a pack of 'em goin' to do if they come across a black man and a white gal layin' around at a picnic in their fields? Ask questions?

Laura Anne apologized as much as she needed to calm J. Henry down, but in her heart she thought he blew events way out of proportion. There simply weren't evil-minded hooligans roaming everywhere around them or hiding behind the trees. Well, maybe there were some here and there, there was bad blood everywhere, and times were dangerous if you didn't mind your own business these days, but murderous peril behind each and every tree? In this downright wilderness? Yes, she determined, timidity was in their blood.

After the relief of the outdoors, the close air in the car was about killing her. She couldn't breathe freely enough to get the sleep she wanted, although she did close her eyes to daydream about the look on Mickey Moe's face when she finally arrived at his mechanic's house. Oh, I'm sufferin' darling, she told him in her mind. You better appreciate this. Then she imagined a dozen ways he could demonstrate he did.

Out of nowhere, the car screeched to a halt. Her body pitched forward, her chin hit the back of the front seat. Ow, she said, ow. What was that? And picking up her head, leaning over the front seat, she looked past J. Henry's shoulder and out the passenger's window. Draped over the car was a beast, a beast bigger than a deer, bigger than a bear on all fours. She stared through the dirt until she realized the beast was a man leaning forward, his two arms stretched out over the hood. His fingers clawed at air and metal. O Lord, she thought, a man. We hit a man.

What in heaven's name happened, J. Henry?

J. Henry's breath came loud and fast at her before he spoke. He wiped his mouth with his sleeve. His hand trembled.

It seems like he just jumped out at us, miss.

Well, you better get out and see if he's alright.

J. Henry gulped twice, put his hand on the door handle. He moved too slowly for her taste. There was a man out there, and he looked badly hurt. In the last few seconds, he'd slumped forward more, and then he stopped moving altogether. She put a little command in her tone.

Go on. Go see.

J. Henry gave out a jagged sigh.

I'm gettin' ready.

Go on. Go on. Go on.

J. Henry went to the man possibly dying over the hood of his car. He tapped the man's shoulder. When his head went up, J. Henry jumped away. Then he inched back. The two of them talked. The man stiffened his arms and pulled himself up off the hood. J. Henry put his arm around his waist and walked him around to the side door opposite Laura Anne, got the door open with his free hand, and more or less tossed the man in beside her.

When she got a close look at her fellow passenger, Laura Anne shrieked. At least she tried to shriek. Her mouth opened, her throat quivered, and the smallest high-pitched whine emerged, like the sound an asthmatic makes when his windpipe gets bothered.

He was a white man covered in blood. It wasn't from any kind of wound the car had made, that much was sure. What bloodied him, she could not say. There were thin red lines all over his face and chest, his hands, too, and Lord knew where else. His shirt was torn, his trousers stained and foul smelling, his shoes gone, and brambles were stuck all over his ripped and filthy socks. Despite the cuts on his cheeks, she could see he was clean-shaven. The fabric of his ruined clothes, she could tell, any woman could, was rich, smartly tailored before he met with violence. He lifted his head, tried to talk, but couldn't. He just lay back down, right next to Laura Anne's left thigh, and passed out.

This poor man is a city boy, J. Henry.

I can see that.

What do you think brought him out here? What happened to him?

I do not know. Who happened to him is more likely. We need to get out of here as quick as we can.

You think he met up with those boys you mentioned?

It's entirely possible.

A tense ring of fear, barbed like wire, circled Laura Anne's throat. She couldn't speak at first. When she could, she tried for bravado, but her tone was shaky, the pitch was off, and it came out false and flat, landing with a thud at her feet. What she said was, Then it's very good it was us he ran into, wasn't it?

And J. Henry said, Maybe for him. For us, could be the worse thing ever happened.

His foot got heavy and he drove as fast as his old rattletrap would allow on a dirt road studded with gullies and ancient roots thick as logs.

They pressed on for what felt like hours and hours. The white man barely moved although he moaned a lot. Laura Anne tried to give him some water, but it dribbled out his mouth. She daubed at the cuts on his face and hands with a dampened lunch napkin, but the blood tracks were dried thick. Since she couldn't do much about them without hurting him more, making them bleed afresh, she gave up and sat back. She took her pocketbook and positioned it square in her lap. She shoved her hand into her purse and found the butt of her daddy's pistol, which she tried to keep tight in her grip. She kept her finger off the trigger, because she didn't want to shoot her own foot or, God forbid, any part of J. Henry up front. She was bouncing a whole lot more in the car now than before, and the whole time, her hand trembled, timid as a field mouse caught in a trap.

XI

Cincinatti, Ohio–Saint Louis,
Missouri–Memphis, Tennessee, 1925–1926

ONCE THEY GAVE UP LOOKING for Aurora Mae, they tried life well
east of the Mississippi. They trekked all the way to Cincinnati, where
they worked for a time in a restaurant, Bernard slinging hash, Horace
cleaning up. They lived in a rooming house near the railway. It wasn't
bad. Bernard had a room next to the bath, and Horace was allowed
to sleep in the basement on a cot set up by the coal pile as long as he
got up a few times in the night to fire up the burner. They made a
few friends. For a time, Horace had a sweetheart. But nothing felt
real to either one of them. It was as if they were suspended in a jar of
jelly, all movement, all emotion blunted. Horace's gal left him for a
man with a proper home, nothing more than a shack, really, next to
the tracks outside of town. The weather got cold, the men got restless, and without even discussing it, they packed up one day and left.
They headed back to the old house in case she was there, but they
found the old house grown over with weeds, its windows broken, the

roof caved in, and no Aurora Mae anywhere. It was like pulling scabs off a half-healed wound. All their misery returned, there was nothing blunted about it. They couldn't stay no matter how kind the cousins were.

They followed the river downstream, because that felt easiest. They were aimless, heartsore, without desire or design. After a few weeks, it rained nearly all the time. They moved on, because they could not turn back. Even when it did not rain, the water was high, angry, impossible to cross. Sometimes it seemed the river was following them. Soup thick and dark, the noise it made to their grieving ears was like a great roar of sorrow. It suited them. They ran out of money. They had no shelter. They slept under the best tree cover they could find.

It wasn't long before the fungus got to Horace's head, so they shaved the hair from it. It didn't grow back. Horace thought he'd become Bald Horace because they'd stolen a bottle of camphor oil from a storage barn they'd come across to treat his naked, sore-covered scalp. A curse came with stolen goods. Aurora Mae always said that. Bernard consoled the man.

Now, I don't want to contradict Aurora Mae, he said. But it ain't pure stolen when you've got as powerful a need and as pitiful a purse as we two. Give it more time. We might see a follicle or two sprout anon.

Whenever his sister's name was invoked, Bald Horace's eyes welled up. He was silent until they overflowed. Tears mixed with the rivulets of rain splashing over his cheeks.

It hurts my heart so to wonder where she is, if she is.

Bernard, tearing up himself, found confidence the way lovers do when all is lost but defeat is inconceivable for reasons known only to them and God.

She is. I know it. And we will see her again. We will be reunited.

Oh Bernard. I fear you are dreamin'.

And what's wrong with that? A dream is a useful thing. Without a dream, Joseph would still be rottin' in Pharaoh's prison. Without a dream, Jacob would not have seen the way to heaven.

Bald Horace fluttered his fingers in the air as if playing a flute.

Up a golden ladder.

Yessir. Up a golden ladder.

Whenever he had his mind to himself, Bernard conjured up scenes in which Aurora Mae escaped her captors. He saw her running barefoot through the woods, hiding out in the same way her men did, under trees, in abandoned farm buildings when she could find one, scavenging, hoping for a run-in with a sympathetic stranger. Other times, he saw her thumping the head of whoever kept watch over her in the night with whatever heavy object came to hand. He saw how she'd pick her way quietly through the house and yard, silent as her warrior ancestors stalking foes through jungle and swamp. She would reach the stable where she'd leap on a horse and ride the wind to freedom. He saw her working cotton fields where she found the roots and weeds required to brew a poison that would kill every one of the monsters who took her. He saw how she'd use what she had to until one of them fell in love with her and gave her gold to buy her way out of captivity, but not before she'd plunged a farewell blade into the bastard's chest as he deserved. This was his least favorite conjuring, for it made a whore of her and his respect for Aurora Mae had not diminished. He still enjoyed tremendously the picture of its final scene: his enemy writhing, suffering, his features twisted in agony that lasted hours, even days, before fire-breathing demons carried him off to hell.

He had no hero fantasies in which he retrieved her himself with or without the aid of Bald Horace. He considered himself a failure in that regard. He'd let her down. He'd not protected the woman he loved from harm. In his worst moments, he figured he was no kind of a hero, no kind of a man at all and never would be. But she! he thought. She was a goddess, an archangel, a queen of the earth and sky! She'd save herself. He knew it. He knew it as hard, plain fact.

They crept downriver. They didn't pick up the volume or type of work they'd expected on account of the rain. What there was amounted to recovery work. They recovered what was left of drowned crops, rebuilt washed-out stone walls, fences, and collapsed roofs, transporting what was saved to where it could be bartered for what was going scarce. Sometimes they caught work shoring up the levees. Everywhere they stopped, the conversation turned to the rain, if people were in the mood to talk at all. They asked how high the river was upstream, did it crest, and speculated on the health of the levees. In general, the consensus was that the levees would hold, they had so far during wretched rain times. There'd be a few breaks here and there, but everyone who studied these things from the local bosses all the way up to President Coolidge said they'd survive. Everyone except crazy old black women, people said, those Obeah Negroes who thought they were smarter than the entire governments of the United States and Canada combined, and maybe a preacher or two, but most of 'em hereabouts been preaching end-times are comin' since Methuselah wore diapers.

As summer bowed to fall, it seemed the whole countryside was on the move. There were days when the river was thick with barges, manned by gunmen fore, aft, and in between, loaded with mysterious cargo, boxed then wrapped in tarpaulin, hiding as much from observation as the rain. There were government boats, packed with surveyors and Army engineers, men who stood on deck under makeshift tents holding their instruments at the ready like rifles in a war. On land, there were the wayfarers, frightened-looking men, white and black, alone or hauling a family, men who believed the preachers and the Obeah women, men who searched for a low watermark along the river near the places where tributaries might drain her off, and wiser men who headed west to high ground. With all the wayfarers about, competition for what jobs might be had was fierce. Even when they reached a big town, no one wanted to hire a funny-looking, little white man traveling with a bald, mournful black, not when there was more respectable-looking labor to be had. As a result, the two friends were almost always on the move.

By then, Bernard and Bald Horace were old hands on the road. They'd set out before the rain started in earnest, when it was just a bother now and again, not the steady, unyielding torrent it had become. They knew how to find the critters who did not flee the waters, the skittering things that made poor eating unless you caught a whole mess of them at once. Sometimes, this took all day, but at least they did not starve. Bald Horace would sit high up a tree. He'd pound and shake a branch while Bernard dashed about in the mud tossing whatever fell down into a sack for sorting out later. Much as water was all around them, there were no fish to catch, not fish they could see, anyway. The river got so dark and brown, they might as well have been looking into the pitch-dark night as the great mother Mississippi. There was refuse floating in it, wagon wheels, window frames, chickens bloated up with drowning, dogs, cats, and donkeys in similar states. Even if they could catch them, they wouldn't want to eat fish from such a source. They tried robbing fields, but most everything cultivated was picked already or rotted under the rain. They got to a point where they would have done almost anything for a job, a hot meal, a spot of dry floor to make their beds. It was October of the year 1926 when Bernard and Bald Horace got to Memphis.

My family's here, Bernard said. They'll help us out.

When they arrived at his granddaddy's store, it was burned out and abandoned. The neighbors told him his mama had gone on a rampage one night years before and torched the place. The flames climbed high, attracting notice. Folk found her before the fire, dancing with a jug and laughing. When they attempted to restrain her, she started in to yell, yell like a backwoods banshee, and she yelled his father's name. Harvé! Harvé! With the strength of ten madmen, she tore away from those who held on to her. She ran directly into the conflagration before anyone could stop her, still screaming, Harvé! Harvé! and she burned up and died. His grandparents passed of heartbreak within the year, one after the other. The county took both the family homes for back taxes and funeral expenses. There was nothing left, neither kin nor inheritance. He might as well have never existed.

Numbed by the news, Bernard told Bald Horace if he didn't mind, he'd just as soon leave Memphis directly after they had a little money put by. Don't get to likin' it too much 'round here, he said. There's bound to be some kind of work down the docks, but I can't think I can stay here in this sorry place, not with times gone by stalkin' me everywhere.

We's both of us orphans now, Bald Horace said. He put his arm around his friend and let the man discretely weep a bit against his chest, but that was only the one, brief time he did so. Neither man could bear to let too much sadness come to the surface or it might bury what was left of their resolve.

There doesn't seem much to live for, does there, Bald Horace remarked when they set off for the docks to look for work. No sun, no work, no people.

There's her.

If you say so, Bernard. If you say so. Oh my. Lookit that.

The Delta is flat everywhere, so they'd scrambled up to the summit of the levee to get their bearings. The docks were below them. Despite the high water, their perch gave them a panoramic view of a bustling, hectic port. Ships, boats, and barges were moored everywhere with their gangplanks stuck straight out. Men swarmed up and down gangways, carrying heavy burdens in both directions. Overseers of warehouses barked orders directing traffic. Ships' captains conversed under umbrellas with men in rubber capes and coats. Papers were signed, moneys exchanged. Behind a row of warehouses facing the docks were men in clusters of twenty or thirty each, crowding about other men with clipboards, who stood under cover from the rain to write down their names, one by one, and send them scurrying into this building and that for a day of labor hauling goods into and out of the ships, boats, and barges cramming the docks.

Work! Bernard cried out joyously as if the word were the name of God. Work!

They scurried down to the docks and took their place in the clusters of men. Their group stood in a jumble in front of a burly man of medium height dressed in a yellow slicker and bonnet of the kind fishermen wore to ride out a storm. His great black rubber boots disappeared beneath the hem of the slicker. All that was human about him poked out of the bonnet's face hole, a grump's mug with fleshy lips and a nose pocked like a pinecone.

When it came their turn in line, the boss asked Bald Horace his name, and he said, Bald Horace. The man wrote it down without asking for a surname, probably because he didn't think Negroes needed one.

Then he asked Bernard his name and Bernard answered, Bernard Levy. The man just about dropped his clipboard.

What? he said. A look of disbelief crossed his stubbly face. What'd you say?

Bernard opened his mouth to speak, but the boss held up a hand to delay him. He called to the other bosses taking names. Hey, Franklin. Get over here. You gotta see this. Eustis, come here! Newel!

While Franklin, Eustis, and Newel disengaged themselves from their respective queues, Bernard's boss gestured for him to stand next to him under the warehouse awning where it was more or less dry. The four bosses squared up around them. Bernard's boss said, Tell these men who you are.

It didn't take Bernard three times to learn a thing. He prepared himself for the derision sure to follow the enunciation of his name. He thought it wouldn't hurt to embellish the revelation. If he gave these men an especially good laugh, it could result in a better detail for him and Bald Horace, a higher-paying one maybe. So he stood straight and tall as he might, scrunched his close-set features up even tighter than nature had done at the moment of his birth, and bowed from the waist with a flourish of arm, the way he'd seen many a dandy bow during his pleasure boat days.

Bernard Levy, he said. At your service. For good measure, he clicked his boot heels.

There was a moment of silence. Then great bellows of laughter, hoots, hollers, and guffaws. Bernard bobbed up and down again, moving his hands in clever arcs then sticking them behind his ears to make those sizable handles look yet bigger while he spouted the pleasantries of swells in theatrical voice. I am enchanted to meet your acquaintance, he said, on this lovely day by this sparklin' shore. The bosses doubled up, holding on to one another's shoulders to keep from falling over. The more they laughed, the more he bobbed. The men from the various queues moved over to see what riotous commotion was going on, and they whooped and whistled as well, though most of them didn't know what the joke was. All they saw was a tattered, dirty man bowing and scraping with a dopey expression writ over an odd assemblage of nose, eyes, ears, and mouth saying things like "I don't mind if I do" and "If it were your pleasure" in an accent none had heard before, but which they would describe later on to those absent as "hoity-toity."

The laughter petered out. The other bosses drifted off, shaking their heads, wiping their grins off with handkerchiefs. Bernard's boss said, I've got a special job for you. Go get in the truck there, and we'll be off soon's I take care of the rest of these here men and square up with the foreman.

Bernard said, May Bald Horace go with us, Boss?

That stopped the other man dead in his tracks. He looked at Bernard as if he were plain crazy. Why? he asked.

With nothing else to say that the man might believe, Bernard said, He belongs to me, sir. He goes where I go.

The boss slapped his head. He looked to be restraining another fit of humor with difficulty. His pocked-up nose wrinkled with the effort. If that don't beat all, he said. Then he shrugged. Yeah, sure. We'll take him in the back. You ride up front. Where we're goin', the big man keeps his own personal niggers. Only his a sore lot luckier than yours, son. I'm willin' to bet they eat and sleep a load better'n that 'un.

While the boss bent over the grille to crank up the engine, Bald Horace climbed into the bed of the truck and wedged himself between two stacks of pallets tied to it. Bernard freed a piece of tarp from a bundle anchored under a sledgehammer and tented it over his friend's head against the rain. You'll be alright back here, he said. I think our luck has begun to change.

They stopped first at the rear entrance of a stately pea-colored house in the city where a uniformed light-skinned black woman handed the driver a pile of letters tied up with string. Then they rode along the river into the countryside north of Memphis. Bernard didn't know the territory very well. He hadn't spent much time in the north country as a child. He lived farther downriver on the south side of town in those days, and what he knew of the places they passed was from leaving home all those years ago and returning with Bald Horace. It was plantation country, some of them kept up with acres of fields and pastures that must be somethin' gorgeous, Bernard thought, in the dry times. The rest crumbled into the earth under the weight of water, time, and neglect.

To his surprise, the boss turned into one of the latter, driving through a rusted wrought-iron gate coming off hinges barely attached to a brick wall riddled with chips and holes. The loblolly pine and red maple at its entryway dipped forward so low from a lack of proper care and abandonment to the wind that their branches brushed the cab of the truck and battered poor Bald Horace about the head. The only element of the place that looked kept up was the road. Planks of fresh wood were laid out over the widest ruts where rainwater flowed through deep trenches as if from underground springs.

Up to this point, the boss was taciturn. A couple of times, Bernard tried to engage him in conversation, indicating that he'd grown up thereabouts, a fact he felt might help warm the man up. The boss replied he was from King of Prussia, Pennsylvania, himself, where it didn't goddamn rain like this ever, though they got plenty of goddamn snow in the winter months. That prompted Bernard to launch into a story about the rare qualities of mountain snow, a story told him by a Frenchman from Switzerland he'd met in a railcar. He wasn't half through when he noticed the boss wasn't paying attention. The man didn't care at all what he said no matter how entertaining the tale. Bernard shut up.

There wasn't another word between them until they turned off the entry road into a clearing of squared-up cultivated bushes and shrubs swimming in mud. This here's what the big man calls his puzzle garden, the boss said, but it ain't goin' too good. They rode a short distance more, made another turn. And there it was.

The big house. Bernard had never seen such a house and by this time, he had traveled some between the pleasure boat and his wanderings with Bald Horace. The house was raised high up off the ground on a brick foundation and had two staircases, one from the north corner and one from the south, meeting up in the middle of a wide veranda that went all the way around to the back. It stood three stories and had balconies from every window, balconies of wrought iron twisted into fanciful shapes that maybe were flowers, maybe animals, he couldn't tell which. It had columns, of course, every plantation house needed columns, and these were thick, fluted, and well spaced. Everything was painted a shining white except the wide oak planks of the veranda floor and the jalousie shutters, which were a dark green. The whole structure looked as if it stretched back all the way to Illinois. Maybe that was it, Bernard thought. Maybe it was the size of the thing that took his breath away. He was taken by the way light radiated from within, light so abundant, so bright, it made him wonder where the dynamo was, how it could be big enough to generate all that light and still hide itself from the eye. There were three chandeliers wired up on the veranda, and these burned brightly, too, so that the house glowed in the rain against the gray sky like a holy place or a magical one.

The boss from King of Prussia, Pennsylvania, left the truck and mounted the stairs on the south side. As he did, the front door with its brass knocker in the shape of a lion's head opened, and a man stepped out in the company of two liveried Negroes. The boss removed his rain hat and stood holding it at his waist. He presented the bundle of letters they'd retrieved in town to the gent, who barely glanced at them and handed them off to one of the Negroes. Obviously, this was the big man. He was dressed in jodhpurs and riding boots paired with a black leather jacket and a turtleneck sweater of the same camel color as his britches. Everything about him was crisp and clean. There was no possibility he had gone riding in a downpour in such an outfit, and it was unlikely he intended to. He was a dramatic type, Bernard assessed, dressing for effect rather than use. His theory was borne out by the man's posture. He stood languidly with a crop in one hand that he beat lightly against the palm of the other as if marking the time of a waltz. His features were undeniably handsome. He had a straight nose, wide-set eyes, chiseled jaw, well-shaped lips coming to a bow at the center. His thick black hair was pomaded to curl over one side of his brow in a studied, graceful dip. In fact, he was so remarkably good-looking and well turned out that Bernard was reminded of an actor on a showboat playing master in some antebellum play. He half-expected an actress in banana curls and hoop skirt to step out on the veranda after him. He rolled down the truck window to achieve a clearer look.

The dock boss smiled at the big man and stretched out an arm, gesturing toward the truck. The big man turned his head to look directly in Bernard's direction, his expression haughty but impassive. Bernard would remember that moment the rest of his life. Their eyes met and a shiver went through him, though not the cold kind. It was a hot, volcanic rush of blood. The big man pointed at him with his crop and circled it in the air, meaning get out of that truck, boy, get up here, and let me look at you.

Bernard's heart pounded, his ears throbbed. He got out of the truck then helped Bald Horace out of its bed as a stalling tactic. He needed time to calm himself. The two friends jogged double-time through the mud and up the steps to the veranda. Bernard felt as if everything was happening in slow motion. Every sound was magnified from the squish of their shoes in the mud to the clap, clap, clap they made hitting the stairs. He could hear every drop of rain hit the ground. He could hear Bald Horace breathe.

They stood behind the King of Prussia man with their heads down. The big man said, I hear you got an unusual name. Let me hear you tell it.

Somewhere in his pounding heart, Bernard knew who the big man was. He couldn't say why. His scalp didn't creep. But he was as certain of the other's identity as he was of his own and so he told his name straight out, without the bowing and mimicry, told it with his eyes squinting against the light of the chandelier under which the other Bernard Levy, his name-twin, stood. Then he made a study of the man before him, a closer study than he'd made from the truck, one which took the measure of the other's character, or at least as much as he could discern. He saw the mark of cruelty in the set of the big man's jaw, the proud heart behind the steel gray eyes, the sensualist in the glossy lips, greed in the soft belly and thighs. He was handsome, alright, but his beauty had a spiteful core that frightened rather than seduced, at least that was the conclusion Bernard came to on that wet afternoon on the veranda of Ghost Tree Plantation as he obediently uttered his name.

Bernard Levy, sir, he said. The other did not laugh but snorted and smirked and proceeded to ignore him as if he were an object rather than a human being.

Quite a find you've made, Carter, the big man said to the boss. My wife will say you've found the mirror of my soul. Let's keep him around for good luck. If the angel of death comes looking for me, it's this ugly pup we'll throw to the old fellow, eh? Now, who's this blackie behind him?

A man named . . . ah . . . dang, I forget.

Bald Horace, Bald Horace offered helpfully.

Bald Horace, yes, thank you. He's t'other's man.

The two exchanged a look of unveiled mockery. His man? Bernard Levy the handsome repeated. His man. Well, then I guess he can stay, too. Looks strong enough. Put them up in the barn or the barracks, wherever there's room, and we'll assign them jobs after supper. Come back up the house after. I want to talk to you.

Carter took Bernard and Bald Horace over to the barn where a horse stall stood empty. He gave them dry blankets.

We'll find you better beds oncet we know if you'll be workin' on the land or on the house. The house workers're mostly eye-talian. We're up to the finish work now. They're layin' tile and carvin' gewgaws into the wood. My, but they're good at that. They're good at brick layin', too. We got 'em in here when we laid the foundation, and they just stayed. Now, the land workers, well, they'd be mostly niggers. You're a lucky boy, he said to Bald Horace, to land here. Plenty of your people goin' beggin' since the rains got bad. Lookie over there next to that first bar-rack, that's the canteen. Supper's in another hour. You go on over there and eat your fill, tell 'em Carter sent you if anyone asks. After supper, I'll come back here and let you know what the big man's decided to do with you. We pay by the job here, so I can't tell you your wages 'til I know what you're doin'. Payday's every other Saturday. Just so you know.

They smiled and shuffled as they were expected to do but after Carter left, Bald Horace whistled and hugged Bernard and clapped him on the back.

Sweet Jesus, look at this. A dry spot to lay our heads, hot food, and steady work. How long's it been, Bernard?

I couldn't say.

Bald Horace walked up and down the barn aisle, marveling at the construction of the place. The aisle was brick, the walls cement, the stalls of the sturdiest wood with iron bars on hinges for windows. The horses in their stalls were quiet and in good flesh. The tack room was immaculate. There was another whole room devoted to carriages, some vehicles made for stylish travel, and others for hauling whatever needed it. The trappings were lush, of the best leather and shining brass.

Must be a dozen men workin' in here to keep her up like this. Where are they all now, I wonder? Takin' a nap? Bald Horace giggled at his own joke. My, oh my, I do believe we landed in the lap of paradise.

Bernard was not so sure. Everything looked fine around him, he could agree to that, but he sensed there was something else going on, something on the rain-soaked horizon, a thing all the hot food, good work, and dry beds in the world would not be worth. He studied his friend, his beloved's brother, a man who had suffered as much as he had in the last year, who carried around a black skin in an unfriendly world the same way he carried homeliness. Bald Horace had wrapped himself up in his blanket and lay down to test the comfort of the stall floor, which was covered in wood shavings five inches deep. His eyes were shut. He was smiling, and a heartbeat later he was snoring. Bernard thought, Bald Horace is happy. He sighed, weighing that happiness against his own anxiety.

A breeze came up and a scent wafted through the barn like perfume. The aroma of rice came from the canteen where supper cooked. Bernard wrinkled his nub of a nose and inhaled the scent more deeply. Yes, rice and beans, for sure, maybe a bit of collard and cracklin' throughout. Oh Lord, maybe even giblets. His mouth watered as if dirty rice and beans were the feast of kings. Alright, he thought, alright. We'll stay here awhile. We'll put a little meat on our bones and fatten up our purse.

He lay down opposite Bald Horace and tried to catch some sleep before supper and whatever work detail might follow, but the unease he'd felt stayed with him and he remained awake.

XII

WHEN MICKEY MOE OPENED THE door to the house next to the junk-yard, Laura Anne just about jumped out of her skin and the car both. She had her hand on the door handle ready to swing it open when J. Henry said, Ho, now, miss, be careful. We're still movin'.

It took centuries for the car to roll to a stop. She feared she'd faint from hyperventilation. And then she was in her lover's arms. He held her close. She let out a little cry of relief. Oh baby, he said. It's alright. You're here now. He kissed her like there was no one else there. Then he moved her aside. She staggered a couple steps, turned around to see what it was distracted him. Mickey Moe had his hands up against the car's rear window, which he stared into drop-jawed.

Who is that? he said, gesturing toward the man collapsed over the seat. He nodded at her driver. I know you must be J. Henry, and how do you do. But who's that?

They told him what they knew, which wasn't much. Mickey Moe

opened the car's door and leaning in, tried to rouse the man, who groaned once or twice but remained immobile with his eyes shut. With considerable effort, he and J. Henry managed to get the dead weight of him into the house.

The mechanic's home was a mean place with scavenged furniture rigged to stand up straight with odd scraps of unrelated furniture lashed on with duct tape. There was an icebox in one corner next to a sink and a kitchen table with a double-burner hot plate set on top. Mickey Moe handed his girl a dish towel and told her to fill it with ice.

Let's see if we can't bring him to.

J. Henry put the wrapped up ice on the back of the man's neck. He moaned and fluttered his eyes open then closed them again while he continued moaning. Mickey Moe dragged a tin tub into the middle of the room from a place outside, then handed J. Henry a couple of buckets.

There's a pump out there. If you could please fill up the tub, my gal here'll heat up a pot or two of water. When everything's nice and luke-warm, we can put him in it without sending him into shock. Gettin' him cleaned up and conscious seems to be the first order of business. Don't you agree, darlin'?

Laura Anne's chest went warm with pride. How could Mama and Daddy not approve of my man? she thought. He's so good in a crisis. He takes charge as natural as a five-star general. She found two big pots behind a chintz-curtained cupboard. She put them up to heat. Once she had the pots going, J. Henry worked at filling up the tub while Laura Anne helped Mickey Moe undress the stranger without shame at seeing him naked or revulsion at the wounds and filth that covered him. It took all three of them to lift him into the tub. His eyes opened for good then. They were wide and fearful. At first, he struggled against immersion, splashing water all around. When he realized they were trying to help him, he quieted. He'd try to speak, and then he'd cry. Speak and cry.

Speak and cry. It took time and patience to soothe him enough to stop his blubbering. The owner of the shack, Billy Dankins, came home from the garage. The sight of Billy, a skinny white man in overalls smeared with axle grease, set him off again. Billy took in the strange goings-on in his living room with a twist of his head and a perplexed pout.

Good evenin', J. Henry, he said. How's your mama doin'?

Good even', Mr. Dankins. I don't know about Mama. I've not seen her yet.

Well, then you'd best go on or you'll be leavin' agin without the time to treat her right. Whatever on God's green earth is goin' on in my own livin' room, I can take care of.

Why, thank you, Mr. Dankins, J. Henry said, taking his leave as fast as he could. He knew what kind of situation he'd landed in thanks to the irresistible temptation presented by thirty-five dollars. It had long passed being worth the trouble.

Laura Anne called out to him. Thank you, J. Henry, she said, but there was no response from him, just the sound of his car starting up outside. She felt a fresh sadness. From the way things turned out, J. Henry had been right about danger in the backwoods, and she should have said something before he left, apologized for brushing off his concerns. Oh, if I had it all to do over again, J. Henry, she wanted to tell him, I would never have put another in danger to satisfy my own desires. But even if she had the chance to do so, she wondered if he would ever have believed her.

Anyone want to explain to me what's goin' on here? Billy asked.

They told him what they knew, which still wasn't much.

And you're the fiancée, I take it?

Laura Anne nodded.

Then I am pleased to meet you. I heard enough about you these last few days that I feel I know you. You're very welcome in my house. Now this fellah . . .

He kicked the side of the tub, which caused its occupant to yelp like a dog.

. . . I'm willin' to bet that this fellah's one of them Yankee agitators come down here to stir up the niggers and have 'em settin' alongside white folks on the bus and in restaurants, have 'em votin' in communists an' whatever riffraff clings to 'em that they may lord over white men. Why, I'm willin' to bet further that he got took from the car he was travelin' in alongside one of his nigger buddies and taught a little lesson or two.

Billy Dankins gave Laura Anne a sheepish look meant to apologize for speaking plainly of matters ladies were better left ignorant of.

Look. I don't appreciate what happened to this boy here. I got the call to join in the fun last night, but I said no. There's a meanness in some men that I just don't want to see or encourage. But I got to believe that this here Yankee interloper had no business at all comin' down here and stirrin' up people's passions like that, and I do not want him in my house. You all got to go, and you all got to go now. I'm goin' back to the garage to bring your car back, Mickey Moe. You was good company these past few days, but your car's done and you'd be leavin' in the mornin' anyways, so get goin' before my people discover he's here.

Mickey Moe's mouth worked soundlessly. Laura Anne knew he was filled up with emotion he fought to keep from spilling out. He shook his head. He raised his hands with palms up in a gesture of helplessness. He looked at Billy from where they knelt washing the wounds of the stranger with much the same expression Billy had when he'd entered his home to find him there. There was the same twist of the head, the same perplexed pout.

It's your house, Billy. We'll be going directly after you return, but I didn't ask this boy to come down here and stir things up any more than you did. I want to be clear about that.

Billy shook his head. Well, alright, then, he said. One good old boy to another, I'll buy that, but there's people here that won't. I got eyes. That boy's buck naked in that tub. I can see he's a Jew, same as you. Nine outta ten of those agitators are Jews. Everybody knows that. Folks say all you Jews stick together. That you got a method of signals and handshakes, and every one of you knows what the rest are up to.

That's ridiculous, Billy. I don't expect you to believe me, but I'd like you to remember I said it.

I will. I didn't say I agreed. But you know, there's people that read their Bible and people that don't. It's the ones that don't who disbelieve me when I tell them the sweet mother of Jesus was a Jew, as you'll recall we discussed t'other night when the subject came 'round. And they'll be the same types you'd best be lookin' out for when you leave here.

It took some time for Billy to retrieve the LTD, but they needed every minute to get the stranger dried off and into Mickey Moe's set of spare travel clothes. The lovers dragged the tub out the back door and dumped the bathwater out. They took a few minutes to hold on to each other and make promises. Feeling the warmth and give of each other's flesh built up their courage. Mickey Moe promised Laura Anne he'd get them out of this mess in one piece. Laura Anne promised she'd use the pistol she'd borrowed from Daddy if need be and not to worry, her aim was pretty good.

The what?

Pistol. Daddy's Colt 45. I somehow knew I should have protection for this trip. Don't ask me how, I just knew.

Mickey Moe suffered a sick feeling in the pit of his belly. Something in there roiled and rose and sought to choke him. Consequently, his voice came out of his throat weak and raspy.

I don't like guns, he said.

Laura Anne looked at him as if he'd just said he didn't care for sunshine or birdsong.

Then it's a good thing one of us doesn't mind 'em.

There are not many things that can pierce the manly confidence of a good old boy, but having a woman best him in an arena that by rights is manly turf is one of them. Mickey Moe's mouth worked. He coughed several times to push down the fear or distaste or whatever it was that sent a burning lump of bile up his throat to begin with. He put a hand out to her, and they both tried to ignore how it shook.

Give it to me, he said.

No.

Give it to me, woman.

Given her generation and geography, Laura Anne felt that she was in one of those moments when a woman says to herself, this is wrong, this is disastrous, this is the most foolhardy, insane decision of my life, but this man, son, father of mine needs me to do this thing for his own sake, and it is my job to put my life on the line for him. In her most salient gesture of love yet, she walked with her head erect, her shoulders square as a queen's, walked over to the kitchen table where she'd dropped her pocketbook, reached into the bag, and produced Daddy's gun. She put it in Mickey Moe's hand, showed him that the safety was on, and then closed his hand over it with her own. Mickey Moe filled his chest with air and thanked her. They kissed.

When Billy returned with the car, they put the stranger in the backseat and covered him up with a picnic blanket Mickey Moe'd kept in the trunk since his visits to Greenville, when he and Laura Anne would lie together by the riverbank planning their future. They settled in the front seat, the pistol on the space between them, and set off for Memphis.

It was night. The sky was clear. There was moonlight all around. Between the moon and the headlights, they managed to ride pretty well through the backwoods, going around the potholes and through fallen branches and puddles that littered the roadway in the manner paper goods and cigarettes litter more traveled byways. They were beyond anxious, expecting sheet-wearing kluckers to pop out of the woods, discover the Yankee in the back, and rain punishment on their heads for helping him. They didn't talk much, but held hands whenever Mickey Moe didn't need two to steer. That warm contact proved stronger comfort than any of dozens of speeches they might have accomplished had the situation been less dire. They weren't five miles from the interstate, which they considered to be heaven's gate to safety, when their passenger spoke up.

Stop! Stop!

Though they refused his directive, they looked in the rear view and turned around respectively in order to pay him attention. He who had been mute, who'd barely moved a muscle since his rescue, was greatly agitated.

Stop! Stop! Stop! This is it! This is where they took us!

Now is not the time, Mickey Moe said.

Oh no, oh no. Stop! Stop! He might still be alive.

It was a terrible piece of news. There was a "he," and he might be alive. Laura Anne swallowed to get her throat wet enough to speak.

Who is "he"?

My partner. Jeffrey Harris. He's one of you. I mean, he's a Negro from Raleigh-Durham. We were assigned together to come out here and canvass the local Negroes for a literacy program. It was great for a while. Everyone was so kind, so hospitable. Then the trucks came. With the white men in 'em. Oh God, oh God, oh God. Please. You have to stop. He could be alive.

Dang!

Mickey Moe stopped the car. He banged his head on the steering wheel three times. He looked at Laura Anne, and there were tears in his eyes, tears of fear and frustration and internal moral combat.

Dang! he repeated. He picked up the gun. Banged that against the steering wheel twice. He left the car. Slammed the door. He paced outside in circles, waving his arms around and muttering in a way that frightened Laura Anne more than the impossible circumstances of the moment. She rolled down a window.

Honey. Honey, she said. What are you doing?

He stood by her window wild-eyed. His shoulders heaved from breathing hard.

Well, I'm about to go into those woods and look around for Jeffrey Harris from Raleigh-Durham, he said. I want you to stay in the car with our guest here. . . .

He hit the rear window with the gun butt.

And what is your name, sir? I'd like to know the name of the man I'm about to give up my life for. . . .

The stranger gulped. Walter Cohen, he said.

Alright. Now, darlin', you stay in the car with Walter Cohen and keep the doors locked. Anyone comes by while I'm in those woods, you take off. Run 'em over if you have to. Now where exactly about here did you think Jeffrey Harris is lying, breathin' his last?

Back there a bit. There's a tree down, a tree with pink flowers. I don't know what it is, but it's lying in a ditch. I remember it, because I was trying to remember everything in case I got out alive. There were seven of them in two trucks, and they parked the trucks there and dragged us into the woods. Not very far in there's a campsite. That's where they took us. They put us against some kind of posts that were there. They made a fire. They drank. They spit and pissed on us, and then they cut us. They had whips, too. Every man took his turn. Then they took Jeffrey off somewhere, and I could hear him screaming. I don't know what they did, but it was awful. I know it was awful from the sound of his screams. He was in agony. His screams went on forever. I never heard anything like that before in my life. I knew I had to get away or I'd be screaming like that next, and I don't know, I guess the bonds they had us in were compromised from the whipping and the cutting, and I was able to break loose. I just ran and ran and ran until I landed on your car, miss. That's what happened, I swear to God.

Mickey Moe walked off in the direction indicated by Walter Cohen to seek out a fallen tree with pink flowers stopping up a ditch. He walked flat-footed with his head down like a child having a temper tantrum. He stiffened his arms and talked to himself. There's not going to be a tree with damned pink flowers lying in a ditch anywhere, he muttered. Walter Cohen has gone crazy from trauma is all, and why couldn't he've just remained incoherent until we got to Memphis anyway? Oh no, Walter Cohen has to perk up and put me and my darlin' Laura Anne in jeopardy for the sake of some dang tortured Negro out here, who brought it on himself, didn't he. . . .

But there it was. The tree with pink flowers stopping up a ditch. And not far into the woods, a campsite with empty whiskey bottles lying around, wood still smoking a little, two bloodstained posts, and Walter Cohen's shoes. Mickey Moe released the safety of his gun and tried to calm himself. They're not still here, he said out loud. No one's stupid enough to hang around and lay claim to this scene.

Unless they were looking for Walter Cohen.

He walked a ways off down a path to find Jeffrey Harris or what was left of him. He walked through brambles and bush with his gun hand shaking and his heart in his throat, his ears pricked for the sound of others. An animal broke a branch, and he jumped, then stumbled to his knees. When he looked down in the moonlight to see what he'd tripped over, he saw a foot. A black, bare foot with its pink sole staring up at him like the face of a living thing. There was nothing attached to the foot, it just lay there along the path in a blackened pool of blood as if someone had dropped it. Mickey Moe didn't have to see any more. He scrambled up and ran back to the car. He banged on the door. Laura Anne unlocked it as fast as she could. He got in, pushed her aside, turned the key, and stepped on the gas.

Did you find him? Walter Cohen asked. Did you find Jeffrey Harris? It took a while before he could respond.

I found a piece of him.

The others tried to ask him what he meant, but he held up a hand to silence them and drove as fast as the road permitted to the interstate. They weren't a mile away from the safety of blacktop and street lamps when a red pickup truck hurtling down the road in the opposite direction nearly ran them into a tree.

Walter Cohen gasped and whipped his head around to stare through the back window. That was them. That was them, I know it. It was a red truck they threw us in and a white one that followed.

Mickey Moe's blood was already up about as high as it went. Walter Cohen's outburst maximized his irritation. Simmer down! Do you know how many red trucks there are around here? Do you? Then set down and stay quiet 'til we get to Memphis. I'll take you to the hospital, and then we'll file a report to the police. After that, you're on your own. I will have gone as far as I can go.

Laura Anne patted Mickey Moe's closest driving hand to show her approval of his plan. She noticed something new that'd gone wrong.

Honey, she said. Where's Daddy's forty-five?

Mickey Moe's eyes near popped out of his head. The gun, the gun, the gun, he thought, what happened to the goddamn gun.

I don't know. Maybe I dropped it back there. Probably when I fell down. Maybe not. It should've gone off if I did.

Well, honey. I'm not so sure it was loaded.

You're not?

I never checked.

You didn't.

I forgot.

He stared ahead at the road with his mouth working a while before sound came out. You sent me back there with an unloaded gun.

Her face wrinkled up. Tears flowed. Her body shook.

He couldn't stand her pain. It's alright, darlin', he said. He reached out and pulled her close to him. It's alright. I'm in one piece.

He glanced through the rear view at Walter Cohen, who had not spoken at all but sat slumped over looking mournful and miserable, when really, thought Mickey Moe, he should be feeling some kind of elated that he's alive at all.

Well, one thing's sure now, son, Mickey Moe said.

What's that?

We will not be going to the police with you. I'll take you to the hospital, but the police, no. I'm not going to put my future father-in-law in jeopardy by having them discover his gun.

I don't understand.

Believe me, if the Memphis, Tennessee, police can find a Jew from Greenville, Mississippi, to blame for body parts turning up in their woods, they will jump at the task.

Then I'll have to tell them, Walter Cohen said.

No, you will not. If you have any gratitude in you at all, you will not.

The men argued. Laura Anne put a hand on Mickey Moe's arm to silence him and took over. No one bests a well-trained Southern girl in convincing a man to do the noble thing. She fixed Walter Cohen with a penetrating look and employed her most honey voice. Mr. Cohen, she said, my fiancé here is right. My daddy is an innocent in all of this. He is a hardworking, generous man who is kind to white men and Negroes alike. Why, he offers Negroes credit in our store and at the same rate as everyone else. My mama is frail and depends on him. If anything happened to him, if he was so much as held overnight in a jail cell, it'd outright kill her.

Laura Anne allowed her eyes to blink as if stemming tears at the thought of her mother's untimely demise. She sighed and put a hand over her heart.

For some coldhearted notion of justice, Mr. Cohen, would you have her suffer?

She was a very pretty woman, and Walter Cohen, ragged and spent as he was, was not made of wood. He relented. He would not go to the police.

It was close to dawn before they found a hospital and dropped their cargo off at the emergency entrance. Once they were rid of him, they checked into the first motel they could find. As soon as the door was closed and locked, they were in each other's arms. She shook against him.

Oh sweetheart, she whispered, a sob in her voice, I am so sorry about the gun. I am so sorry I never checked it. Everything seems to be happening so fast. I just didn't think.

Mickey Moe took her face in his hands and held it a few inches away from his own.

But the way you handled Walter Cohen, darlin'. That was perfection.

They beamed at each other. They kissed and did not stop 'til they hit the bed backward, falling onto it laughing. Laura Anne swore it was a wonder they could laugh after the day they'd had. Oh, that's not the only wondrous thing we can do after a hard day, Mickey Moe said, undressing her with one hand and stroking her with the other.

Later, they fell asleep entwined. They were so worn out not even the frequent sirens of ambulance after ambulance screeching outside their window woke them up.

They planned to head over to Aurora Mae's at the address Mama Jo Baylin had given them the next day. After what they'd been through, they figured that part of their journey would go easy. When he opened his eyes at high noon to the sound of his beloved taking a shower, the first thing on Mickey Moe's mind was not joining her or getting coffee from the machine down the hall. His first thought complicated matters. His first thought was of her daddy's gun lying in the dirt next to Jeffrey Harris's severed foot.

XIII

Memphis, Tennessee, 1926–1927

BALD HORACE HATED THE FIRST job they set him to. While Bernard lolled around at a house job, for the first two weeks Bald Horace filled bags with wet sand then trekked them up to the flat of the levee wherever the river fronted the property. He did it bone cold and in the rain. Sometimes he was told to load the bags onto a truck for sale at neighboring farms where men more flood fearful than Ghost Tree's owner and without his workforce paid jacked-up prices. The men working side by side with Bald Horace cursed the big man as a greedy Jew.

Who else could profit over a neighbor's despair? they said.

Bald Horace defended his friend's race. They not all like that, he said.

How do you know? they asked.

Big man's not the first I ever met.

That night, he looked for Bernard outside the white men's barracks.

They're talkin' about the boss bein' a greedy Jew, he said. Better watch out.

Bernard heard his granddaddy's voice. Don't forget who you are, son. Alright, he wouldn't. But he wasn't sure what he was supposed to do with this intelligence now that he had it. Watch out, he guessed. Like his friend said.

Sandbag detail was the worst backbreaking job on the farm. Every bone and muscle Bald Horace had ached so much, he could not sleep at night. It got so bad, he thought about leaving Ghost Tree even if he left alone. One morning, he was about to pack up his kit and tell Bernard he quit when the rain stopped and it stayed stopped. Every day, the sun shone, and the sky was a hard, brilliant winter blue.

It didn't take long before folk stopped caring about sandbags. Fresh opportunity knocked, and Bald Horace answered. Much of the help had been wayfarers working at Ghost Tree as shelter from the deluge. Once the rains stopped, they went back to their homes with a little coin in their pockets and the intent to rebuild what they'd lost. Bald Horace had his pick of the vacancies created. He chose to take care of the farm animals, which meant everything feathered or furred except the horses and hunting dogs. He looked after donkeys, chickens, cows, pigs, and goats. He watched them mate, argue, and play to learn their individual natures and habits. He knew when one of them was footsore or bad in the belly. When feeding time came around, the joyous way they ran to him braying, clucking, lowing, bleating, or grunting filled his heart. He named them, cared for them, and they cared for him, too.

His work was so pleasant, he saw Aurora Mae's hand in things. Though Aurora Mae was surely dead, he felt that she hadn't forgotten her brother and his friend, that her spirit was close and blessed them both. How else to explain how they'd wound up at this paradise called Ghost Tree where they paid the help on time and didn't skimp on the vittles, either? To think he'd been this close to leaving. It was as if Aurora Mae saw his misery and plugged up the hole in the clouds with one hand then grabbed his shirt collar with the other to pull him back. Yessir, he told whoever would listen, Ghost Tree Plantation was a sacred place for all those who mourned someone. His own sister's soul was set down by the hand of a merciful Lord in the forked arms of one of the willow trees that draped the border of the puzzle garden. He'd seen her there one morning when the fog lifted. Day and night, he could feel her like she was in the next room. This gave him peace. In fact, for the first time since Aurora Mae went missing, he was happy. His friend said that was because he didn't have much to do with that other Bernard.

Once it was established that Bernard could read and write, he was made a secretary to the big man himself. He didn't have to wear the Negroes' livery, but he was given three fresh shirts and two pairs of pants in the plantation colors, crimson red and the near black green of the shutters, a pair of paddock boots and a red-and-green cap with a short visor. He was told to keep these and himself clean. He reported to the big man himself on the front porch every morning. He knew it was not his place to question why he was not allowed over the threshold. Depending on the terrain, the name-twins made inspection rounds together in a truck or on horseback. They were together so much, people all around started calling him Bernard the ugly to differentiate him from the big man. Bernard didn't like that much, but he understood the joke and tried not to take offense.

Together, the two Bernards inspected the cotton fields, the rice fields, the vegetable fields along with the various stock barns, the tannery, the smithy, the silos, the millhouse, all of which were in the process of rehabilitation. Bernard the ugly wrote down whatever he was told without knowing why because Bernard the handsome didn't think him important enough to explain things to. He didn't converse with him at all except to command. Bernard the ugly made lists of mysterious percentages and inexplicable dollar figures, the names of people he did not know and of equipment of indeterminate function, comprehending little. Every two weeks, he rode in the front seat of the big car next to the driver and delivered envelopes to the bank and to the pea-colored house in town. He never questioned what was in them, because he never would have gotten an answer.

Two years before, Bernard the handsome bought Ghost Tree Plantation from a family of blue bloods gone to ruin with war, gambling, and disease, dragging the property down with it. Soon after, he purchased a few hundred acres of abutting land and set about creating the finest plantation Tennessee had known since Grant's and Sherman's men destroyed them all. It was his great dream, what he saw as his life's work. His ambitions were stuck in a vision of the past, when a man might behave like Caesar on his own property and get away with it. Ever since his granddaddy died, leaving him a fortune in the family agricultural supply business, he desired to use that fortune to make himself a mighty lord with the power of life and death over man, beast, and the river. He thought such his birthright because of his good looks and the size of his purse. What's more, he thought his vision an ideal life, worth resurrecting from the boneyard of history.

Although he had a pretty wife of excellent lineage, he loved nothing so much as his gold, of which he had a great deal since he did not like nor trust greenbacks. He preferred fondling his chests of coin to his wife. This was fine by her, as she didn't much like him. They argued often about the way he conducted business or the way he treated the help. He told her she was a soft-headed nag, who didn't understand commerce. She told him he had a tiny soul, small and hard as a pebble, and the heart of a devil. He made his name-twin his secretary to irritate her. When her local friends telephoned with social invitations, it was his delight to send Bernard the ugly over to their farms with handwritten notes of acceptance or regrets and instructions to announce himself by name as he did so. This proved more annoying to his secretary than to the lady of the house, who'd long ago given up caring what her husband did. She was more interested in the work of the young Italian stonecutter who chiseled lions, stags, and cupids for her flower garden. She couldn't get enough of them. Once the garden was stuffed with more figures than rosebushes, winged cherubs appeared on the lintels of doors all over the big house. Her husband complained that her decor was too funereal. She countered that if a plantation named Ghost Tree was to be her home, it should be festooned in a manner that reflected the death of her innocence. When she ran out of doorways and windows in the big house, winged cherubs appeared over those of the workers' barracks and even the latrines.

Sometimes, when he was feeling particularly happy, Bald Horace would point at one and tell Bernard, Look, you see? We were led to paradise by our own angel.

And Bernard would answer, No. We have wandered into an asylum for the insane.

Christmas of '26 came and went. New Year's followed. Bernard tried to convince Bald Horace it was time to move on, but Bald Horace said it was cold and travel would be arduous. It made more sense to wait 'til spring. Bernard agreed, and they missed their chance. Long before spring, the rains returned. Once the deluge started, it was relentless.

Most days, the rain came in sheets, making work impossible. Every day, the skies were dismal, the hard sparkling blue of December and January was completely bled out. The only relief from the gray, wet canopy overhead were lightning storms that robbed everyone of rest. Buildings too wet to burn were struck by lightning bolts and sputtered smoke. Bald Horace's critters weren't so lucky. He lost three chickens and a baby goat to fiery bolts. With great effort, he managed to make a hole in the heavy, sodden earth to lay their poor singed bodies down.

Soon as his back was turned, the mud collapsed in on them. Wild dogs feasted at compromised gravesites in the night, scattering feathers and goat hair all over.

Those poor little things, he told Bernard. They never did the world a lick of harm. I think Aurora Mae's traveled on. She's not lookin' out for us no more. No matter, I still feel her as if she was standin' next to me.

She's in our hearts, is what it is, Bernard offered. I've been telling you, she's no ghostly presence. She's still alive. I know that in a way no rain can erase, no run of luck can alter.

Have it your own way, Bernard. I don't know much anymore.

By the end of February, the wayfarers came back. The Negro barracks were full again. Bernard the handsome had the workers filling up sandbags. He rode out every morning to the levee first thing to satisfy himself all was under control. The river was higher than ever, but his levees looked in good shape, so he sent Carter around again to sell bags for cash money to panicked croppers. The other Bernard went with Carter to collect the money and make out receipts. They took a couple of Negroes along to unload the bags and free up the wheels when the truck got stuck in the mud. It was nasty work. Bernard the ugly had a small measure of influence with Carter. He made sure Bald Horace was never among the conscripted.

The day came when Bernard the handsome went into town alone and came back pale and shaken. He went to his treasure room up in the attic of the big house and stayed there all night. In the morning, he summoned Carter and Bernard to him. Never had they seen him in such a state. He was disheveled. Great chunks of his thick black hair stood on end. Dark rings had formed under his eyes. His clothes stank of sweat and hooch. He looked at them with the fixed, bright stare of a cornered animal. His voice started out soft, but by the time he came to his final avowal, he was nearly shouting.

There's flood up north, he said. There's a crest coming. Seven feet high they say. And two behind it. It's too late to dynamite. In the town, they're saying we are doomed.

He pounded his desk with a fist and his voice rose.

But I am not giving up. From now on, all hands are on sandbag detail. I will shore up the levees, and I will beat the tide that's coming. I promise you, I will not be conquered by this goddamn river. Now get out of here both of you and get those lazy bastards to work.

When they left him, Carter and Bernard went directly to the levee. Bernard climbed up its walls, slipping in the earth twice, rolling back down, getting up again, climbing, climbing until he was high up at the flat. He looked upriver. He saw the crest. It wasn't a wave, but a slow-moving wall of water, from his vantage point, a ribbon maybe two inches tall on the horizon. The sight struck a spear of ice-cold terror through his heart.

That day every worker on the plantation took up a shovel or held open a bag. There wasn't any sand left anywhere. They shoveled wet Tennessee clay instead, one murderous shovelful after another. It took three men to carry a full bag up the levee. When night fell, not two dozen bags had made it to the flat.

The next dawn when Bernard woke up in the white man's barracks, all the Italians were gone. So was the big man's wife.

They needed more workers. Bernard the handsome and Carter drove into town to comb the docks for labor and returned with a truckful of Negroes. Once those were unloaded, Carter went back for three truckfuls more. Where they got them, no one knew. Bald Horace determined they got them from the jailhouse. The workforce was now comprised of a few dozen old hands and one hundred convicts. There were fifteen white men left on the farm. Each carried a rifle everywhere he went with instructions to shoot any able-bodied man trying to run off. They wore yellow slickers and hats to help identify them through the veil of constant, blinding rain. Two ran off themselves. To keep the rest on hand, Bernard the handsome showed them thirteen bags of gold coins, one for each, bags he kept in a strong box he carried around most days under his arm. When the rain was especially thick and the crest crept forward, he'd take one out of the box and shake it at men with rifle butts balanced against their yellow slickers at the hip, their white faces poking out of yellow bonnets.

Stay with me, he'd yell over the roar of the river, his forelock drooping over his eye, his beautiful lips glistening. Stay with me, and I will make you rich men. Leave me, and the river will still rise. Leave me, and you shall surely die.

After one such occasion, Bernard sought out Bald Horace, whose look of pain as he tried to dump yet another shovel of dirt into a bag put him firmly in mind of engravings he'd seen in one of the doctor's books on the *Delilah's Dream* all those years ago. It was not a medical book but one of poetry, poetry Bernard could hardly fathom, except for the engravings, which were startling, exquisite. The look Bald Horace had that day was precisely that of the picture labeled PORTRAIT OF THE DAMNED. The damned had the same hollowed cheeks, the same agonized grimace. It was as if the artist had known Bald Horace personally.

His heart melting with compassion for his dearest, his only friend, Bernard said, At least if we get out of this, we'll be rich, we'll have our bags of gold.

Bald Horace responded, I didn't notice the mister including Negroes in that distribution.

Bernard blushed. Don't worry, he said, I swear by the head of Aurora Mae that whatever I get from him I will share with you equally, and she, too, should she appear.

Every day the river got higher. It rose well beyond the flat of the levee, lapping at layers of sandbags, when the rains stopped. The first crest was still coming. It was a ways off yet and didn't look to be the seven feet reported, even if one accounted for the distance, but three feet would swamp them. Everyone feared a crevasse erupting. Meanwhile, the river spit out geysers or twirled around everything from wagon wheels to hogs in its eddies and whirlpools like it was playing a game of ball 'n' jacks. One of Ghost Tree's laborers, a man conscripted from the town, fell in the river and got sucked down before any of them had a chance to throw him a line. He shot back out one hundred feet downriver, crashing to his death on the far bank. The only thing Bernard the handsome could do to keep his men on after that was to shoot his guns at random morning, noon, and night and have his armed men do the same. It kept the others more frightened of death in the next minute than death next week. He had tents pitched up at the flat, so men could work around the clock and he could keep them in his sights. They slept in bedrolls laid directly on the cold, wet ground. He never slept himself. He drank out of a leather sleeve he wore around his chest like a bandolier and paced up and down the levee barking orders no one could hear above the river's screams. He shot off his pistols to get their attention as much as to intimidate them.

The sandbags ran out. Carter was sent into town to acquire more, but he returned within the hour to report that the main road was washed out from the rain. The earth had had so much, it couldn't take any more. Run-off ditches overflowed. The mud was like tar. Nothing could get through it. He tried alternate routes, and they were in worse shape. He set out again, this time on horseback, and he was gone three hours. While he was gone, everyone at Ghost Tree felt a fresh surge of hope as each hour passed. Men who'd never had much affection before for the King of Prussia man slapped one another on the back and exclaimed, That Carter. He's a right clever one. He'll bring the goods on home, and we'll be saved. But Carter came back on foot without his horse and in such a condition that no one dared ask what had happened.

The crest was two bends of the river away. It moved slowly enough to rouse the workers to the point of rebellion. Everyone knew when a crest moved that pokey it was because the water beneath raged. Without bags to fill, there was no work. Men sat on the levee staring upriver complaining about the goddamn Jew bastard who'd corralled them and kept them there. Bernard the ugly patrolled the levee with a tighter grip on his firearm when he listened to them talk so. He knew if they ever decided to rebel, he'd be floating downriver along with his name-twin.

We're all dead men, they said. The boss goin' to get us all killed. Someone chimed in, I'd rather take a goddamn Jew bullet to the gut than drown like a pig. Others cheered him and concurred. When Bernard the handsome paraded his domain with pistols raised, they cowered instead. Bernard the ugly couldn't help himself. He was glad about that.

One morning, the men woke up in wet beds. The floors of the tents were puddled. The men of Ghost Tree rose as one and staggered like an army of drunken ants out to the levee's edge to watch the Mississippi raise a great fist to them. Water spilled over the top of the sandbags. The crest was very close, within the day's reach. The levee could spring a rip any moment. If they were lucky, it'd happen on the opposite bank. Otherwise, the water was sure to wash them away. There was nothing to do but stare, weep, or pray.

Bernard the handsome had other ideas. He called a meeting of his white men, leaving a skeleton crew to guard the labor. He spoke to them from the front veranda of the big house, using a megaphone so they could hear him.

I've studied a remedy they used over to Washington County in the flood of 1912, he said. It'll save our side of the river, I am certain. What I want you to do is order those niggers to lay down. Lash them together if you have to. They're the best goddamn thing next to sandbags we got. They're probably better. Now get back there and get to it.

His men stood before him in shock. Carter was the first to speak. They're not going to do it, Boss.

Then shoot them. A cadaver's as good.

No one moved. There was a rumble of discontent.

Bernard the handsome roared displeasure. Do I have to show you how it's done? Alright, I will.

He went to the back of his house to the outbuilding where the dependency was and returned dragging a mammoth black woman behind him. She was barefoot in a huge apron and dress made of odd swatches of material sewn haphazardly together. Her hair, pulled back by a piece of string, sprouted foot-long spikes in all directions behind her. The big man had her in a death grip by the wrist. Her free arm was up over her face protecting it from the rain that coursed over the roof of the veranda and splashed all around her. The sight of her stilled the men. No one had ever seen a woman that tall, that wide.

She's like a corn-fed ox, Bernard thought, like John Bunyan's Babe Blue. She must be six and a half feet tall and hundreds of pounds on the hoof. And because the mind comes up with its own considerations without regard to logic, especially in times of imminent disaster, he thought, she's like the generator up at the house. How does he hide a thing that big?

Bernard the handsome saw the effect his cook had on the assembled and gave them a mad, drunken smile. This one will do to start, he said.

They made a most unwholesome parade. Bernard the handsome dragging that poor confused woman through the yards up to the levee, his raggedy contingent of rifle-toting men in yellow rubber behind him. They trekked up the wooden planks laid for that purpose to the flat where more than a hundred Negroes gathered, most on their knees praying to Jesus. The big man raised the hand of his cook high in the air as if she were a prizefighter. Her head was down, her clothes were plastered against her. Her free arm bent over her breasts in a futile gesture of protection. She might as well have been stark naked. Her posture made clear she was frightened to be on display in such conditions before a hundred men. The men themselves were as wild and mad-eyed as Bernard the handsome. Some of them stared at her and put their hands down their pants. Surely, she was some kind of offering. Surely, they were meant to feast on her before dying.

Lay down, woman. Bernard the handsome shouted. Lay down and marry the goddamn river.

Her head snapped up. She backed away from him. He smacked her head hard with the butt of his handgun. She fell down to one knee.

A voice cried out. Stop! Stop! and then, 'Rora! 'Rora Mae!

It was Bald Horace who recognized his sister beneath the enormous cloak of flesh she'd amassed over herself like a disguise. 'Rora! 'Rora Mae! he shouted, while Bernard opened his mind to see that Bald Horace was right. It was her. His love. His goddess. On the ground being beat by his name-twin. His heart swelled so, it felt it might break through his ribs. His rifle butt found its way to his shoulder. He took aim.

Let her go! Let her go! Let her go! he said, but Bernard the handsome could not hear him or did not want to.

He continued to beat Aurora Mae over the head, on the shoulders, on the back between her shoulder blades. When still she would not lie down, he yelled out, A cadaver is just as good! and shoved his handgun deep between her massive breasts. Before he could pull the trigger, there was what sounded like a crack of thunder, and he crumbled to the dirt with a large bloody hole trailing smoke at the center of his chest.

Bernard the ugly shot his name-twin twice more, a second time to the chest and once in the head. No one tried to stop him. Afterward, everyone, all 125 human beings assembled on the flat of the levee, took off running. Everyone but Bald Horace, Aurora Mae, and Bernard

Levy. The two men helped Aurora Mae to her feet. The three stood clinging to one another over the body of Bernard the handsome. Bald Horace kicked him, and he didn't move. He's real dead, Bald Horace said. The other two shook their heads. Without speaking, they bent and rolled Bernard the handsome into the river, watched him bob and sink and reappear until he was no more.

They headed for the big house where pandemonium reigned. Convicts and free men, black and white, ransacked the place, tearing whatever looked precious off the walls, the sinks, the banisters. They tossed clothes through the air and threw any container that might hold jewelry onto the floor to break it. Someone upstairs yelled out, That man, that man there, he hit the jackpot!

There was the sound of a first-class scuffle, a banister cracked, and then the air rained gold coins from Bernard the handsome's strong box. Men scrambled for them on their knees. Ignoring them, Aurora Mae led Bald Horace and Bernard to the pantry, where they filled their arms with canned goods, knives, whatever was cooked and whatever they could eat raw. They went to the attic, stopping first in a bedroom on the second floor to pick up blankets and pillows. They made a camp up there to ride out the crest. In the next hour, they were interrupted a couple of times by men bursting in to see what they could find, but when they saw Bernard the murderer, their liberator, they backed out bowing as if he were the king of Egypt. Then it was quiet. Even the roar of the river seemed subdued. The men were gone.

Aurora Mae wept in her brother's arms. Bernard wanted to comfort her himself. He longed to hold however much of her he could grasp and never let go. He wanted to tell her he didn't care if she'd got as ugly as him. He loved her, he'd always loved her, and if he'd been brave enough to declare himself in days gone by, maybe they'd have found a way to avoid all the tragedy that pursued them. He wanted to apologize for letting her down. He wanted to weep a little and be comforted by her, too. He wanted all of that, and he wanted to know exactly what had happened to her.

There was a horrible noise, a noise none of them had ever heard before and hoped never to hear again, a noise that crashed against the eardrums and ran its talons against that tender tissue drawing blood. They screamed and covered their ears with their hands. It was the sound of the levee dying. A crevasse broke through earth and rock to flood the Delta in mere moments. The currents conquered everything in their path, ripping ancient trees from their roots, swamping whatever man-made object lay ahead. But there was luck in the reunion of that strange little family from Missouri, of Woodwitch, her herdsman brother, and their devoted friend. The crevasse had broken on the opposite shore. The pressure on Ghost Tree's side of the river was released.

They were saved.

Aurora Mae and Bald Horace fell to their knees. Thank you, sweet Jesus, they said, thank you.

Bernard Levy fell to his, also. It was a position he'd not held often in life, and it felt awkward, shaky. He murmured as he recalled his grandmama did years ago on the mornings her daughter returned home in one piece after a night of carousing with her no-good lovers. *Baruch Ha-Shem,* he said and a warmth, a strength surged through him. He studied his friend and his love where they knelt next to him.

In a flash, he remembered Bernard the handsome's treasure chests from which the thirteen bags of gold had been but a pittance. He remembered where they were stored, there in an attic corner behind crates of hooch. Visions came to him of the place that money could find for the three of them to live together in as much peace and security as nature would allow. For the first time since the night he and Bald Horace returned home to find Aurora Mae gone, he had hope.

XIV

Memphis, Tennessee, 1962

THE LOVERS AWOKE THAT MORNING with a grim sense of purpose. They were priests before the sacrifice, boxers before the match. They did not make love, they did not so much as kiss. They showered separately and dressed back to back in silence. Although they were pure, intense, determined, there were doubts. Laura Anne contemplated her parents' reaction to her return with her loss of honor as well as Daddy's gun and wondered if she ought to go home at all. It wouldn't matter if Mickey Moe's family turned out to be directly descended from every prominent Jew in America from Alexander Hamilton to Judah P. Benjamin. Mickey Moe braced himself for disappointment if Aurora Mae would not tell him what he needed to know. He recalled their first encounter and feared she could be neither bribed nor intimidated to candor.

They had breakfast at a diner. Their waitress was a buxom blonde matron with a starched-lace handkerchief popping out of her right breast pocket with a name tag that read HAZEL B. pinned to it. Mickey Moe asked her how to get to Orange Mound.

Hazel B. raised thick, penciled eyebrows and pursed orange-stained lips at the inquiry. Are you all sure that's where you want to go? She jabbed her order pencil in Laura Anne's direction. It's not a neighborhood you want to take that nice young lady, boy. When Mickey Moe assured her it was exactly where he wanted to take her, Hazel B. tsked her tongue and gave him the most direct route.

Once they entered Orange Mound, they understood Hazel B.'s caution. There was not a white face in sight. Everyone gave the young couple suspicious looks, some of them downright hostile. Not a one had the shy, subservient gaze they were accustomed to. Mickey Moe reached for his girl's hand and found it trembling. Are you alright, honey? he asked.

Her chin went up. Of course I am, darlin'. Her tone was confident, brave despite the damp, quivering palm. His eyes went moist and his puffed-up chest nearly burst his buttons with pride.

They drove down dirt streets 'til they came to Carnes. Three cross streets down from Mount Moriah Missionary Baptist Church they arrived at an unassuming storefront on a corner lot with living quarters in the back. The curtains of the store were drawn, there was nothing to indicate what type of business was conducted within. A sign hung from a post by a short iron gate, but its script, THE LENAKA, meant nothing to them. They parked across the street to steel themselves for what was to come and watched Negroes enter and exit the place more or less rapidly. Whatever went on in there didn't take long. Mickey Moe brought his girl's hand to his lips and kissed it.

You ready?

Yes, I am.

Then let's do this thing.

They opened their doors and slammed them for courage. They

crossed the street arm in arm, firm of stride, jaws set, their eyes straight ahead to ignore the passersby who slowed down or stopped to stare at them. Every stare shouted out, What are you all doin' here, in the very heart of negritude? When it became obvious where they were headed, Laura Anne saw from the corner of her eye that people shrugged or smiled. They pushed open The Lenaka's door. Entry bells chimed. Vibrant colors and scents assaulted them.

Why, it's an apothecary of some kind, Laura Anne said. Look.

Inside were floor to ceiling shelves on three walls, and all of them were covered with bottles of colored liquids in varied sizes. There were tables supporting honeycombs of open wooden boxes in which fragrant herbs released their perfumes making the air heady and thick. A glass case with a cash register on the countertop displayed rows of vials filled with powders underneath. Another table held packets of bandages in a rainbow of colors. To the rear of the store was a curtain made of strung glass beads, which cast prisms all over the walls. Its valance was made of dangling chicken bones knit together with multicolored yarn.

Laura Anne picked up a yellow bundle of braided cloth from the bandage table and held it to her nose. This one has witch hazel, she said. She picked up a puce one, then a blue. And this one, this one's sage, I just know it. And the other I believe is garlic and mustard. And that one there that's got green bits stuck to it. Looks like slippery elm to me.

The beaded curtain jingle-jangled. Prisms shimmied up the ceiling and back down again. A deep feminine voice said, You know quite a bit for a white gal. Your people mountain people, dear? Or were you cared for by a woman from the islands as a child?

A huge shadow cast itself over the wall, and a person emerged sideways from the beaded-glass doorway. It was herself, Aurora Mae, in all her enormity. She was everything Mickey Moe remembered only more so: impossibly tall, broad, even her face seemed out of human scale with its huge widespread black eyes, its nostrils like caves, its mouth a red wellspring at the center of the earth. She wore a turban made up of bands of red, gold, and green cloth. They crisscrossed over her brow and were bound by a starched coxcomb in the back. Her dress was a plain black tent with a V-neck, and she wore long ropes of periwinkles over that.

Laura Anne took color. She was not accustomed to being questioned by a Negro in such a tone, let alone a Negro of majestic proportion.

The latter, she said with difficulty.

Aurora Mae's lower lip jutted out, and she nodded. Alright. Well, what can I do for you two? What has brought you to such a far-flung place in a foreign land?

She laughed at her own joke. The bottles on shelves vibrated and knocked together. Mickey Moe coughed to gain control of the anxiety and excitement carousing through his blood. He asked his question in one breath without a hint of the turmoil troubling him.

Are you not Aurora Mae Stanton, sister to Bald Horace of Guilford, Mississippi?

Aurora Mae tilted her head back, narrowed her eyes to study him. This made her appearance more disturbing as there seemed to be threat in her posture as well as the power to carry it out.

Who wants to know?

He squared his shoulders, took a step forward so that Laura Anne was behind him, protected.

Mickey Moe Levy, son of Bernard.

Aurora Mae lowered her head, tucked in her chin, opened her eyes, and grinned. She clapped her hands in delight. Her voice boomed. Why, sweet Jesus, so it is! I been expectin' you. I should've known who you were, but no one told me you'd have a pretty little gal with you.

She pulled back the beaded curtain, gesturing for them to enter her inner sanctum. They shared a certain trepidation, but they walked through. She followed behind, reaching up and tapping the row of valance chicken bones lightly with her fingertips as she did. The beads made a soprano music, the bones a baritone. Mickey Moe wondered what kind of outlandish home lay beyond. He expected wooden masks, drums, straw mats, whatever he'd seen of Africa or the Caribbean in the movies. Instead he found a quotidian 1962 kitchen with linoleum of a tiny yellow-flower design, a chrome and Formica table with chrome, leather-seated chairs on three sides and a chrome leather-seated bench on the fourth. The refrigerator and oven were newer than his mama's. The wallpaper was fairly plain except for its border of crowing red roosters with bright green tail feathers. The white lace curtains on the windows were drawn but billowed gently in a cool breeze that floated in, accelerated by a reed-and-wood ceiling fan.

Sweet tea? Aurora Mae asked, motioning for them to sit. They took opposing chairs, leaving her the bench, a wise move considering it was the only seating where she might fit. She huffed around the kitchen, getting their refreshments, tall iced glasses of sweet tea and a plate of homemade ginger cookies. They waited for her to settle down, which she did with an exhalation of breath, as if the act of serving them had about done her in.

Oof.

She took off her turban and plopped it on the table. The hair beneath was gray, wiry, and cut close to her head like a man's. She twisted her head from one to the other, waiting for someone to speak.

Well, children. Why are you here?

It's my daddy.

She leaned away, gave him that slit-eyed look again.

What about him.

I need to know who he was, why everything he told my mama was a lie. Most of all, I need to know who his people were so that this very fine young lady and I may marry with her parents' blessing, a blessing they will withhold from us 'til doomsday itself if they cannot be convinced my lineage is a righteous one. One day when I was a child, you said you knew my daddy better than anyone else, so I am hopeful you can put an end to the miserable mystery that is my origins. Please, m'am, he said, since he knew no other way to address a female he was required to beseech, can you tell me that? Were you truthful all those years ago when you spoke to a young orphan befriended by your brother? Were you?

Aurora Mae heaved a great sigh, which fluttered the pile of paper napkins she'd set in the center of the table when she'd brought in the tea. You need to hear that old story. Mmm-mm, children. I'm not sure I'm goin' to tell it.

Mickey Moe reached forward and grabbed one of her colossal hands with two of his own. Calling upon the spirit of his daddy—help me out here, you lying son of a gun, help me out if ever you loved me—he gave Aurora Mae the sales pitch of his life. While he did, he squeezed. He squeezed then raised the hand off the table and placed it down again repeatedly, making emphatic thumps.

Have you never loved someone? he asked. Has no one ever loved you? Do you know the torment of love denied, whether by sickness, by death, or the slow cruel tortures of fate? I have seen with my own eyes and have felt with my own heart what such has done to my mama, for she is a mean, withered tyrant to my sisters and a spiny, clingin' vine to me.

Look at this gal beside me. Look at her! She is as pure and lovin' a miss as a man could dream of, one who has risked her life to be at my side this moment—and I do mean that literally, Miss Aurora Mae— yes! risked her life and her honor. Would you see her denied? Would you see her turned into my mama? That is what your refusal will do to her.

And me. Doesn't a man have the right to know who his father is? As much as he has the right to breathe, the right to stand up to the world and say, I am here, and this is who I am?

He went on for some time, abandoning his code of ethics by stretching the truth wherever it occurred to him it might be helpful. He threw every argument he could at her, even if they contradicted themselves, principally because her impassive flesh gave no clue to his effect. According to him, Laura Anne was at first a victim of unreasonable parents who could be rescued from them only by the truth and later a virago who would not and never had taken no for an answer. He was by turns a humble supplicant and next a righteous inquisitor. He told stories, just as he might in the backwoods at the derelict home of a sharecropper he sought to woo out of a dollar fifty a week in premiums. He told her about his childhood, of following big Roland about with the toolbox in hand, of traipsing after her brother, Bald Horace, and learning from him the ways of earth and the river. Thinking that all women had a maternal streak and that she'd warm to his need somehow, he gave her a tough little boy who struggled against the chasm of loneliness that inhabited his riven soul, but still Aurora Mae's expression did not change. It remained flat, curious for just an instant maybe, or amused about as long by some pitiful revelation before her features returned to deadpan in the blink of an eye. At last, Mickey Moe ran out of story or knew he would compromise himself if he went too far. He stopped, heaving hot breath. A tear ran down his cheek, which he did not move to wipe away as that tear was his last ditch, his final hope to reach her hard, iced-up heart.

She studied him and snorted.

Man, oh man, she said. You think you know what sufferin' is? Well, you do not. Let me tell you, your daddy was an orphan, too, with his daddy disappeared downriver when he was hardly more than a baby and his mama no kind of mama at all. That man knew how to work cold, hungry, and out of luck for a crust of bread, and that's just the beginnin' of it. He knew how to love, too. He knew how to love, come hell or high water, and I can testify to that. A li'l thing like you all are worryin' about, her people, my Lord, her people! wouldn't have made him lose a wink. Try havin' the whole damn world against you and nature, too.

Her speech perplexed him. What was she talking about? As far as Mickey Moe knew, his mama and daddy were lovebirds and never had so much as a bump in their road until World War II. His brow knit while he tried to puzzle it out. He looked over to Laura Anne for help. She stared straight ahead, bug-eyed. Slowly, her hand went up. She pointed with a rude, straight finger to a small table in the corner holding a telephone and a single gilt-framed photograph. She tugged on Mickey Moe's shirt and pulled him over to him to whisper as if Aurora Mae had her back turned or was incapacitated in some manner and could not hear her.

Eudora Jean showed me pictures, honey. Isn't that your daddy there? Next to that tall black woman? There. Three people down on the right-hand side of the bride.

Mickey Moe got up and took the photograph in two hands. It was antique, tinted sepia, apparently a family portrait of about forty individuals sitting on the front steps of an old plantation house and spilling out over the front lawn. A bride and a groom stood in the middle. Everyone was dressed in Sunday clothes. They were all Negroes but one. His daddy. His daddy stood down some from the bridal couple, shoulders back, chest out, proud as punch, with a smile of pure delight over his face. Next to him was a magnificent Negro woman with a head of hair like a black Rapunzel's, thick, curled, long, luxurious. She was as tall as Bernard Levy was short, as beautiful as he was funny looking. Bernard was the only subject in the photograph who was not staring straight ahead at the cameraman. Instead, he gazed adoringly at the creature beside him. Mickey Moe studied Aurora Mae. He studied the woman next to his daddy. Realization crept over him. By the time it was done, his throat was so dry he could barely get the question out.

Is this . . . is this some relative of yours? he asked.

Aurora Mae laughed. She laughed as if she'd invented laughter, that is in a dozen ways, all of them big, hearty, loud. Everything in the room felt electrified by the sound of it.

No!

Laura Anne's and Mickey Moe's scalps tingled. Their hair stiffened at the roots.

It's me!

She leaned forward with her mouth open, ready to join with them in a second round of mirth, but they were plain dumbstruck with disbelief.

Me. It's me.

She pointed to the woman in the photograph and then to her own chest.

Me.

Because they continued to sit there immobile, wondering if she was crazy or they were themselves, she relented and told them most of what they'd come to find out, at first hesitantly, then as she warmed up to her task, in a rush. She told them about herself and Bernard Levy, about their time together with her brother Horace up near Saint Louis on the family compound. She told them how happy they were, how close. To prove it, she told them everything Bernard ever told her about his background. She told them things even Horace did not know. She did not tell them about the night the kluckers came and abused her and took her away. To cover that episode, she made up a story, told them Bernard and Horace were conscripted by a landowner who transported them downriver by force. In this tale, she left the family farm soon after to search for them. She had many adventures, she said, most unpleasant. After a time, she gave up the search. She was alone, heartbroken.

She wanted nothing of men, having experienced more than she wanted of them out in the world without her brother's protection. In the course of avoiding them, she discovered the best way to rid herself of their attentions was to become, well, this! she said, slapping her thighs, and this! her breasts, and this! her close-cropped hair. One by one, I shed the things that made them go after me. I found other pursuits until all by accident, or you might say by an act of God, after nearly two year, in a wet season, I landed at a plantation close by here, a place called Ghost Tree. Your daddy and my brother worked there, too, only we did not find one another on its grounds for quite a while.

When she told them about the flood, she told as much of the truth as she remembered, which was everything. She told them how Bernard was a hero that day, who saved a hundred souls and murdered a monster bent on killing her along with all the black men on the levee. He was a brave man, your daddy, she finished. With the heart of a titan. He was a saint. A saint.

She stopped. Mickey Moe frowned, trying to absorb her narrative. Laura Anne, knowing he was expecting a different kind of story, stroked his back in comfort.

So. My daddy was a poor river rat who murdered an evil man to save the love of his life, which would be you, not my mama, and together with Bald Horace, you stole all the victim's gold and went, where? Your separate ways? After all that?

Aurora Mae clammed up.

Not at first. Later on.

Well, what happened? What?

She put her two hands on the table and raised herself up.

I ain't talkin' about that. I have no desire to revisit that particular piece of time. You don't know what the world was like after the flood. So much destroyed. So many dead. The ones alive were homeless. Negroes were mostly stuck in labor camps where they got paid in food if they were lucky. If you tried escapin' and were caught, they just killed you. No questions asked. Life belonged to those with a gun and those with gold. We had both. Then there were things happened it's not my place to tell. Let's just say for now that I came here. The men went elsewhere.

But you were in Guilford that time when I was a boy. You lived there.

No. I didn't. I was visitin'. I'd do that from time to time, startin' with that occasion I showed up a mess at your mama's house while she was havin' a party. You couldn't have been more than a baby that time. Oh yes. That was some occasion. But that's her story to tell, not mine. You want to know that story, you ask your mama. Tell her I told you to ask her. Yes, you tell her I told you.

It was as if she'd punched him in the gut with all her considerable might. He could not speak. He sat open-mouthed, crumpled over, a hand holding his belly. Laura Anne spoke for him.

His mama knows about you?

Oh yes. You ask her. You ask her about Aurora Mae Stanton. You'll see.

Stunned, shaken, Mickey Moe got up. He felt caged by all this knowledge, as if the truth were pressing in on him from every side. He had to get out of there or be squeezed to death.

Thank you, m'am, he said. I need to go absorb what you've been tellin' me. I confess it's been a shock.

Aurora Mae rose also. Of course, she said. It's a lot to take in. I understand that, son.

They said their good-byes, which to Mickey Moe sounded hollow, as if he lived inside a great bell and the words he spoke reverberated back at him through still air. Laura Anne put her arm around him and guided him out as she might an invalid.

They were out in the street, squinting into the bright Tennessee sun.

They walked to the car fast, in a hurry to get away from all the terrible news they'd just had land on their heads like a tree limb in a hurricane.

All along your mama knew, Laura Anne said in disbelief after they were back in the car with the doors locked. I am dumbfounded by that. Dumbfounded. We have to get back to Guilford and ask her about it. Right away.

Mickey Moe was in tears. He laid his cheek down over the steering wheel pointing himself in her direction. His damp face, his red eyes twisted up her heart.

If you wish to separate yourself from the son of a murderer thief, one with deranged tastes in women as a bonus, I completely understand, Laura Anne. I set you free without bitterness.

Now don't get yourself in an uproar, she said. I'll still marry you. Who your daddy was makes no difference to me. I told you that on the day we met. I'll marry you today. I don't care what my parents think.

And for the first time since she'd fallen in love with Mickey Moe Levy, she felt 110 percent released from her parents, her upbringing, and her social caste. Liberation exhilarated her. It was one thing, she realized, to voice modern opinion about a woman's place, quite another to seize control of your own fate. She was doing it, really doing it and how about that? she thought, how about that? She gave her lover a bright, shimmering gaze of triumph, but Mickey Moe surprised her.

No, darlin', he said, taking up her hand and kissing her fingertips. I thank you. We'll do that but not today.

No?

No.

He straightened up. Put the key in the ignition and shifted into gear.

I'm taking you back to the motel, he said. And then I'm goin' back to the woods for your daddy's gun.

Oh honey, I don't think so. The police could be there by now if

Walter Cohen's told them anything at all. How can we trust him, you know? We don't know him.

Mickey Moe pulled out of the parking spot and into the street. That's alright. Didn't you hear, Aurora Mae? I am the son of a man of action. A hero. And I'm going to do what the son of such a man does.

I don't understand.

I'm going to protect my woman's family. That's what.

With extraordinary courage filling him up in that place Aurora Mae had utterly depleted with her story, he drove Laura Anne back to the motel.

XV

Memphis, Tennessee–Saint Louis, Missouri–Kansas City, Kansas, 1927–1930

THE THREE OF THEM LIVED up there in the big house attic for a time, waiting for the second crest and the third to pass on by. After that, they waited for the waters to stabilize. Day after day, they huddled together on the upstairs balcony, leaning against the wrought-iron gazelles that supported them. From high up, they could study the Mississippi and the new routes the floodwaters cut through the countryside. They watched the bloated bodies of livestock and humans float by along with rooftops, tires, whole ancient trees with their roots sticking up like the hair of a crazy man, wooden barrels, plows, machinery parts. They made a guessing game of identifying the mangled ruins of civilization, the way one conjures objects out of passing clouds on a fair afternoon. They went downstairs only so far as they had to, to the second floor for the bathroom or to gather more furniture for firewood, as they found the nights damp and cold like wintertime. There wasn't any reason to hide, not to go all the way downstairs or even out the door. The rains had ceased, the river quieted. There wasn't anybody around. It shouldn't have mattered how they carried on in the buildings or on the grounds of Ghost Tree Plantation, but it did.

Sometimes at night, Bald Horace would get up and pace and fret over how his critters might be getting along until Aurora Mae or Bernard reminded him he'd opened their paddocks and coops the day the crest came, thinking they'd have a better chance free. Once they jogged his memory, he imagined all his babies out there sorting for themselves. Now they are prey to wild beasts and hungry humans, he thought and sat down and cried.

Aurora Mae developed a habit of standing in front of Bernard the handsome's wardrobe mirror, running her hands over herself, clucking her tongue, murmuring to herself things like "Well, lookit here" and "This sure is somethin', ain't it" in a manner that awed the men. They didn't interrupt her or comment. They tried not to watch, but it was quite a spectacle. She'd pass by the mirror, then stop, go back, make her repetitive self-examinations, talk to herself in wonderment. It was as if she'd never before comprehended what had become of her young, strong, and magnificent self.

Bernard was the happy one. Details of the trauma he'd experienced, that of the flood combined with the haunting guilt of murdering his name-twin, faded away each time they rose up to enslave his mind. In an act of will, he pushed all ugly, fearful questions aside and focused on the future when they'd leave Ghost Tree and find a home together. What joy that would be! Aurora Mae would have housemaids to wait on her, ten little dogs to cuddle. Bald Horace would have all the goats and chickens and pigs a man could desire to dote upon. And he, Bernard Levy, would keep his love by his side where he would never lose track of her again. Out of all past misery and terror, untold delights would blossom beneath their feet and buoy them to a heaven on earth. In the meantime, he busied himself sewing gold coins into their clothes and making backpacks that would hide more in clever compartments a Pinkerton couldn't find.

Early one morning, a wayfarer showed up on the property. He strolled right up to the front door and knocked. They waited upstairs to see if he'd go away, but he did not. He'd noticed the smoke coming from the chimney and knew there were people about. He banged away, relentless. Eventually, full of dread, they trooped downstairs en masse and opened the door. The man doffed his hat, taking Bernard for the original Bernard Levy whom he'd never met.

Sir, he said, kind sir. My brother worked for you. The family's lookin' all over for him. His name was Carter. Do you have any word of him, any at all?

No one had seen the King of Prussia man since the day of the first crest, which is how they chose to recall events. It beat recalling the day of the murder of Bernard the handsome.

I don't know what happened to him, Bernard the survivor said. He was here one day and then there was the crevasse and he was gone. I'd go into the town if I were you and inquire there.

That's where I come from, the man said.

Then we cannot help you.

They gave him a packet of food and a bottle of spirits to help him along his way. They watched him walk down the road.

Bald Horace said, I guess that's it, then. If they're lookin' for Carter, they'll be lookin' for the big man soon enough. We'd best be gone.

His sister and the man who loved her agreed.

The next morning, they put on the clothes Bernard had altered and tried on the packs he'd salted in gold.

It's a heavy burden, Bald Horace said.

Can't be helped, Bernard responded.

They set out.

Any other time, they would have made a strange procession. There was Bernard in his service livery and one of the big man's panama hats, Aurora Mae in a fresh costume fashioned out of Ghost Tree bedsheets and table linens, and Bald Horace tagging along, bent over from the weight of his backpack plus that of the goat cart he pulled behind, which was loaded high with everything they thought might be useful on a trip to nowhere in particular. Any other time, local authorities coming across their path might've stopped to ask them who exactly they were and where they got a cart full of goods. But these were flood times, and they were not the only motley crew on the road. There was a great crush of humanity on the move, remnants all, odds and ends of half-crazed folk with water still in their ears, most either homeless or scavengers. Among those legions that emerged in that time from out the Delta's sodden skirts to wander or pillage, Bernard, Aurora Mae, and Bald Horace were flyspecks, passing curios in a great and desperate parade.

They trekked along the riverbank, looking for transport. One time early on, they met up with a steamship loaded with refugees run by a hard, stout man with three weeks' worth of scraggly beard. Bernard waved his hat at him until he steered close enough to converse.

Where you headed?

Up north. There's not much left south of here.

Might you be goin' to Saint Louis?

I might be. If you got the fare.

They negotiated a price, but when the captain saw that Aurora Mae and Bald Horace were part of the deal, he balked.

No niggers, he said. They's swarms of 'em tryin' to get north, and I ain't takin' any of 'em. They's enough white people on the move. Don't need no trouble takin' thievin' niggers.

Bernard insisted. The captain stood firm. Bernard offered him double his price per head. The captain weakened.

But she's a big'un. You pay three times for her.

He would not take on Bald Horace's cart for any amount of money.

The three stuffed their pockets with whatever small things they found most necessary—shells for their handguns, a few toiletries, a hunting knife, bits of wire and rope, a flint—and abandoned the rest.

It was hard traveling. There was so much debris in the river, below and above the surface, the ship went slowly. There were times Bernard thought they'd make more progress if they disembarked and walked. The other passengers were restless and argued with the captain and with one another. They argued about how to judge where they were with all the changes in the river's course wrought by the flood. They fought over food. They fought over where they slept. If the sky took on a darkness in the daytime, they argued about whether it would rain again and for how long. The captain took to wearing a handgun in a holster under his arm and shot off rounds into the air to quell their noise and agitation, just as Bernard the handsome had done. Bernard, Aurora Mae, and Bald Horace kept to themselves, their own firearms hidden in their clothes.

They came upon a fragment of a levee holding twenty Negro souls. Whatever shore the levee once graced, it now stood in the middle of the river, like a tiny island sprouting human beings instead of trees. When they saw the ship coming toward them, they raised their hands and praised Jesus and waved back and forth, hoping for rescue.

My Lord, Bernard said to Aurora Mae. Can it be these poor people have been stranded here these last weeks?

She shuddered and turned to him with teary eyes.

Looks like. Looks like. And there's babies there. Scrawny, little, faint-lookin' babies. Sweet Jesus, they look half-dead.

The captain steered the ship away from them, making as wide an arc around as he could maneuver. Bernard and Bald Horace with Aurora Mae a great hulking shadow behind went up to the wheelhouse to confront him.

What are you doing? Why don't you help those people?

The captain grunted. I told you. No niggers. Besides it don't look to me like they got the fare.

I'll pay for them. Double.

The captain looked out his window to where the people stranded on the levee continued to wave, hop up and down, bang together whatever was at hand hopeful they still had a chance to win the attention of the steamship. With a wry smile, he lifted a finger and counted them, calculating. Dang that's a lotta juice, he said. But I ain't haulin' 'em. And I wouldn't be lettin' anybody know you got that kind of money on you, boy.

He laughed. It had a coarse, bitter sound. He took one hand off the ship's wheel then pushed the brake lever. He turned to face them and put the other hand on the grip of his gun.

I wouldn't be lettin' me know that.

His hand moved to pull the gun from its holster. A shot whizzed by so close to Bernard's ear, it burned his skin and singed his hair. The captain's face blossomed in a jagged red pulp. He twitched, gurgled, crumbled, and was still.

The wheelhouse, thick with gunsmoke, went quiet 'til the air gradually cleared like fog on a day that warms slowly. Bald Horace spoke first. Now we both murderers, he said.

Bernard stepped back to avoid a widening pool of blood at his feet.

Why, oh why, did you do that?

Bald Horace's eyes went round as two moons. Lordy, don't you know? First off, he won't let those poor sufferin' people on board. And second, he was gettin' ready to shoot you dead, Bernard. Maybe you didn't notice.

Oh Horace. We don't know that. Maybe he was just fixin' to rob me. I would've given him everything I got. He never would have thought you two had gold. We'd still have plenty between us. Oh, this is terrible, terrible. What are we goin' to do?

Now Bald Horace was crying. Aurora Mae put her arms around him and glared over his head at Bernard. You know how fragile he's been since the flood! her look said with electric clarity.

Bernard's own eyes welled up. He paced from one end of the wheel-house to the other, slapping his head with two hands repeating over and over, Oh, what a mess, a mess, a mess, we're in a royal mess.

Outside the hand of God was at work. As soon as the steamship braked and came to a grinding halt, the strongest men stranded on the levee jumped off and swam over, risking life and limb to submerged perils none could see. As they climbed over the side, the passengers on deck swarmed near and came this close to running them back off the ship into teeming, brackish water littered with debris. But these men were not the submissive, shuffling Joes they might have pretended to be before the flood. They stood desperate, hunched over, feet planted wide, arms curled, hands out, ready to attack. Their eyes were on fire, their wet clothes plastered against bodies made hard and lean by life-times of work and weeks of disaster. They looked like the nightmare savages the white people on board had feared rising up against them since childhood. None dared confront them. Directly, the Negroes took the lifeboats, lowered them down into the river and went to fetch their half-starved women and babies. When these were all transported back to the ship, they went about demanding food and fresh water from the others who scurried about, trying to appear charitable instead of terrified. Night fell.

Under cover of chaos and a starless night, Bernard, Bald Horace, and Aurora Mae wrapped the captain's corpse in tarpaulin with the ship's heavy brass compass for company and lowered him overboard with a gentle, sinking plop. They took possession of one of the life-boats and paddled the great distance to shore, dodging obstacles in the dark. Once ashore, they ran off into the woods.

They continued north. The siblings' plan was to go back to the old house to see if it stood and if the cousins were still there. Maybe they believed if they went back to their old life, they could put all the horror behind them, forget about it, like it never happened at all. Bernard disagreed. He wanted to go someplace new, out west maybe or Europe, someplace a trio as odd as they were might find their place, renew their spirits, and redeem their sins. They had enough money to go anywhere. It felt as if they had all the money in the world. But the others insisted on returning home. Bernard went along. For now, it was enough to be near her, to sleep on the ground with Bald Horace on one side and his beloved on the other. The great warm mass of her while she slept enthralled him. He loved the way she smelled, the way she moved, the big throaty music of her snores. When she woke up, it was like a whole new planet arose with the sun. Once, when they came upon a freshwater lake and they all took baths, he hid behind a rock above the spot she chose to wash herself in private. He noted the changes in her body since that first time he'd spied upon her. He marveled at its undulations, the way the trails of soap disappeared inside one fold of her flesh and rolled out another. Though there were acres more of it, her skin was still resplendent, iridescent, and her hair, no longer unkempt as she'd left it during her servitude to the master of Ghost Tree, remained a living wonder. His desire knew no diminution. He was as much in love with her as ever, while she, though grateful and tender, kept as much distance from him as she could during a long trek in the backwoods with only her suitor, Bald Horace, and wild beasts for company.

It was high summer by the time they made it back to the family farm. The house and the lands around it had been spared the flood, but the house was nearly as much a wreck as they were. There were cousins still living on the property, but not so many as before. It was like the soul got ripped from here once you all was gone, one of them told Bald Horace. People left. Even before the rains.

Little by little, they built the place back up. Afraid to attract too much attention, they spent their gold sparingly and hoarded the rest. The only extravagant thing they bought was a truck, and they took care to buy one secondhand. Everything should have been fine. Bernard was content to worship his goddess without satisfaction. Bald Horace tried to put his life back together, gathering a little herd of goats and a coop full of chickens. He had his times of torment, dark and flammable as the creosote they scraped from the old chimney. The blown-up face of that captain would come to him in the night, waking him from sleep, and he'd pace the kitchen floor, pounding his fist into his palm, mumbling, Kill you, I'll kill you, I'll kill you again, I'll kill you a thousand times, you bastard, one for each time you raped my sister, you bastard, I'll kill you, proving that he'd got everything mixed up in his sleep or in his conscience. In the morning, Aurora Mae would find him asleep sitting up at the kitchen table, and he'd wake smiling and remember none of it. She fretted over him some, but Bernard told her not to worry, it was alright, it was the way his mind needed to heal. They needed to give him time.

Aurora Mae was miserable. Country life irritated her nowadays. She couldn't figure out whatever made her want to come back in the first place. Everywhere she looked, there was something she'd struggled to forget. It didn't matter that the men plastered up the wall where Maxie's brains had splattered or that they put down a new floor where her own blood had spilled. It didn't matter that they put up headstones over the graves of her old yard dogs and bought her new ones, more docile creatures given to staying close by the house and barking up a storm if a stranger came by. The only thing that made her halfway happy was concocting her powders and potions in a room they added to the house with its own lighting and plumbing so she could work alone and undisturbed. All that did was give her solitude enough to come to a few conclusions and make a new plan. When she built up a stockpile of wares large enough, she called the men to her.

I am leaving here, she said. I'm loadin' up the truck with my herbals and whatnot and goin' back to Memphis. I'm goin' to Orange Mound, where the black people live, and open up a store there. And I need to do it alone. Don't ask me why. It suits me, is all, it suits me. You all can stay on here. I don't care. I'm goin' back to Memphis. I'm leavin' in the mornin'.

Bernard was stunned. He stared up at her dumbstruck. Bald Horace, on the other hand, had something to say.

I think I'd like to move on, too. I don't know if you all noticed, but there's some things that happened recently I just can't get out of my thoughts, awake or asleep. I believe I need to do penance for my sins. So, 'Rora Mae, I want you to take my share of the gold. I don't believe I should profit by it. Lord knows, the white world owes us both, but it owes you a heap more than it owes me. I think I should sell my flock and my herd and head on to wherever God sends me. Mornin' does me fine as well.

They embraced.

Bernard snapped himself out of shock and argued with them. He made pleas to their sense of family, to the foolishness of splitting up again when it had required so much grief to bring them back together, to the bonds they shared from the antediluvian past up to that very day. When all of that did no good, he played his ace. How could they leave him when he'd saved their lives?

And I thank you, Aurora Mae said, meaning her gratitude should be sufficient. In any case, it was all she was prepared to give.

I saved yours back, Bald Horace said. And it's killin' me.

They were at an impasse. Bernard felt as if a pile of rocks crushed his chest. He'd run out of argument, bribery, and blackmail. He felt a husk of a man, light as milkweed. His heart was too dry to break. When the others went to sleep, he sat alone on his bed and stared into darkness. Just before dawn, he got up and walked flatfooted through the house to Aurora Mae's bedroom. The door was open. He went through it. He could see her, lying there, naked under a sheet, bathed in moonlight. He sat on the edge of the bed. Quietly, so as not to wake her, Bernard wept. She opened her eyes.

There was no surprise in her expression. It was as if she'd been expecting him. Out of kindness, out of affection, she lifted her arm and put a hand behind his neck, drawing him down beside her to comfort him. He felt like a child next to her. She was that big.

I'm sorry, Bernard. I got to go. I got to be alone.

Words he'd kept inside for years spilled out.

I love you, Aurora Mae.

I know. I know.

He propped himself up on an elbow and tried to kiss her, but she turned her head and his lips landed on her cheek.

I can't do that, she said softly. Maybe once upon a time I could. I always had feelin' for you, Bernard. I did. But them crackers ruined me for that.

He cried out and sobbed, the great ragged sobs of a rent and tortured soul. The sound of it roused her brother, who was suddenly at the doorway in his nightshirt, his mouth dropped open at the sight before him.

Help him up, Horace, she said. He's at least as broke down as us.

The next morning, after Aurora Mae packed up the truck bed and Bald Horace sold his goats and chickens to a cousin, Bernard stood on the porch watching them leave, she in the truck and Bald Horace on foot with two days' rations and a staff, which he believed was the only way a penitent should travel. After a handful of months, Bernard realized they weren't changing their minds and coming back. Staying there without them made no sense. The cousins were kind but kept a cautious distance from him now that Woodwitch and her brother were gone, because you never knew with white people. They could be sweet all their lives long and then just like that turn on you. Their reserve dug the pit he was in a little deeper. Bundling his broken heart together with his memories and his gold, he left, too, without plan or purpose.

The first thing he did was find a place to bury half the gold. There was that much of it. He could not carry it all for long. He chose a high place at the outskirts of Saint Louis in a graveyard flanked by a great stone church, thinking it unlikely to be disturbed by flood and impossible to forget. Then he headed west for no particular reason other than to fight the temptation to follow his lost love south. Besides, he'd had enough of the North in Cincinatti. Despite the gold sewn inside his jacket and the false pockets of his pack, he'd been poor too long to know how to be rich. He rode the rails where he could or walked. Boxcars were stuffed with black folk. The first car he hopped, he threw his pack in ahead of him, and the weight of it slamming against the floor created a great cloud of dust. As he hauled his limbs up and in, a multitude of coughing fits welcomed him. He looked up through the settling air to see what appeared to be two dozen Negroes ranging in age from toddlers to ancients.

At the sight of him, women shrunk back against the walls, grabbing their children and holding them close. Most of the men clenched their fists, the rest looked to be reaching behind them, for what Bernard did not care to find out. He gave them his most practiced good-natured smile. He doffed his hat. Ladies, he said. Gentlemen. He bowed a bit from the waist, but not overly low or they'd think it mockery. He smiled wide and open. Wiggled his big ears for the amusement of the children. Then he settled into a corner of the car far from everyone else and whistled a popular song. In short, he did everything he could to make himself seem friendly. It didn't help much. The women eased the pressure on their backs and the men loosed their fists, but no one gave him welcome. He opened up his pack and produced what he had to eat: a few potatoes and onions, three tins of sardines, one of salmon, and two cans of tomatoes. He cradled them in two arms and held them aloft. The body helps cook these up will surely share them, he said.

The ice broke. The wall tumbled. So many voices chimed in together, he didn't know who was talking when. The men made a fire in a metal tub and the women cooked a stew over it, adding their own stores of turnips and spice to Bernard's cache. There wasn't much per head, but it was more than many of them had eaten for a time. Soon a festive air replaced suspicion, and Bernard felt comfortable enough to pull out of his pack what his riverboat ancestors would have called the pièce de résistance, a bottle of bourbon. It was turning dark and cold. Everyone took a sip—men, women, and children all. There was a second pass about just for grown-ups, a third just for men, then Bernard got an earful.

Down in the Delta after the flood, they told him, life was as cruel for Negroes as life could get. There was plenty of work digging out, cleaning up, rebuilding, unloading, and distributing federal aid, but it was miserable work, conscript labor performed under rifle and whip. Wages, when they were given, were worthless chits. There was typhus, cholera, dysentery and no medicine unless you worked like your granddaddy slave, while the whites put out a hand and got it government-free.

Time has passed, they said, the waters have drawn back and things are put back together some, but still there's lynchin' in the wood and murder at the work camps. Every morning the sun shines down on more black men turned up dead of gunshot and knife wounds, and heaven help every woman, whether good lookin' or plain, once that day is over and darkness falls. The bosses suffered terrible in the flood time, and we did, too, but in our case, it was more of the same, and in theirs, trouble newborn. They had not known the Lord's rod in times gone, only His velvet glove. The devil's anger took hold of 'em. Someone had to pay. We are the scapegoats, they said, striking chests made scrawny from illness and hunger, just like in the Bible. We cannot survive it. We are on the move. Going north. Going west. Don't matter where. Anywhere that ain't the Delta.

Every car he rode, he found Negroes with like stories. It seemed God had rained down the flood on them, after which white men rained down the fire and brimstone. Bernard could not rest thinking of poor, fractured Bald Horace with no gold and nothing but the hate of others and his heart's desolation to keep him company. He did not care to think of Aurora Mae. When he focused on her possible fate, his fancies met up with the horror of what was told him on the rails, and he could not bear the pain of it. He consoled himself with the thought that at least she had two portions of gold. There was always the possibility she'd convinced Bald Horace to stick with her after all, and the two of them were safe, protecting each other however they may. Then he'd think of how they'd both abandoned him and grieve.

He put down stakes for a while in Kansas City. When he got to town, he went first to a bathhouse and washed the road and rails off. He obtained the address of a good haberdasher, who outfitted him in a respectable wardrobe from drawers to fedora. After noting the way the tailor's eyes lit up at the sight of payment in gold coin, he went to a bank next and got himself several safety deposit boxes as his gold would not fit in merely one or two. Then he checked into the best rooming house in town. There he slept and ate well and found he liked it. If I am not to have love, he thought with more resignation than bitterness, then I shall have luxury and the company of fine folk. So he studied the ways of the guests of Mrs. Karp's Home Away from Home on Blossom Street, a steady stream of salesmen, married couples on a honeymoon, schoolteachers, well-heeled tourists all on their way to someplace else, and learned a thing or two about how to speak and hold his fork properly. He was a favorite of Mrs. Karp, mostly because he stayed on while others passed through and was never late with the rent. Mrs. Karp was a blonde, rosy-cheeked widow not much beyond forty, plump and pretty, who did not know how lonely she was until Bernard Levy came to stay. She found herself drawn to him, because he was a strong, quiet type of independent means, always clean and never rude. Looks aren't everything, she told her cook, Lulu, in fact, looks can deceive when homeliness masks a noble nature and beauty a base one.

It wasn't long before she made her move.

Bernard sat on the back porch in a rocker smoking a cigar. It was a warm night. He'd chosen the back, because the kitchen windows and door would be open while Lulu and her husband, Daniel, the general caretaker of the place, cleaned up after dinner. He felt more at home listening to those two squabble and gossip than he did in the front parlor where he was still a little afraid of opening his mouth and saying something to a fellow guest that would label him the low-class son of the Mississippi he was.

The screen door opened and fell shut in a clatter of noise that stirred him from thoughts of Aurora Mae in better times, which was why his eyes were damp. Mrs. Karp noticed.

Why, Mr. Levy, are you feelin' well? she said. You look about to come down with a cold or worse. I could get you some tea with honey. Maybe spike it up, too. It'll help you sleep.

She didn't wait for an answer but called out to Lulu to bring the drink for them both, easing herself into a rocker set close by Bernard's with just a tiny wedge of table between them. She dismissed Lulu and Daniel, shooing them away from porch and kitchen with a waved hand and harsh looks. She leaned over and touched Bernard's arm while she murmured pleasantries. She wasn't but halfway through with her tea and admiring the moon when Mrs. Karp pronounced herself feeling chilled, and why didn't they move indoors.

This was a surprise to Bernard. Her flesh radiated heat. He should have been forewarned, but he'd been so awful lonely that her company proved welcome. Once they settled on the second parlor couch in a room that was vestibule to her private quarters, she poured them both a second cup, spoke to him softly about the death of Mr. Karp in the Great War. And me, she said, a child bride, suddenly alone in the world. Then came tears, followed by a clumsy effort Bernard made to comfort her. He really didn't know how it happened, but a hand he thought he'd placed around her shoulder for a good pat found itself under her left breast after she'd twisted around unexpectedly. Then one of her hands fluttered about as deft as butterflies, clever as monkeys undoing all his buttons and ties while her other hand took care of her own. Come the dawn, he found himself being served breakfast in bed by a flushed, robust blonde, old enough to teach him a thing or two and young enough for him to like it.

He lived with Mrs. Karp just shy of two years. He grew fond enough of her, as he'd nothing else to do. He ran her errands, patched her roof, evicted tenants, bought whatever she claimed she could not live without. They became an item in the town, an odd couple who amused their betters. Though no one expected the widowed operator of a rooming house to be as respectable as her lodgers, her choice of lover invited fun. Inevitably, women being what they are, she began to demand avowals from him he could not give. He gave her the best he could and remain honest, but he disappointed. She nagged him constantly. He thought often of leaving her. If he'd had somewhere else to go or an ambition in the world beyond one day hearing from Aurora Mae or Bald Horace, he would have. The stock market crash came next, landing like a wall of bricks across their bed. Her clientele dried up. The lodgers she did have were less and less well heeled, and her resentment grew that Bernard did not give up his amatory reticence nor wholesale his gold. Her breath went sour with whiskey at odd times of day. Her hair was always loose and wild. It did not occur to Bernard that he was breaking her heart, indeed that he could break anyone's heart or that anyone would offer him her heart to begin with. But he was.

On a certain Saturday morning, he woke up to the sight of her standing over him in her duster, a paisley scarf tied around her head. Get up, she said, get up. We've somewhere to go. He did so, because he was accustomed to obeying women, from his mama to Miss Maple, from the riverboat dolls to Aurora Mae. There was no other reason. Without complaint or question, he dressed in the clothes she told him to wear, his corduroy suit, flat cap, and his sturdiest boots. He followed her to the Packard he'd bought her used for her birthday. I'm drivin', she said. He got in from the passenger side.

He thought to ask Mrs. Karp where they were going, but one glance at her white-knuckled grip on the steering wheel made him reconsider. It was possible she was in one of those moods becoming more common every week when her nagging turned to yelling and her voice screeched. Times like those, it seemed she was halfway to the madhouse. He kept mum.

She started up the car without another word. They drove deep into the Osage plains. Once, she stopped and sweetly asked Bernard to refill the gas tank from the canisters she had in the back. He complied, wondering what it was he didn't like about her tone, sweet though it might be. When he got back in the car, he fell asleep.

Bernard woke up when the car came to a halt with a jolt. They were in a tallgrass prairie full of bluestem and switchgrass. Far off on the horizon was a blue line of hills rolling there like a tide of tiny waves.

Now put up or get out, Mrs. Karp said. Her eyes were wide and round. They bulged a little. Her lip quivered. She sprayed when she talked. At last, she'd achieved a primary goal. She frightened him.

He backed against the car door to get as far away from her as he could without leaving the vehicle. What are you talking about?

You heard me. Put up or get out, get out, get out. You like it out there? She gestured in a grand way, encompassing the whole of the wilderness. Better than livin' with me? Because that's your choice, Bernard. You can either marry me today at the first justice of the peace we can find, or you can make a new life here. Find out if you prefer the company of prairie dogs and snakes to me.

She laughed in a maniacal way that, whatever her intention, had Bernard running from the car at top speed. He ducked down in the grass. She howled and drove the car around in mad circles looking for him. He crawled on his belly zigzagging and hoped for escape. Eventually, she stopped the car. Wept. He could hear her cries, and each one was like a knife to his gut. He thought of getting up and seeing if he could comfort her, coax her back to sanity somehow, but by then her cries had turned to sniffles and whimpers. Just as if he'd never existed, she started up the car again and slowly drove off.

It took him three days to walk back to Kansas City. He had three days of walking, of begging for scraps at the farms and towns he passed through along the way, three days to review his life so far and how it all had come down to the vengeance of a woman's unrequited love. He could not decide if all his times of glory and all his times of pain amounted to a tragedy or a comedy. He vowed that he would marry one day. It seemed far too dangerous to remain single, and the idea of children had begun to appeal. He vowed to marry as soon as he found a woman who was as unlike Mrs. Karp and as much like Aurora Mae before her troubles as he could find. Respectable, he decided, a virgin, strong in her opinions, with lots of thick black hair, yes, the hair would be nonnegotiable. Whoever she was, he wanted to lie in bed with her and bury himself in her hair and maybe then he might catch the scent of Aurora Mae once in a while and be happy.

When he got back to town, he went to the bank and emptied his deposit boxes into a flour sack he'd come across on the way. He went to a livery, decided to buy a car instead of a horse. He bought a battered

Model T with a reconditioned engine, as it suits a wanderer with a flour sack full of gold to be nondescript, and left his home for the past two years without a plan, without direction.

Somewhere out there a new life beckoned. What it was mystified him completely.

XVI

Memphis, Tennessee–Guilford, Mississippi, 1962–1964

IT WAS AFTER DUSK BEFORE Mickey Moe drove far enough along a certain wooded dirt road to find the knocked-down tree with pink flowers sitting in a ditch next to a path strewn with acorns, pinecones, empty beer bottles, and one or two jugs of hard liquor. He found the air crisp for a summer night. He shivered as he exited the LTD and dropped himself into the darkness of a night lit only intermittently by the full moon as there were clouds above that shifted constantly, jockeying for dominance over that old man and his silver light. One minute he could see before himself plain as day, and the next hardly at all. So he walked then stopped as the light permitted. When he was still, he looked up to see when the clouds might part again. It took time to come to the place he sought, the spot where a fire had burned and men had been tortured not three nights before.

The first thing he noticed was that Walter Cohen's shoes were no longer there. Hope rose in this throat like a sob. The best scenario was that someone, with luck not law enforcement, had already been to the crime scene. If they were friend to those who'd done it, evidence would be secreted or destroyed. That might include Laura Anne's daddy's pistol. He could replace the gun as a gift for his future father-in-law and apologize for losing the original during a scuffle with a snake they'd encountered on a picnic during their honeymoon in Memphis. Yes, he thought, that would work well enough to sow the peace. During his solitary ride, he'd decided he'd marry his girl as soon as this unwholesome chore was over. He was not going to repeat his father's mistake of moving too little too late. He walked down the path where he'd tripped over Jeffrey Harris's severed foot, hoping that was gone, too.

No such luck.

There it was, looking just as gruesome as it had the night before, only more so, because now it looked chewed up along the edges by the Lord knew what. Mickey Moe swallowed bile, shivered in the night air, and looked around for Lot Needleman's gun. Clouds came to cover him in darkness, and he knelt down in the dirt to feel about with his hands. It wasn't long before he hit cold metal. The joy that surged through him was as powerful as a shot of morphine. Flush with the exhilaration of success, he hopped up and started to walk as fast as he could down the dark path when he heard movement in the brush and voices. He spun around seeking their source and saw two round shafts of light scouring the path ahead maybe twenty yards behind him.

Terror struck him down to his knees again. He crouched low and listened. The first voice was male, but young, a tad high-pitched. A teenager's. I know it's here someplace, Wesley. It's got to be.

An older voice, gruff, gravelly, mean-sounding answered the fairer one. That's if some wild dog or bobcat didn't carry it off. Keep lookin'.

They were close enough so that Mickey Moe could see their shapes in outline behind the flashlights' beams. One was tall and thin, the other short and round. Both wore hats. The first wore a cap, the other a fedora of some kind. As they got close, Mickey Moe's heart beat so hard, his ears throbbed. He wanted to tear it out of his chest before it betrayed him. He didn't know who these men were. They could be FBI for all he knew. They could be the dirty kluckers who'd killed Jeffrey Harris and tortured Walter Cohen. Whoever they were, he didn't need an introduction.

I'm gettin' tired, Wesley. Why'd we have to put the truck so far away?

Christ, boy. Think I was sober enough to know exactly where we were? Wesley laughed in a thin, nasal way.

I wouldn't think nobody was. This is gonna take all night.

I tole you bring the dogs.

Glinda had the bloat last week, you know that. I didn't want to stress her. And the others. Dang, but they won't go nowhere without that bitch.

They were very close now, and the moon had peeped out from cloud cover enough for Mickey Moe to see the men had a large canvas bag with them. It was at least a quarter full of something that rounded out its bottom. O Lord, Mickey Moe thought, I do not want to know what's in there. Please do not let me have to see it.

This thought more than any other coursing through his head made him stand up suddenly in the nearly full light of the moon and run like heck toward his LTD on the road by the downed tree with the pink flowers lying in a ditch. He knew the men would see him, but he figured he could outrun them. That's all he had to do. Run very, very fast. A shotgun blast rang through the air. Then another. The kluckers were yelling, and he couldn't tell what. He prayed it wasn't for reinforcements. Their voices were louder than they should be. They were closer than he'd hoped. He must be slower than he'd thought. O Lord, he thought, O Lord.

Without determining whether Lot Needleman's gun was loaded, he did what instinct told him to do. He turned, still running, and pointed the gun in the general direction of his pursuers. He pulled the trigger. God was with him. The thing went off.

There was a crashing sound, the sound of a heavy object falling into the brush and the yelp of a high-pitched teenaged voice screaming, Wesley! Wesley! You've been hit! as if the man now groaning loud as a bear did not know it.

He got my shoulder, boy! Git him!

But the boy didn't move, or at least Mickey Moe didn't see or hear him move. He did not even try to git him, either out of fear, or because he did not want to leave Wesley on his own. It really didn't matter which as far as Mickey Moe was concerned. He kept on running. When he reached his car, he jumped in and floored it. He roared out of those backwoods like the hounds of hell were following him, and in his mind they might well have been.

When he got back to the motel, it was ten o'clock in the evening. Laura Anne was sitting up in bed in her nightgown reading a magazine with the TV on. Pack it up, honey, he said. We're leavin'. Right now.

She saw the way he looked. He was half-crazy, his shirt all sweated through with leaves and dirt sticking to it. She saw her daddy's gun dangling from his right hand. She didn't speak. She didn't ask questions. She just got up and did what she was told.

Well, at least you didn't kill him, she said once they were on Highway 61 and he'd had the chance to get his story out.

He took his eyes off the road to give her a wild-eyed, half-second glance that gave her gooseflesh.

But I could have. I would have.

If you had to.

That's right. If I had to.

They were silent awhile.

I guess your parents are right. Blood will tell. I'm just like my daddy.

Oh now, darlin'. . .

I could be a murderer.

If you had to be.

That's right.

They didn't get married on the way back home to Guilford, although they did spend the night just over the Tennessee border, because they felt safe in Mississippi though neither of them could tell you why. They felt safe, and they needed to catch their breath and clean up before their next hurdle, that of confronting Beadie Sassaport Levy. There was more to the life of Bernard Levy they wanted to know. According to Aurora Mae, Beadie knew it.

They pulled up to the old house on Orchard Street. Mickey Moe surveyed the front yard with its purple hydrangeas and blue creeping phlox, the broad-columned porch in desperate need of whitewash, the lion's head door knocker his mama said Daddy had affixed there just after he was born. Home the place said to him, only it didn't feel like home anymore. It was a place built on blood money and lies. It wasn't that he blamed his daddy for what he'd done. He could see the reason in it and the love. It was that it'd been kept from him his whole life, as if he wasn't worthy of truth, and couldn't be trusted with it. Why had his mama done that to him? Hadn't she seen how he'd suffered growing up the son of a scoundrel? Especially in that place and in that time? Hadn't she cared?

Those were his feelings as they walked together, hand in hand, from the driveway up to the front door. Laura Anne held on to him tight. She sensed his turmoil and wanted to help. Her loyalty, her affection was what she had to offer. He squeezed her hand back.

No one came to the door to greet them, which struck Mickey Moe as odd. Where was Sara Kate? Where was Eudora Jean? Where was Mama? He always thought those women had secret antennae for company. They were headed to the door before visitors finished framing the idea of paying a call in their minds. How many times did people drop by to find them sitting there on the porch with a tray of sweet tea, lemon slices, and extra glasses at the ready? It was too early an hour for a lie down. So where were they?

The foyer was unlit, dim, quiet. They set their luggage down and poked their heads into the sitting room and the dining. No one.

Mama? Mickey Moe called out. Mama?

I'm in here.

Mama sounded faint, feeble. They found her in the kitchen, sitting at the table all alone polishing silver. She wore rubber gloves and an apron over a blue dotted-swiss dress. She had jewelry on, a pearl choker and her good gold watch pinned to her chest like a brooch. Her hair was done up as if she was going out. She looked at them with an expression of long-suffering despair. Her greeting was delivered deadpan, without nuance or spirit.

So, she said. I have not been entirely deserted after all. The prodigal has returned. One of 'em anyway.

Dismayed as he was with Beadie, Mickey Moe, like all good old boys, loved his mama. Her demeanor alarmed him. Mama, what's wrong?

Oh, nothin' I suppose. Nothin' a woman accustomed to abandonment might not have anticipated. I could take it when you up and left without a word. I figured, well, Mickey's a man, can't tell those creatures what to do in the best of times, let alone when they're head over heels with a rebellious young girl who'd crush her parents' hearts again and again like they were crumbs underfoot. I put caution in my heart and wished you wisdom.

She saw they were hanging on her every word, and so she paused to punish them. She thought about insulting Laura Anne a little more directly but then considered that after recent events, she might need her around. Of course, she couldn't have her under her roof in their current state of sin. She'd have to insist they correct their situation. Maybe they already had. She squinted up her eyes and made a grim line of her lips.

You all get married or somethin'? she asked.

No, Mama. Not yet. But we will very soon.

She sighed, looked down, and muttered. Mickey Moe wondered if she'd had some kind of breakdown.

Where's Eudora Jean? he asked, thinking she must be at the pharmacy getting whatever it was Mama needed to help her through.

At his question, Mama started to bawl into her rubber gloves.

She left me! She left me with that traitor, Sara Kate! The day after you took off she announced out of the blue that she and Sara Kate were leaving together! I had to let Roland go the next day. I couldn't have him stayin' here with his wife run off with my daughter! People would say we were . . .

She shuddered, unable to utter what calumny the neighbors might spread.

Mama, what do you mean they run off together?

She put her hand to her chest.

Do not make me say it. Use your imagination. I had to. All she said was that she never had such a good time in her life as when she went to the village to spend time with Sara Kate and her people. That she felt like she belonged there with them. Once she mentioned to Sara Kate how she felt, a dam burst. For both of them. Now what do you think that meant? Hmm? What do you think that meant?

Mickey Moe and Laura Anne were speechless.

Exactly, Mama said. Exactly. It's disgustin'. Now I'm afraid to go anywhere. My canasta ladies came by this afternoon to pick me up, and I could not go. What would I do if they asked for Eudora Jean? Tell them she'd discovered she was a . . . she was a . . . oh, I can't say it.

Her son sat down in the chair beside hers and put an arm around her while she whimpered.

Well, Mama. Now this is a shock, of course it is. Best you can say is it was in her blood. From Daddy's side.

Beadie Sassaport Levy froze. She went stiff and still as a board. When she spoke, her voice was again flat, barren of inflection.

Whatever are you talking about.

I know everything, Mama. I spoke with Aurora Mae Stanton.

My stars, she said after a bit. My stars. And where did you find that . . . that . . . person?

In Memphis.

Mama shook her head. Of course you did. Of course.

It all came out then. The full story of what happened the day of Rachel Marie's sixth birthday party, when Aurora Mae emerged from the cornrows, demanding to see Bernard.

She'd been on the road three days, I think, Beadie said. Lord, she was a dirty, ragged mess. She needed to know where Bald Horace was. He's her brother. You know that now, right?

We know almost everything, Laura Anne volunteered.

Beadie gave her a low, level-eyed stare, trying to decide whether an interloper ought to be there, listening to all this. Her eyes went from her son to his beloved, and she saw that he'd tell her everything anyway. She took two noisy little breaths and continued.

There was some fish story about a cousin, Mags, I think was the name. A cousin who died unexpectedly. Mags's grown-up daughter, Sara Kate, and her son-in-law—that'd be Roland—needed jobs after their mama's farm went to payin' the medical and the funeral bills. Your daddy said they could work here, never mind that I had a perfectly good couple already. Findin' jobs for those two was only an excuse. That Aurora Mae came here to get him back.

Your daddy told me all about his past that day. Everything. Endin' with how she walked all the way here to bring him back to Saint Louis with her. I suspect life without a man got tough for her in some way, don't ask me how. And who else would have her? But, you know, Daddy had me by then, and you and your sisters. It was too late. He told her she had to go. And she did. Every once in a while, I happen to know, she'd visit her brother, that Bald Horace, and your daddy would sneak out and meet the two of them. I know that for a fact. And don't you think I didn't make him pay for it, too.

It was a lot to absorb all at once. Mickey Moe didn't ask the questions he should have immediately. They came out in dribbles and drabs. He asked, Why did Daddy come to Guilford in the first place?

Because he found out Bald Horace was here, she answered.

He asked, How'd he find that out?

I do not know.

He asked, Why did Aurora Mae tell me her visits to her brother were your story to tell, not hers?

How would I know.

He asked, Why did you never tell me all this?

She answered, Lord, I've raised an idiot child! Are you aware of the country you live in, boy? Are you at all familiar with a little thing called race relations? Exactly what do you think our lives would have been like if your daddy's origins and attachments got around? I'll tell you one thing. We would not have been livin' here. And I like it here. It's where my people are. No, no. It was better no one knew. I kept his secrets. Do you think that was easy? It was not, especially after he died. My heart was bereft, completely. But I put on a good show the only way I could think of. I took all his secrets and buried them in a bundle inside a bigger one. Yes, I did. I kept his secrets every day of his life and beyond. No matter what it cost.

There were other holes in her knowledge. She was sure there was more of Bernard the handsome's gold around but did not know where. She knew nothing of how Daddy spent those years between splitting up with the Stantons and arriving on her doorstep, of how he transformed himself from a murderer, thief, river rat to a well-groomed, well-spoken gentleman everyone in Guilford knew as the heir to Levy Agricultural Supply. She suspected there was yet another woman mixed up in it.

Once he realized he got everything he could out of her, Mickey Moe got up and poured Mama a glass of sherry. She looked like she needed it. She thanked him. Her eyes were red-rimmed from crying, her cheeks stained with tears and silver polish. She was a most pitiful sight, and it was pity he felt most deeply for her. He put an arm on her shoulder, bent, and kissed the top of her dolled-up hair.

Mama, it's alright. We'll take care of you. You don't need Eudora Jean anymore. You've got a good new daughter who understands what you've been through. Don't you, honey?

Laura Anne quickly assented. You'll never be alone again, she said, kissing Beadie's cheek.

Beadie drank in her son's affection as a desert flower does rain. The few days she'd spent in despair over the flight of Eudora Jean with Sara Kate had terrified her. Mickey Moe now came with an encumbrance named Laura Anne. She realized she'd have to like it or lump it if she wanted to live out her days with her blood taking care of her. The alternative, living alone for all the world to think no one she'd borne and raised cared two figs what happened to her, inspired her to accept Laura Anne's kiss and decide there was something admirable in her. She'd brought Mickey Moe back, hadn't she? And she looked ready to face the clamorous music her adventurous nature had struck up with her own folk. Another girl these days might have set up house with her lover in Jackson and avoided the families the rest of her life, wallowed in scandal, and dragged Beadie's son down in the dirt with her. But not this one. How could she be the mad slattern she'd first assumed and bring Mickey Moe back home? Maybe she'd been wrong. The conclusion that Laura Anne wanted very much to win her affection hit her next. Well, she thought, if she's eager to have my approval, then I might retrain her some. Why I could mold her more to my own design. The idea that here was another chance at having some kind of a daughter live with her until she died was the most encouraging thought yet. She even smiled.

Mickey Moe complained to Laura Anne one night soon after. Look at all we went through, he said, and still I don't know everything about my daddy. There's some very important leftover information to be had. I haven't a clue how to get at it.

Maybe you don't need to know everything, honey.

Huh?

You know enough. Let it go. We have a life of our own to live.

Mickey Moe went back to work directly after his first night home. By 8:00 a.m., he was out and about on his sales route, catching up with his roll of 'croppers and gentlemen farmers. He left the women alone together and was much relieved when he returned at the end of the day that no blood had been drawn. The women cooked a meal together. Laura Anne insisted on serving. You've had a long few days, she told Beadie. You need your rest.

The next day, Mickey Moe told them he needed to go on an over-night trip to continue collecting premiums from all over. Collections had lapsed to near ruin for policyholders since he'd gone off on his quest. When he drove up to the house thirty-six hours later, he found his women sitting on the porch rocking, relaxing together. Laura Anne served another meal and at Mickey Moe's quiet suggestion, poured Mama wine in such amounts that she slept early and soundly enough for the lovers to enjoy some time together uninterrupted and unobserved.

They drew the window shades in the living room and curled up together on the couch. Just before their fond embrace and sweet kisses got more serious, Mickey Moe pulled away.

I have something important to tell you, he said. But first, let me ask you this. Don't you think you need to get in touch with your people? They must be worried sick about you.

Laura Anne winced. You know what? I did call them. From the road when we were in Memphis and you were out, you know, retrieving Daddy's gun.

He sat up. What happened? What'd they say?

She looked away from him, embarrassed. She shifted her weight around as if she was trying to get away. Mama just cried and cried. I tried to soothe her, but Daddy grabbed the phone. He had a few choice words for me and hung up. I had a good cry myself after that. Then you got back to the room and said we were leavin' fast, so I put it out of my mind. Your mama asked me about them this mornin'. It preys upon her that I'm here without their knowledge. I confided in her how sore it all made my heart. She thinks they'll forgive us if we go to them hat in hand and humble. I'm not so sure.

Mickey pulled a folded-up paper from his back pocket. And what if we go to them hat in hand and humble with this?

She sat up and unfolded the thing carefully as though it was an artifact of some kind that might crumble to dust. Then her brow wrinkled. That other Bernard Levy's birth certificate, I assume? I mean, the address is in the city at a hospital and your daddy was born outside town, poor as a church mouse, probably at home.

Oh, my love is so clever, thought Mickey Moe with pride, can't put a thing past her.

Yes, yes, it is! he said. I got it yesterday from the town hall in Memphis. Can you believe our luck? It survived the flood! Look here's what we'll do. We'll present this to your parents and say that my daddy was who he said he was after all. We'll tell them that everything mysterious about my daddy had been a colossal misunderstanding. His Memphian people were estranged from him over his choice of a bride out of their sect, just as everyone believed before the war. Then after his death, they were pitiless, unrelenting, and refused to accept Beadie Sassaport Levy out of spite. It was not the quality of his blood that was questionable only that his blood had been cruel.

She took his face in her hands to study him. There was a matter of seminal importance to discuss about the foundation of her love for him.

But darlin', it'll be a story we're tellin', that's all. You told me the day we met that truth was important to you, that you needed to atone for your daddy's lies. What happened to all that? I fell in love with you because you were an honest man.

Sweetheart. You're the one who shut the door on your daddy's love with your deceptions. Can you really be asking me this?

She blushed. He continued.

Now that I know about my daddy's life, it's affected my judgment. Look at the lies he had to tell to find love and then protect it. Was he wrong? Should he have confessed to the authorities and left that gold to gather dust in Ghost Tree's attic? Should he have turned in Bald Horace for murder? Should he have announced to the world of Sassaports that their prize daughter was not his first, abiding love? Besides there aren't any Memphian Levys left to argue another side. It's a good plan, and it's foolproof.

She grimaced and shrugged, unsure. He kissed her again in a way that blotted out care. Alright, she thought. I've made my bed here. This is a good, brave man I have in my arms. We sealed our fates early on in that old sedan of his by the river. I love him whether he's completely honest or only mostly.

When they got ready to depart for Greenville to confront her parents the following morning, she went shaky. She embraced Beadie farewell and clung to her in a way that both pleased and confounded the other. What's the matter, child? Beadie whispered into the girl's ear.

Oh Mama, she said, addressing her as she'd been requested to do, I'm afraid a little of what's going to be.

If she'd had the courage, she might have confessed that she was more frightened on that day at that moment than she'd been the whole time she was up in Memphis and Littlefield with Mickey Moe facing the threat of arrest or death together. It was one thing to love her man from the security of her bedroom at her parent's house and dream of liberation, another to experience crisis at his side in parts unknown, wild and violent, and yet a third to embark on a life of day-to-day living with perhaps—if her parents continued to reject her choice—only this woman she clung to for stability outside her man's arms.

Beadie understood all this without requiring an explanation. Everyone's scared at first, she said. Don't worry. It'll pass.

It was a Sunday. Laura Anne and Mickey Moe drove past Needleman's Furniture to make sure her daddy wasn't there, doing accounts. Satisfied both her parents would likely be home, they went directly to the house on Elton Street, parked, and gathered courage to walk up to the front door. You know, honey, she said, I always thought of this as a big house, but it looks so small to me now. Is that a good sign?

He gave her a quick peck on the cheek. Yes, darlin', I think it is.

Rose and Lot Needleman caught wind of their arrival before they reached the house. The front door opened when they were halfway to it. Laura Anne kept her eyes down while Mickey Moe, holding her hand as they advanced, gave the pair a bright, bold as brass smile. Rose shrunk behind her husband as if requiring a shield against all that light. Lot, dark and immobile, glared.

So, he said through the screen door. You've come back.

The sight of her mother cringing behind her father jolted Laura Anne. The pose distressed her immensely, broke her heart with guilt and another emotion hard to name. Maybe it was a new fear that beset her, fear that she'd turn into her mother one day, unable to help herself, cringing behind a man. It was a breathtaking thought. One that renewed her courage. She dropped Mickey Moe's hand just as he was about to speak up and spoke for herself.

Yes, Daddy, I have, she said. Mama, please don't be afraid. We're not here to argue with you, we're here to reconcile.

Reconcile? Lot snorted. Reconcile? Next you'll be expectin' a fatted calf.

Oh com'on, Daddy. Just let us in. The neighbors have had enough speculation to chew on, don't you think? Want to give them more?

Rose Needleman sprang into action. She pulled backward on Lot's belt. She's right, she said. Let them in, Lot. Please.

The four of them settled down in the front parlor. The young people sat side by side on the settee, the elders in two winged armchairs opposite. There was a heavy wood coffee table in between. Amid a silence as thick as gumbo mud, Mickey Moe reached inside his jacket's breast pocket and pulled out a bundle wrapped in a white linen handkerchief. He laid it on the table. It made a little clunk, louder than it needed to be in all that quiet. With the delicacy of a man defusing a bomb, he undraped the object within, corner-by-white-linen-corner, exposing at last in all its majesty Lot Needleman's handgun. There was a deeper silence, and Lot said, Where'd you get that.

Laura Anne's daddy was confused. Turned out, he never even missed his pistol. Hadn't had call for the thing. So Laura Anne started to laugh. Here they were so concerned about his reaction, and there really wasn't much of one, was there? Then she told them everything about their time in the backwoods. About Mickey Moe's quest to find Aurora Mae and about J. Henry and Walter Cohen and poor Jeffrey Harris and poor Jeffrey Harris's severed foot. She told them about losing the gun and Mickey Moe gambling his life to find it again, the shots that were fired, and the interview with Aurora Mae. Well, she only told part of that last. Whatever parts fit with the next revelation they had to spill.

Rose Needleman listened with a hand on her heart and her eyes wide, so enthralled by her daughter's courage her twitch ceased for the time being. Lot Needleman's eyes welled up with tears, his hands clenched and unclenched with frustration as he imagined his baby girl in mortal peril. Somewhere in there, gratitude to the man who'd protected her headstrong self from harm was born.

When it came time for the final disclosure, Mickey Moe reached again into this breast pocket and pulled out Bernard the handsome's birth certificate. He laid it out on the surface of the coffee table, smoothing out its wrinkles with two hands before giving it to his future in-laws to view. And that's all there is to tell, he said, after they'd absorbed the paper's contents and his story of the Memphian Levys' hardness of heart. Accept that I love your daughter and she loves me, and we're getting married with your approval or without it. But we dearly hope and pray that with both explanation and evidence, you will see your way to remove your objections to my bloodlines and accept us.

Rose Needleman, who'd had just about enough of suffering, looked over her shoulder twice in rapid succession. It was out of habit, for her nerves were now calmed for the first time since that Sunday supper when they'd insulted Mickey Moe on purpose. Then she opened up her arms and said, Oh my sweet girl! How I've missed you!

That nearly shocked the pants off Lot Needleman or so it seemed as he grabbed onto his belt at the sound of her words and hitched his pants up twice, roughly, as if about to undertake heavy lifting. Rose! he said. Rose! He wasn't sure they should let the young people get away with their rebellious and wounding deeds so easily.

It was too late. The women were in each other's arms, weeping the kind of happy feminine tears women reserve for such full moments.

Lot fumbled and hmm'd and looked to the only other man in the room for a witness to such unseemly behavior, shaking his head and hands as if to say, You see that? You see that?

And the only other man in the room smiled back at him with great delight, his shoulders shrugged, his palms uplifted in that age-old posture of his people that said, Yes I do, but so what? Really, so what?

Six months later, they married under a chuppah in the Needlemans' backyard.

They lived with Beadie at the old house at the beginning of their marriage, but after Aunt Lucille passed on, Mickey Moe took over her farm, and they lived there with Beadie in her own suite of rooms off the second drawing room. They raised some livestock, enough to keep them in eggs and milk, and Mickey Moe bought a horse to drive a Sunday cart purchased from a farmer on his insurance route. They hoed a few rows of vegetables and a couple of acres of cotton. They let out the rest of the property to sharecroppers. They were generous to their tenants and didn't overcharge. Once they convinced Mama Jo Baylin it was a good idea, they moved her and Bald Horace to a spare house among the 'croppers and bought them a couple of goats to cheer Bald Horace up. It was a fine life, a happy life. Then all of a sudden, Mickey Moe was drafted due to the chicanery of the Guilford draft board, under pressure in that time to draft more white men rather than so many blacks. They started with the whites they knew couldn't complain. They started with the Jews. Which meant that Mickey Moe was off to Vietnam.

Laura Anne would never forget the day they said good-bye before he went overseas. She tried as hard as she could to be brave, but nightmares tormented her. Perhaps because she was pregnant, she went weak and told Mickey Moe about the dreams.

I dream of your daddy a lot, she said through tears that shamed her. I dream of him in that foxhole leaning up against the roots of an old, dead tree and then his face starts to turn into yours and I run up to him in my housedress and I have an apron on and I try to rub your face out of his head. Then your skin starts to come off, and you bleed like you were just about bathed in a chemical, somethin' really harsh.

She shivered as much with humiliation that she'd voiced her terrors as with the terror itself. He wrapped her in his arms, stroking her back until a great moan came out of her, one not so much of misery as relief.

Don't worry, he said to her, pulling her in closer, making his voice as steady and reassuring as he could, I am nothing like my daddy. I do not share his fate.

And because she had to, she believed him.

XVII

Saint Louis, Missouri–Memphis, Tennessee–
New Orleans, Louisiana–Guilford,
Mississippi, 1930–1941

ONCE HE GOT FAR ENOUGH out of Kansas City that he could be sure Mrs. Karp hadn't caught wind of his return and followed him, Bernard went back to Saint Louis for the rest of his gold. After he dug that up, he stashed his treasure in a secret compartment he'd crafted in the boot of the Model T. Since he could not resist the call of the past, he went to visit the old house, currently inhabited by Cousin Mags.

Cousin Mags treated him like royalty. She kicked her two sons out of his old bedroom off the kitchen and installed him there with her best linens and fresh flowers in a vase. He wasn't going to stay more than a night but lingered a week for the pleasure of listening to stories of Aurora Mae and Bald Horace in their childhoods, many of which he knew already from the lips of those two, but all of which he delighted in hearing again and again. His heart, he realized, had begun to heal. It gave him pure joy to hear Aurora Mae's name spoken aloud where once he'd felt only sorrow. Cousin Mags told him she'd opened a botanical shop in Memphis just as she said she would and did fairly well by all reports. It was like waving a bone in front of a dog. A dangerous idea pestered him like hunger.

By the end of the week, he decided. He would visit Aurora Mae in Memphis, and they would be like old loving friends who meet to reminisce and share the warmth the past had knit between them. Nothing more. It would be an occasion of peace to him, a way to let old love behind, so's he could search unencumbered for the new. He hoped she'd know where Bald Horace was and how he fared. Then he could look him up, too.

Before he quit the place, he put a handful of gold coin underneath a bell jar in the kitchen on a shelf that held Aurora Mae's germinating herbs in the old days before the flood. He touched the shelf with two fingers and then kissed them, as if that simple plank of wood were a mezuzah. The gesture felt strange to him yet familiar also, and he questioned himself on the whys of that. He'd had acquaintance of mezuzahs at his grandparents' home all those years ago though he couldn't recall anyone ever caressing them. Maybe five times in preparation for his bar mitzvah, he'd visited the traveling rabbi's horse-drawn caravan, which was graced with mezuzahs at every portal, exterior and interior both. It was likely he'd learned the devotion from him and had forgotten it until now, when moved by an object he found sacred in its own right for who had used it. He smiled and shrugged at himself for being a sentimental man. He set off for Memphis for a reunion with someone he pretended to himself was nothing more than an old, beloved friend.

In those days, Orange Mound was largely a shantytown, home to the Great Depression's most down-and-out. Hobos arrived and quit the place after a sniff of air knowing the pickings there were worse than slim. There were shotgun houses, narrow boxes of undressed lumber, all in a jumble, as there were not so much roads connecting them as paths and sewage pits. Canvas tents were pitched all around the churches as shelter for those without, and everywhere there were men and women congregating outside, watching the children, flirting, arguing, trading whatever they could, praising Jesus. There was no work, and nothing else to do.

Three times, Bernard stopped to ask directions of men surprised by the sight of a vehicle driven by a white man in those parts, even one as beat up as the rattletrap he drove. Men approached him with hats in hand and bug-eyed smiles as they hoped for a handout. He'd describe Aurora Mae and mention she had a business, The Lenaka, somewhere thereabouts. They'd say, oh yessir, the shaman lady, why you just keep goin' south, and you'll find her, can't miss her place, no, not even if you tried.

Bernard gave them a nickel each and meandered on until at last, just as they'd said, there arose from out of the dung heap that was Orange Mound an oasis of prosperity, a shining white shingled house with an iron fence all 'round. Within the fence was a garden green with tall, feathery herbs and flowering bushes. A small glass dependency for growing things stood out the back as well. The house had lace curtains on the windows and a big bright door of haint blue with a brass knocker in the shape of a ram's horned head. A sign on a post just outside the front gate read THE LENAKA. As an aid to those who could not read, a variegated leaf dangling above a mortar and pestle was painted underneath the words. He parked his car around the corner where it would not be seen.

Bernard huddled in a doorway across the street for a few moments, trying to still his wildly pumping chest. He laughed at himself. The mere sight of the house filled him with excitement and the heat of an infinite tenderness. She is near, he thought, she is within those walls that sparkle like a palace in the desert. Whatever made him think he'd traveled there for the sake of nostalgia, love's lukewarm cousin? Love is eternal, he thought, why, everlastin'! It didn't matter how many Mrs.

Karps his life acquired—although he prayed to the Lord there'd only ever be just the one—or how many wives—same prayer—the woman in that house over there had a leash around his heart. He continued to marvel at true affection's mysteries when the door to The Lenaka opened.

A tall, broad black man in a charcoal pinstripe suit, spectator shoes, and a bold red cravat to match the hatband of his gray fedora exited. He held the bright blue door ajar with one gloved hand and twirled an ivory-topped cane with the other. Bernard watched him, fascinated. What kind of a man is this? he wondered. He looked like a riverboat swell, but those types didn't come in Negro that he knew of. Maybe he was some kind of actor or a landlocked gambler. Then Aurora Mae Stanton came out join him for a promenade down Carnes Street.

At the first glimpse of her, Bernard gasped. Fresh tears sprang to his eyes. She looked the same and yet completely different. She was still big. That hadn't changed, but everything else had. When he'd last seen her, she was wounded, haunted. The woman who strolled down the street escorted by an Orange Mound dandy was restored to glory. She wore a turban of red and black and gold, a turban that tied in the back then again in the front so that a vibrant floppy bow sat on her crown like a diadem. At her nape beneath its hem, a cascade of waist-length braids snaked down her back like a thing alive. Her eyes and lips were painted, not in a garish way but in a soft, appealing manner. Her bearing, the way she carried all that weight, reminded him of the Aurora Mae he first knew young, unscarred, imbued by nature with grace and power. She was in a dress of the same vibrant cloth as the turban and wore a pair of high-heeled boots laced with red ribbon on her feet. Bernard followed the couple down the street taking care to remain where he could see them but not be seen himself. He wanted to hear her voice. Her companion spoke to her constantly while they walked. He spoke in a low tone Bernard could not distinguish. Aurora

Mae did not speak. She shook her head or inclined it toward or away from him in response to whatever it was he told her, and Bernard was frustrated in his desire.

From as great a distance as he could manage, he followed them to a low brick structure not far off. When they entered, he came out of hiding and looked the place over, discovering it was an office building. There were four nameplates on it signifying that a doctor, a lawyer, an accountant, and a bail bondsman worked out of the place. It was Orange Mound's one and only professional building if you didn't count the bank up the way that had few depositors and functioned more as a telegraph office for wired funds than commercial institution. Bernard waited outside 'til Aurora Mae came out alone. He chose that moment to approach her, popping out of a bush more or less and scaring her. A hand flew to her chest. It was full of rings set with gemstones of every color. Bernard, she said. Is that really you?

He shook his head and opened his arms, expecting or hoping for a welcoming embrace, but his hands trembled with emotion, so she grasped them instead and held them close together between her own to still them, to comfort him while they stood there in the street, a public spectacle. Come with me, she said, and they walked arm-in-arm back to The Lenaka, entering through the back where the living quarters were. Once they were inside, she guided him to a brocade settee and sat him down as if he were enfeebled or a child. She stood in front of him, wide-eyed with her ringed hands over her mouth and spoke.

I never thought I'd see you again, Bernard.

He looked around the room, took in the lamps with cut-glass shades, the heavy wood furniture, the gilt mirrors. He said the first thing that came to his mind.

How can you live like this with so many poor folk around? I would think they'd murder you from envy.

She shrugged. I'm their medicine woman. I help their sick babies and ease their old ones into death. I don't charge but what they can afford. It's like it was back home. Most of 'em think I can put a hex on 'em. Then Bailey helps me, too. Most of 'ems afraid of Bailey.

Bailey? he asked, thinking correctly that she referred to the man in the pinstripe suit. But what was this man's role in her life? he wondered. Business partner? Bodyguard? Her answer broke his heart.

Bailey's my man, she said.

At her words, he deflated, sunk into himself. His head drooped, moving slowly side to side in amazement. He studied the swirling pattern of her carpet without seeing it.

She looked out a window so as not to have to watch Bernard try to gather himself, a sight that broke her heart in turn. Then since she knew he deserved an explanation, she gave him one. I found I needed a man after all, she said. It's a hard world, and a hard time for a woman to be alone. All my life I had Horace, you know.

How is he?

Oh, Bailey don't bother me much. He's happy long as I keep him in grits and gabardine as they say.

Bernard's head snapped up. His eyes were shiny with tears.

I meant Horace, he said.

They both laughed. Despite the terrible burdens they carried on each other's account, Aurora Mae sat down next to Bernard, and they held hands and talked. Bald Horace lived in a small town in Mississippi, she told him, doing what he loved best, raising goats and chickens and tending his garden. She sent him money regular though she thought it likely he just turned around and gave it away. Bernard had her write down an address so he could go visit. They talked about her shop, and he told her about Mrs. Karp. Aurora Mae asked him if he wanted to stay on awhile, and he said he didn't think that would be a good idea. He got up when it felt like time to be going, who knew when that Bailey might be back. She walked him to the door. They continued to hold hands the entire time. He was about to drop her hand when she said, softly, I don't love him. I only ever loved one man in my life, and he ain't the one.

Oh 'Rora Mae.

It's true.

He squeezed her hand, thanking her for that, and left with shoulders square as a general's to keep him from turning around for a last look, because if she was watching him he might never leave at all. He'd live in the outhouse and shine Bailey's boots if he had to, and that would not be good for any of them. A crowd of children milled about his car, standing on the running board and staring in the windows. He gave each one a nickel.

The second time a woman breaks your heart, he found, the healing comes quicker, because you're used to having that sodden place in you, heavy with sorrow. He toured around some, stopped in Biloxi and New Orleans. In the latter city, he set up shop for a while. He sold tobacco and moonshine out of a truck just to have something to do. His fortunes increased. He made a friend or two. He learned about finance and invested in real estate. He employed three lawyers, and to one of them, a man named Joshua Stone, he told all his story one night when they were holed up together during a hurricane with a bottle of bourbon. Joshua never told a soul, likely because his own sins were spilled that night, which gave the two a mutual bond of silence.

When he decided he was strong enough for it, Bernard made a trip to Guilford, Mississippi, and looked Bald Horace up.

I been expecting you for two and one-half years, Bald Horace told him. Ever since 'Rora Mae made mention that you'd been to see her. What took you so long?

Bernard sighed. I needed more healin', he said.

He found he quite liked Guilford. It was good to live near a man he thought of as his oldest and dearest friend, one who could keep him up to date on Aurora Mae's goings-on as well. A town is not the country-side, so they couldn't live together as they had outside Saint Louis given the difference in their race and class, but they could visit from time to time without causing talk. Bernard cast his eyes over the women of the town and knew which was his bride the first time he saw her leaving Sassaport General Emporium in the company of her mother. Beatrice Diane Sassaport was dressed in a striped blue-and-white frock with flounced sleeves and wore Mary Janes with a short stacked heel. She was beautiful, of course, and her carriage, her dignity bespoke the propriety he'd longed for since his liberation from Mrs. Karp. What stole his heart in an instant was her hair. It was thick, black, abundant, tied back away from her face that day with a white ribbon so that it rolled down her back in waves reminding him powerfully of Aurora Mae.

They were married the next year. Everything went well between them until the day Aurora Mae showed up at Rachel Marie's birth-day party. She'd been abandoned by Bailey, who'd run off with all her money and a young chippie born and bred in Orange Mound, and just when she'd taken charge of Cousin Mags's orphaned girl and her hus-band, promising them jobs she could not now provide.

Bernard staked her for a new start and hired Sara Kate and Roland on the spot. He wanted to do more. If he could, he would have kept Aurora Mae in Guilford, supported her and loved her from a distance, the way he was used to doing all his life, but she was having none of that.

You have your family to think of, she said. Three girls and a baby boy! Take care of them the best you can, and don't let what happened to me happen to none of them or theirs.

He took her words to heart. He put it about he was traveling to Memphis to confer with his family on business and went to New Orleans as usual. He visited his bank and transferred the usual amount of gold coin from a safety deposit box to his cash account for distribution over time by Joshua Stone, who sent him money as he required it. He took the rest of his gold and divided it into two piles. One pile he left in a deposit box, the other he packed in the false compartment of his car. When he got home, he buried it on a dark moonless night in his own backyard. He told no one, not even his wife, Beadie, it was there. One day, he dreamed, when their children were old enough, getting married perhaps or graduating college, he'd produce it and stun them all. Until then, he didn't want them feeling too at ease in the world or they might grow up like Bernard the handsome, spoiled and cruel. When the war came, he thought about digging up the gold or telling Beadie where it was, but that felt wrong, like he was extending a branch across the Mississippi for the ghost of Bernard the handsome to hop upon and curse his family in his absence. He decided to leave for war with his secret intact, refusing to entertain the idea he might die in battle. If the great river couldn't kill me, he thought, a Nazi can't do it, either.

Before he left New Orleans, he had Joshua Stone draw him up a trust that would husband the remaining half of his treasure for the future of his children's children as a safeguard. He named Aurora Mae and Bald Horace trustees.

Joshua Stone returned wounded from his war in Burma to discover that Bernard died in the Ardennes. Right away, he contacted Aurora Mae and Bald Horace to give them instructions. When the grandbabies come, he told them, you are to telegraph me two code words, and I will contact Bernard's children for birth certificates and such and release the grandbaby gold to their care accordingly.

What are the code words? Aurora Mae and Bald Horace asked.

Ghost Tree, Joshua Stone said, letting the words sink in as he knew their significance to those two. Then he repeated them. Ghost Tree.

It was twenty years gone before the code was needed. By then, Bald Horace had lost his mind. That left Aurora Mae to see Bernard's wishes carried out, a duty she held solemn and sacred. The Levy girls had been barren, which meant that the child of Laura Anne Levy, the sole grandchild of Bernard, was a lucky child in some respects long before he was conceived let alone born.

XVIII

Nah Trang, Vietnam, 1965

THE DAY AFTER CRACKAH MICK was wounded, the battle of Chu Lai came around howling like a pack of bad dogs full of long teeth and rabies. Forty-six dead and two hundred wounded and Field Hospital 8 was the only place they had to go. The bunkers were stuffed with mangled and dying men. The docs were in high-gear triage. They put the stabilized, Crackah Mick among them, outside in the grass under tarp on poles in case the rains started and left them to speculate on what came next.

He spent his week at Nah Trang trying to comprehend what had happened to him and always came up empty. He knew his legs didn't work, although one of them seemed to twitch now and again, and both of them hurt like hell sometimes, especially when he tried to sleep with or without the drugs. They sure wouldn't do anything he told them to. He didn't know if this was because they were healing and needed time or if it was because they were gone for good and would never come back. He grabbed the coattails of his doc, a Lieutenant Stein out of New York, as Lieutenant Stein was rushing past his cot and asked.

The doc said, What do I look like, a neurosurgeon? Hope for the best, son. You'll find out when you get back home.

Mickey Moe didn't believe he was going home. He didn't see anybody in a hurry to ship him there. He saw other boys go off to general hospitals in country or in the Philippines and Japan. Some of them went directly home. It was as if they'd forgotten him with all the commotion going on. For all he knew, they'd keep him there in Field Hospital 8 until his tour was over. Certainly, he did not seem to be anyone's priority.

For days, helicopters dropped off the wounded. Orderlies lined up corpses in bags near the makeshift tents of the stabilized. After a couple of days, they started to transport the bags to an amphibian hospital from which they'd be flown back home to their families and Arlington. Mickey Moe thought about crawling inside a bag himself. At least it would get him out of Field Hospital 8.

The only good part about waiting was they let him call home. He called twice. The first time, his mama fainted dead away at the sound of his voice. The second time, he reached Laura Anne before the first ring was over. She told him she loved him, and he told her he loved her. He asked for the baby. She told him the baby was fine and dandy and must be a boy, because he kept her up all night hopping around in her belly. Her words made him moan, which made them both teary. Oh Lord, they swore, I miss you so!

He told her he'd been wounded and that he'd soon be home, he couldn't exactly say when, but maybe she knew something from the Army, what had they told her?

They didn't tell me a thing, Laura Anne said. All I know is there's been some fierce kind of bloodbath goin' on out there. I've been tryin' to figure out where your hill is exactly and how close your unit is to all the fire, but I still don't really know.

I'm sorry, sweetheart. You have no idea how screwed up the Army is until you've been in it awhile. This doesn't surprise me. I'm sorry if my call has shocked you and Mama.

She laughed in a short, sharp way that brought to mind how strong she was. At the sound of it, he felt proud as a Spartan warrior of his Spartan wife and his heart warmed.

It didn't shock me at all. I knew something had happened to you. I been a wreck wondering what. Where are you hurt, darlin'? How bad is it? Oh, I know it must be bad if they're not just patchin' you up and sendin' you back in. Please tell me. I can take it.

What about the baby, can the baby take it?

It was a dark and dreadful joke that he regretted as soon as it left his lips. He heard her draw in a breath. There was a piece of quiet between them that would have split open with a kiss or a tender glance if they'd been together. But they were not.

The baby is ours, she said at last. The baby can take it.

So he told her about his legs, how maybe he could use them again and maybe he couldn't. That they'd best anticipate a long, hard haul ahead. There was another piece of quiet, only this one felt long and jagged and not even the sweetest embrace would shatter it. This quiet needed something hard, exceedingly hard, to break.

Then Laura Anne said, We'll do what we have to, Mickey Moe Levy. Don't you worry about it. Everything's going to be alright. You know how I knew something happened to you? I had a dream about a week ago. I was at the edge of the backwoods up there by Littlefield, and I was dressed in these black pajamas. And you were there, in your uniform, lookin' so smart and handsome. I pointed into the woods. You followed my direction. You went into the brush. I couldn't see you anymore. There was a riot of noise. There was fire, there was smoke, and I was terrified, terrified you wouldn't come back. But you did. Upright on two legs. I swear to God, Mickey. This is the truth.

And I just know it means that no matter what, everything's going to be alright.

He didn't tell her about his own dream, the one with herself in black pajamas and the severed foot in the jungle, but he'd bet dollars to *pho ga* that she'd had her dream the very same night he'd had his. This seemed more than a coincidence. It felt prescient. He decided to go with her assessment. At the end of the day, didn't a man and his woman know more than Lieutenant Stein and a boatload of neurosurgeons about their own dang lives?

You're right, he said. Everything's going to be fine.

And when they got off the phone, he lay back on his cot under the tarp across from the row of body bags to consider amid the echo of far-off gunfire and the stench of death the wonder that was love.

Acknowledgments

I WOULD NOT HAVE WRITTEN *One More River* were it not for my husband, Stephen K. Glickman, a voracious reader with a mind that is always percolating with something new. He took an interest in the Great Mississippi Flood of 1927 and infused me with his enthusiasm. The tragedy of that spectacular event, the greatest natural disaster in American history, expanded my literary themes of the Southern Jewish Experience and American racism in a way I could not have anticipated, as it came to focus on the mysteries of love and friendship in the face of extreme adversity. So my first piece of gratitude goes to him, who has never bored me, not for an instant of our thirty-nine years to date.

I must also rush to thank my agent, Peter Riva, who counseled me so wisely before presenting this novel to my publisher. I might yet be struggling in a "what the hell comes next" moment without his advice. And of course, I must thank my editor, Diane Reverand, who parries my pouting protests with grace and never gloats when I give in to her wisdom. Thank you, Peter and Diane, thank you.

But I would not be thanking any of the above if it were not for Open Road Integrated Media. For their expertise in shepherding my two novels across all media, I am deeply indebted to Jane Friedman, Jeff Sharp, Brendan Cahill, Luke Parker Bowles, Rachel Chou, Danny Monico, Greg Gordon, Andrea Colvin, Nicole Passage, Laura De Silva, Ann Weinstock, Jason Gabbert, and Lisa Weinert. Their support of both my first novel, *Home in the Morning*, and now *One More River*, has been phenomenal, their energies on my behalf boundless. In today's publishing world, when so much is expected of authors that is not writing but working in entirely different disciplines, for which we are often poorly prepared, the genius and commitment of these brilliant teammates are priceless.

cover design by Jason Gabbert
interior design by Danielle Young

ISBN: 978-1-4532-5816-3

Published in 2011 by Open Road Integrated Media
180 Varick Street
New York, NY 10014
www.openroadmedia.com

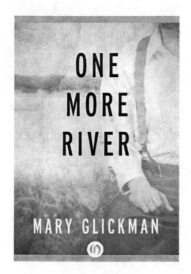 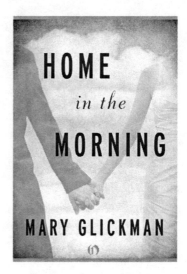

INTEGRATED MEDIA

Videos, Archival Documents, and New Releases

Sign up for the Open Road Media newsletter and get news delivered straight to your inbox.

FOLLOW US:
@openroadmedia and
Facebook.com/OpenRoadMedia

CPSIA information can be obtained at www.ICGtesting.com
Printed in the USA
LVOW111322160412

277784LV00002B/7/P